A groundbreaking book, black soldiers in the *Vessels* is peopled with flesh and blood characters and true events that not only inspire and entertain but educate. Well done!

— LAURA FRANTZ, CHRISTY AWARD-WINNING
AUTHOR OF *AN UNCOMMON WOMAN*

While America fights for freedom, a young widow fights her feelings for the sergeant who delivers the news of her husband's death. Micah Hughes just might have more of a task winning the love of Lydia Saunders than he does in preparing a regiment of freed slaves for combat— especially when Lydia's dark family secrets surface, pushing them into desperate decisions and danger. Elaine Marie Cooper has delivered her most gripping, heart-warming story yet. You won't rest until Lydia and Micah find forgiveness and freedom in each other's arms.

— DENISE WEIMER, MULTI-PUBLISHED AUTHOR
OF *THE WITNESS TREE*

Head to 1778, and immerse yourself in Elaine Cooper's heartbreaking, fast-paced story of one woman's saga during the Revolutionary War. Readers will connect with Lydia Saunders' losses, new love and family guilt on the road to her redemption. A historic tale of how our ancestors suffered to form a new country, it's a study in love, slavery, the fragility of life, and one woman's enduring determination to do the right thing.

— CAROL GRACE STRATTON, AUTHOR, *LAKE SURRENDER*

Elaine Cooper's latest release, *Scarred Vessels,* is a poignant, realistic depiction of war's losses for those left behind to tend families, farms, and businesses as well as for those on the front lines of the battle. Vividly set during a crucial period of the American Revolution, the story doesn't dwell on the scars tragedy causes. Instead, Cooper portrays in a very affecting way the grace and blessing God pours out amid great trial and how He uses the storms we endure to not only grow us spiritually but also satisfy the deepest longings of our hearts. *Scarred Vessels* is a gripping story full of both action and deep reflection that entertains even as it inspires readers to trust God through their own hard struggles.

—J. M. HOCHSTETLER, AUTHOR OF THE AMERICAN
PATRIOT SERIES, AND, WITH BOB HOSTETLER, THE
NORTHKILL AMISH SERIES

Scarred VESSELS

Elaine Marie Cooper

Scrivenings
PRESS
Quench your thirst for story.
www.ScriveningsPress.com

Published by Scrivenings Press LLC
15 Lucky Lane
Morrilton, Arkansas 72110
https://ScriveningsPress.com

Printed in the United States of America

Paperback ISBN 978-1-64917-002-6

eBook ISBN 978-1-64917-065-1

Library of Congress Control Number: 2020947124

Cover by Linda Fulkerson, bookmarketinggraphics.com

All characters are fictional, and any resemblance to real people, either factional or historical, is purely coincidental.

All scriptures are taken from the KING JAMES VERSION (KJV): KING JAMES VERSION, public domain.

This book is dedicated to my son, Commander Benjamin Cooper, USN.

ACKNOWLEDGMENTS

I am grateful to so many who have shared information and offered support during the writing of this novel.

First I want to thank my son, Commander Benjamin Cooper, Commanding Officer VAQ-130, who gave me the idea for this story line. From the moment he suggested writing about the black soldiers in the American Revolution, I knew he was inspired. What I did not anticipate was the research journey this story would take me on. As a girl who grew up in New England, I was left astonished by some of the facts I gleaned from my studies of black people in the Revolutionary War—facts that were often difficult to swallow about the slave trade in the north.

My friend, Cherrilynn Bisbano, who is from Rhode Island, practically begged me to visit her home state. I was so glad I took her up on the gracious invitation. She took me on tours of several important locales presented in this book. We even traveled to Aquidneck Island where the Battle of Rhode Island occurred. I walked atop the rampart that protected the Continentals from the Brits. It was ... awesome! Thank you, my friend!

The gracious and knowledgeable member of the Portsmouth

Historical Society who escorted us on the tour of Fort Butts was Gloria Schmidt. What a fascinating tour she took us on, transporting in our minds the now grass-covered fort into a soldier-filled den of war activity. Thank you, Gloria!!

I also wish to thank the other members of the Portsmouth Historical Society who gave of their time and knowledge to help me in understanding the events of that battle. Such a kind and helpful group of historians they all are.

A great "Huzzah" to Jennifer Hayden Epperson, a fellow author who I met at a writer's conference. She was a descendant of a Rhode Island "Swamp Yankee," which introduced to me the concept of the backwoods Patriots from Rhode Island during the American Revolution. We had delightful conversations and these talks led to create a couple of my favorite characters in *Scarred Vessels*.

Thanks to my son, Nathaniel Cooper, for my new author photo!

Many thanks to Rei Battcher of the Bristol (RI) Historical and Preservation Society. Rei was generous in giving of his time and knowledge to this history-hungry researcher/author. Thank you, Rei!

Thanks to editors Alycia Morales and Kathy Cretsinger! Thanks to my editors/publishers at Scrivenings Press, Linda Fulkerson and Shannon Vannatter. Authors with wonderful editors are so blessed, and I feel very blessed, indeed!

Thank you to Hope Bolinger and Cyle Young of Hartline Literary Agency.

Thanks to author Christian McBurney who researched in great detail the Battle of Rhode Island and provided key understanding to the framework of its history. I encourage you to seek out his wonderful book, *The Rhode Island Campaign: The First French and American Operation in the Revolutionary War*.

There are so many fellow authors, friends and family to whom I owe so much in supporting my writing and my research. Thank you all. You are the heartbeats behind my words.

Mostly I want to thank my Lord and Savior Jesus Christ, from Whom all blessings flow.

1

Bristol, Rhode Island, March 1778

Dawn spread faint beams across the sky. Lydia scanned the gray horizon from her bedroom window as though her hopes for an early spring would materialize with the intensity of her gaze. But it was not to be.

Bare trees topped countless snow mounds that clung to the frozen acres of land. All life awaited the coming thaw.

The long, bitter winter brought storm after storm, pummeling the rafters of the barn and Lydia's two-story home. Comfort, her four-year-old daughter, slept most nights in bed with her, the child's small hands gripping the quilt tighter with every creak from the roof. Lydia treasured her daughter's presence, truly a solace while Jeremiah served with Washington's troops in New Jersey.

Through his letters, her husband tried to reassure her all was well. But unsettling news of little food and even less fuel for warmth filtered from neighbor to neighbor through correspondence from other sons and husbands. They revealed more than Jeremiah wanted her to know.

Her mind drifted to their final evening together on his brief furlough October last. If she closed her eyes, she could almost taste his kisses that still sent chills of pleasure through her. She smiled despite the gloomy day and prayed God would bring her husband home soon.

While she relished the sun rising over the snow, a slight movement caught her eye. She leaned into the windowpane and squinted. *Jeremiah?*

As the two figures rode their mounts closer, Lydia's heart sank. Strangers. Continental soldiers. Fear gripped her. Were they deserters? Could they be trusted? She moved with caution so she would not disturb her still-sleeping daughter, then closed the bedroom door behind her before she hurried down the staircase.

"You should not be hurryin', Mrs. Saunders. Take care of yourself and that babe you be carryin'." Hannah took her arm when she reached the first floor and led her to a chair.

"Two soldiers are coming in the distance."

The young maid's eyes widened with fear. "You stay here. I'll go fetch Ezekiel."

Before Hannah left to search for him, Ezekiel burst through the front door. "Strangers. Two soldiers. Want to be certain they mean no harm." Ezekiel grabbed the musket from over the fireplace and went back outside.

Hannah squeezed Lydia's shoulders, but the trembling in the maid's fingers belied her calm expression. Lydia reached up and touched Hannah's brown fingers. She wasn't sure who comforted whom.

The men arrived and spoke with Ezekiel. Lydia strained to hear their conversation, but the wind prevented her from discerning the message through the manor's walls.

Lydia took a deep breath, released Hannah's fingers, and pushed herself awkwardly from the chair. Her belly had seemed to enlarge overnight, and an awareness that her steps resembled a waddle made her self-conscious.

She and Hannah reached the front entrance at the same

moment. They both gripped the handle, but Lydia released her hand and allowed Hannah to open it. Both men turned their gaze toward the women while Lydia stood behind her servant, hiding her pregnancy from them.

"Good day, Mrs. Saunders. Miss."

The taller of the two men tipped his black tricorne hat and tugged at his neck cravat. His blue woolen coat, covered with dirt and splatters of mud, looked clean compared to his boots, which bore so much mud they seemed more brown than black.

He appeared to be in his twenties, but his eyes bore wrinkles brought on, perhaps, by too little sleep and too many battles. An ugly scar marked his forehead, yet his eyes were kind and his voice kinder yet.

The other soldier, dressed in a similar uniform, bore the darker skin tone and features of an Indian.

"I beg your pardon, Mrs. Saunders, but may I speak with you?"

She shivered at the tone in the taller man's voice. "Of course, please come inside." Lydia turned and went back to the parlor while Hannah opened the door for the men.

Before they entered, the men pushed the soles of their boots across the iron scraper on the porch. The man who spoke wore a higher military rank. He surveyed the interior, taking in the high ceilings and elaborate furnishings.

"You have a beautiful home, Mrs. Saunders." He clutched his hat with nervous fingers. "Forgive me. I ne'er introduced myself. I'm Sergeant Micah Hughes, and this here's Private Henry Bearslayer. We ..." He cleared his throat. "We're from Lieutenant Saunders's regiment, ma'am."

Her heart leaped, whether from fear or joy, Lydia could not be certain. "You know my husband! Is he well?" She stood from the chair, and the two soldiers stared at her enlarged belly.

Sergeant Hughes's face paled, and he swallowed. Private Bearslayer glanced downward then turned away.

"We ..." Sergeant Hughes paused. "We were not told you

3

were with child, Mrs. Saunders. Your husband ne'er said a word."

"Aye. I did not tell him for fear he would worry. He had such unease with my first confinement, and I did not wish him to be concerned." When the men remained quiet, Lydia's breathing increased, and moisture covered her brow. She found her voice. "How is Jeremiah?"

By now, palpable tension permeated the room.

"Perhaps, Mrs. Saunders, you'd best have a chair." Sergeant Hughes's voice sounded low and strained.

Unaware that Hannah had already grabbed her arm, Lydia plopped back into her chair.

"Please." Her voice caught, for ill tidings would surely be in their reply. "Please tell me my husband is well."

"I wish more than anything I could. But Lieutenant Saunders succumbed to fever in the service of General Washington's Army. I am so very sorry, ma'am." The soldier's gaze dropped to the carpet, and he swiped his hand across his face.

Lydia could not speak. A salty taste filled her mouth, and lights flashed in her eyes. She inhaled slow breaths and fought the sensation. Hannah placed a cup of cider in front of her and held it so she could sip the sweet liquid.

When her vision cleared, she noticed both soldiers sat on the edge of their seats and leaned toward her.

"Are you well, ma'am? Shall we fetch a doctor?"

A small voice came from the stairway. "Mama?"

Lydia gasped and turned toward Comfort. "Come here, my sweet."

The small bare feet pattered across the wooden floor, and the child climbed onto her lap.

I must be strong for her.

She forced a smile. "Comfort, these nice men are here to visit. They know your papa." Lydia threw a warning glance at the soldiers. She preferred to tell her daughter the news in private. And perhaps, if she put off telling Comfort for a long while, she could convince herself it was just a bad dream. A very bad dream.

Private Bearslayer nodded at the child. "Pleased to meet you, Miss Saunders."

"I'm pleased to meet you as well, sir." Her tiny voice held all the purity and sweetness of childhood. An innocence often lost in times of war. How long would Comfort continue to see life through her uncorrupted view? Lydia remembered she had been Comfort's age when her own world shattered.

Sergeant Hughes sat taller. "I am pleased to meet you as well, miss."

Comfort's eyes squinted, and she walked over to his side. She placed small fingers on the scar on his forehead. "Does it hurt?"

He grinned. "Nay. Not a bit."

"Did it hurt when you got it cut?"

"Aye, it hurt a fair bit." His face clouded, and he glanced to the side.

Comfort put her hands on his cheeks and pulled his face down so she could kiss his scar. "Mama says that makes it feel better."

Sergeant Hughes struggled to keep tears at bay. "Well, your mama is right. It feels better already."

"Comfort, thank you for tending Sergeant Hughes's wound. But we must get these gentlemen some victuals and tend their horses." She regarded the two men. "You will stay at least a day and night? And rest? And mayhap, you might tell me more about my husband." She pulled her lips inward.

"Aye, Mrs. Saunders, we shall. You can feed us in the barn. We are not dressed for dining." Sergeant Hughes straightened the facing on his coat.

"Nonsense, gentlemen." She arose with difficulty.

The men stood as Lydia rubbed her lower back that ached more each day.

"You are our guests. Ezekiel will show you to your room where you can wash up. Breakfast will be ready forthwith." She took Comfort's hand and walked the child back upstairs. If Lydia did not think about the message these soldiers brought, she might survive this day.

~

THAT EVENING, Lydia lay in bed next to Comfort. She had yet to tell the precious child about her beloved papa. Every time she'd seen an opportunity, her own distress overcame her ability to share the tragic news. It was difficult enough to deal with her own grief. The anticipation of her daughter's emotions would push her own over the edge of reason.

War kept her on the brink of fear at all times. She thought it would be over after the Battle of Saratoga in 1777. But here it was, '78, and the conflict raged on. Would it never stop?

And now, with Jeremiah gone, a part of her died as well. How would she overcome the loss of this man who stole her heart in Newport so long ago? Just then, her unborn child pushed outward against her firm belly. She touched the spot through her thin shift and felt the outline of a tiny foot press back against her finger.

How she wished she had told Jeremiah. The knowledge of another child—perhaps a son—might have filled him with enough hope to survive the terrible sickness he endured. Had her secret kept him from surviving? She forced these thoughts to flee, lest they drive her mad.

She lightly touched Comfort's soft hair while the child slept. Her daughter took after her husband in so many ways—not just with her russet hair and blue eyes but her sweet personality. She could make friends with anyone, unlike her mother.

Ever since Lydia had discovered the truth about her father, she'd withdrawn into a shell of guilt. Jeremiah had been the only one who could draw her out of her mind's darkness and help her realize the guilt did not leave its stain upon her soul. Her husband could always shed light in the darkness. And now? Who would encourage her in her desperate moments?

Lydia sat up and placed the quilt snugly around Comfort. She glanced around the empty room, then realized she'd never heard the soldiers return from tending their mounts in the barn.

Panic seized her. Had they left? She'd never know the details about Jeremiah. And she needed to know.

Tiptoeing across the room, she grabbed her shawl and left her bedchamber. Lydia closed the door behind her, making every attempt to be quiet. She saw streams of light from underneath Hannah's door and knocked with a light touch.

Hannah answered with widened eyes. "Oh, 'tis you, ma'am. I thought ... never mind."

Too preoccupied with her own fear, Lydia didn't question Hannah about her apparent worries.

"Hannah, where are the soldiers? I didn't hear them return from the barn. And I see their doors are open." Open, with no light within.

"I don't know, Mrs. Saunders. I never heard them return from tendin' their horses."

Her breaths quickened, and she spun toward the stairs. Hannah cautioned her to be careful on the steps that led to the main floor. Clinging to the rail, Lydia descended as quietly as she could. She grabbed her woolen cloak from the hook near the front door then placed it over her shawl.

Barefoot, she left the house. When her feet met the snowy ground, she didn't stop in her quest to reach the barn some fifteen rods away. Lydia opened the creaky door and slipped inside. The scent of fresh hay and horses filled her nostrils. She prayed it would be the soldiers' mounts she smelled and not her family's mare and gelding.

Lydia trod across the crunchy straw on the wooden floor and exhaled with relief when she saw the military horses still in their stalls. Where were the men?

Feeling like an intruder in her own barn, she waddled with careful steps down the row of stalls. In one horse stall, she saw Private Bearslayer asleep. In the next lay Sergeant Hughes.

She feared breathing too loudly lest she awaken them. She thanked God they'd not left. But why did they not accept the warmer accommodations within that she'd offered?

While she observed the sleeping sergeant, her thoughts traveled to Jeremiah. In the dark of night, she could imagine the man's hair could be russet in color and the uniform that of an officer. She clamped her hand across her mouth and spun toward the entryway. Moonlight shone through the still-open portal.

When she neared the door, she fell to her knees and sobbed into her hands. Her grief, once allowed to emerge, transformed into an unstoppable flow of memories. Any hopes for a future with Jeremiah dashed with cruel force upon the rocks of eternity. Spasms of lament seeped out of her tight grip covering her mouth as she attempted to smother them.

"Mrs. Saunders."

Lydia gasped and peeked toward the voice.

"I'm so sorry I awoke you, Sergeant Hughes." Her face, covered with tears, must be swollen. She felt him touch her hand with his handkerchief.

"Please take this, ma'am."

She unceremoniously blew her nose then handed the wet linen back to him.

"Please keep it. You may have need of it in the future." He grinned and combed his fingers through his long hair, which had come undone from his military queue.

"Thank you," she whispered.

"Might I help you up, Mrs. Saunders? The floor is mighty cold, and you are without shoes."

"Aye."

Sergeant Hughes pulled her up with strong yet gentle hands. "Let me take you back to your house."

He gave her his arm, and she clung to him, surprised by the thinness of his muscles.

The rumors must be true about insufficient victuals at Valley Forge. No wonder Jeremiah succumbed. He'd likely shared his portions with his regiment. She inhaled and swallowed with force to keep from crying again.

She made a checklist in her mind of the stores from last year's harvest. These soldiers would return to camp with bulging knapsacks overflowing with victuals.

When they reached the house, she invited the sergeant indoors. He declined, but she urged him to comply.

"Please, Sergeant. I need to know about my husband. I need to hear from those who knew him ... in his last days."

"Very well, ma'am."

"If you like, I can awaken Ezekiel to be nearby, in case you deem that more proper."

His face reddened in the candlelight of the foyer. "Very well, ma'am."

There was no need to awaken Ezekiel since her servant had already lit the candles. The distressed man walked into the parlor.

"I was worried about you, Mrs. Saunders." Concern etched Ezekiel's furrowed brow. "I heard you get up in the middle of the night and came to fetch you. It's still freezin' out there."

"Aye." She turned toward the sergeant. "Which is why I welcomed you and Private Bearslayer into our home, Sergeant. Hughes. The barn is fit for beasts, not men."

He sniffed and glanced to the side. "I fear years of war have gotten us used to sleeping in all manner of places. Most, none too comfortable. Me and Henry—Private Bearslayer—didn't want to bring our dirty uniforms into your rooms upstairs. Seemed more fitting to sleep in the barn."

The realization of what the army endured on a daily basis enlightened her sympathies. "I'm so sorry, Sergeant Hughes. Truly. I would not have minded one bit. You have served our country with much sacrifice, and I thank you. Please. Come sit in the parlor. Ezekiel, can you bring us biscuits and coffee?"

"Yes, ma'am."

"Ezekiel, bring some for yourself, too. I know you are

interested in the army and our cause."

His white teeth shone in his dark face. "Thank you, ma'am."

When he'd gone to the kitchen, she sat, then motioned Sergeant Hughes to sit on her right.

"Please, tell me about Jeremiah. I wish to hear anything— whatever memories you have."

"Well, he was one of the bravest. And kindest. Always seeing to our needs. When victuals were low in camp, or there were none at all, he managed to scrape up a few morsels for his men." Sergeant Hughes stared down at his hands, and his hair almost covered his face from the side. "That's likely why he could not fight off that sickness. We thought he fed himself enough. But 'twasn't so. He looked as skinny as the rest of us."

He sniffed and wiped his face. Before Lydia could respond, Ezekiel strode in with biscuits and coffee.

"Thank you, Ezekiel. After you've served, please sit down and join us."

Sergeant Hughes looked surprised but not displeased. "Not used to white folks being kindly to their slaves. 'Tis pleasant to see. My family—we came from simple farmers in Connecticut and never owned Negroes. Don't think my pa ever wanted any. We had a small farm, and our minister preached against the sin of slavery. We managed okay."

Discomfort needled her conscience, and she shifted in her chair.

The sergeant's cup clattered into the china saucer. His face reddened. "Not that you don't fear God, ma'am. I greatly apologize for my thoughtlessness. I meant no offense."

She cleared her throat. "No offense taken, Sergeant. I have long abhorred the practice of slavery. I grew up with this sin and prayed God's forgiveness on my family." She paused. "My husband felt as I do. We kept on a few Negroes to work here and help in our house in Newport."

"When the King's Army took over that city, we escaped here to Bristol and settled on my parents' farm. 'Twas deeded to

Jeremiah and me in my father's will." She glanced up at the flushed face of the soldier and smiled. "Again, I know your words to be both true and in no way improper."

Ezekiel sipped his coffee. "Mrs. Saunders and her husband have always taken care of me right nice. They've been kindly to all of us—Cuff, Hannah, Miriam, and Rose too. Even let Miriam keep that baby. Not all masters be that way."

"I'd never have let Miriam's baby be sold." Darkness threatened to consume her as memories flooded her thoughts. Her mother's gut-wrenching pleas for the baby to be sent away revolted her still. The nightmare visited her again and again. She resisted the memory and begged God to clear her mind of that recollection. She forced herself to focus on Ezekiel.

"I just wish there's somethin' I could do to avenge my master's death." The slave's countenance sobered, and he stared down at his hands. "Fill in for him. I know how much this cause meant to Mr. Saunders, and I feel like I should be doing somethin'." Ezekiel's eyes widened, and he stared into the distance, his hands folded into a tight fist that he held against his mouth.

His fiery words surprised Lydia. Ezekiel's distress over the loss of Jeremiah seemed to incite a passion for war.

"Beggin' yer pardon," Sergeant Hughes said, "are you aware your state passed a law that allows colored men to join a new regiment—the 1st Rhode Island? I'm here in Bristol not just to deliver your news but to recruit slaves for this regiment."

"Slaves? Their own regiment?" Lydia rarely read the papers, since she avoided news that filled her with anxiety.

"Aye, just last month. The State of Rhode Island will pay owners and, once the soldier passes muster with Colonel Christopher Greene, each man will be free. A full-fledged soldier in General Washington's Army."

"Free." The awe in Ezekiel's voice was undeniable.

Words choked in her throat. The vision of hope shining in Ezekiel's eyes thwarted all her attempts to speak.

All Ezekiel knew was slavery. The son of two slaves carried over as human cargo on one of the dreaded ships from Africa, he'd been torn from his mother's desperate arms when he was less than a year old.

Jeremiah's father purchased him then gifted him to his son when Lydia and Jeremiah wed. And even though she made sure Ezekiel learned to read and write, he still bore the color that labeled him as less than human in the eyes of many. Mere property to be used by others.

The injustice threatened to overwhelm her anew. She swallowed with great difficulty.

"Is this what you wish, Ezekiel?" Her eyes met his, and she knew the answer.

Ezekiel shook his head with force. "I promised Mr. Saunders I'd take care of you and the farm. I can't go and leave you and your children. Especially not now."

The thought of living without his protection began an uncomfortable racing in her heart. And how she would manage the farm, Lydia had no idea. If she could not keep up, would she be forced to move in with her Tory mother on the coast? She rebelled at the thought.

God, what should I do?

In a whisper to her heart, the answer came. *Let him be free.*

"I want you to go." With a firmness in her voice she did not feel, she stared straight at him. "You will be free. And you can fill in where my Jeremiah cannot. We will manage here. And we shall pray for your safety every day."

The thought of her beloved Ezekiel facing danger almost forced her to change her mind. But she could not disobey the whisper. Surely God must abhor slavery more than she did.

In the silence that followed her declaration, peace filled the room. And Jeremiah's baby kicked gently within her womb. It seemed like an affirmation to Lydia, even when confronted by the greatest challenge of her new life as a widow. She sensed there would be more difficult challenges ahead, and she shivered.

2

Micah Hughes could not have been more surprised if Washington's troops had just declared victory. He sat speechless, both distraught and in awe of the widow's bravery.

To free her best farm overseer overwhelmed him with both respect and concern for Mrs. Saunders. Ezekiel's presence likely kept the farm going. How would she survive? Especially since she would soon birth another child. This was madness.

He tried not to stutter. "Mrs. Saunders, are you certain? You're making a grave decision."

"I'm aware of the solemn nature of my decision." When she met his eyes, she bore an expression of calm and peace. "Yet I must follow my conscience. And my God."

What could he say? How could he argue with a belief he agreed with? Yet he had earnest concern for her well-being.

"How will you manage, ma'am? With only one field worker?"

"I do not know, Sergeant Hughes." She gripped her china cup so tightly it seemed it would shatter in her grasp. "I find I must take a step of faith, however uncertain my future is." She gave Ezekiel a tentative smile. "I'm certain you have preparations to make. Please feel free to take your leave and get ready, Ezekiel."

"Thank you, Mrs. Saunders. I am eternally grateful. May the good Lord bless you." He gathered the empty coffee cups and plates and hurried toward the kitchen, balancing the china in his strong hands.

When Ezekiel left, Micah leaned forward in his chair. If it would have been deemed appropriate, he'd have reached for her hands and made an earnest plea for her to reconsider.

"Sergeant Hughes, please do not fear. Whatever happens will be God's will. I feel that most deeply in my spirit."

"You ... you have already been through so much, Mrs. Saunders. Your husband told us about the attack on your home in Newport before you escaped to Bristol. Who will defend and protect you? Who will attend your crops and horses?"

"We will manage. Somehow." She averted her gaze, then stood. "How do I sign the papers necessary to free Ezekiel?"

"This must be done at the county seat." He rose from his chair. "I can follow your carriage there." No sense in dissuading her. She'd made up her mind. "We'll post the recruit signs there and accept signatures within. Once Ezekiel passes muster, the officials will render payment to you."

"No payment is necessary."

"Please, ma'am, 'tis the only way Ezekiel will truly be considered a free man. If there is no exchange of shillings, 'twould not be legal."

She bit her lower lip and frowned. After a moment, she said, "Very well."

A sudden sensation must have occurred in her large belly as she grasped it and inhaled.

Fear prickled through him. "Do you need a doctor, ma'am?"

Lydia grinned. "'Tis quite normal that infants kick."

Heat rose in his face. "I'm sorry, Mrs. Saunders, I don't know what I imagined."

A quick squeeze of her fingers on his hand left him with a strange sensation that confused yet pleased him. The smile on her face entranced him.

"You really must not fear so," she said. "God will watch over me."

"Aye." He cleared his throat. "I must get a few nods of sleep before dawn. We will have much work to do then."

He turned and almost tripped over his own feet, increasing his embarrassment. Micah hurried out the door, took a deep breath, and ran toward the barn.

MICAH AWOKE at dawn to the sound of sobs. He heard a female voice speaking amidst tears.

"Hannah, I must do this." The deep and unique tone of Ezekiel's voice pierced the quiet. "They need soldiers to fight. And Mr. Saunders, he can't help in this cause for freedom no more."

"And just whose cause is this, anyway?" The woman's voice grew angry. "I don't see no one offering to free us colored folk if we win this war. What's to become of us, even if you be free?" She resumed her heartrending cries.

"I don't know, Hannah. But I promise, I will come back to you. Maybe Mrs. Saunders would free you too, so we can start a family of our own."

In the quiet that followed, Micah could hear sounds of the couple's affection, then passion. Embarrassed, he stirred so they would know he was awake. He heard them leave the barn in a hurry.

Since he shared quarters with his regiment for so long, Micah kept thoughts of women and their finer ways at bay. Until last night.

What sort of madness prompted these feelings of attraction to Mrs. Saunders? She may be a widow, but he felt ashamed of his reaction to the touch of her fingers. What sort of man is bewitched by the widow of his newly deceased officer? He must be desperate. Or a deeper sinner than he thought.

Not to mention, foolish beyond comprehension. What wealthy woman would glance twice at a simple farmer from Connecticut? Being a soldier for so long must have rendered him on the verge of insanity to think Mrs. Saunders would be attracted to him. Though proficient at combat, he came across as a complete dunderhead in social circles.

Focus on this war. Indeed, he might never return home from future battles, which made any hopes of sharing love with a woman a complete farce. For the first time, that thought left an emptiness in his spirit.

The rooster had already crowed, so he pushed his weary frame up from the straw.

He packed up his gear then took note of the recruiting posters Washington had entrusted to him. Micah still could not understand why the general had requested he and Henry to do this mission. Perhaps they were some of the healthiest in the regiments. That did not speak well for the condition of the rest of the troops.

When he walked past the stall where Henry had slept, he saw his Indian friend had already risen. Grateful for the man's tracking skills, Micah knew Henry's abilities had saved their hides on more than one occasion on the 300-mile trek from Valley Forge. And with Henry's hunting expertise, they'd probably enjoyed more food on that journey than they'd eaten all winter at camp.

As he approached the stately Saunders home, he saw Ezekiel emerge from the front door.

It was evident the gravity of his decision had hit Ezekiel. The serious set of his eyes and steeled jaw revealed no less determination to go to war than Micah had seen in the man last night. But the slave's reddened eyes affirmed the pain this decision caused.

It weighed with heaviness on Ezekiel's heart. The slave would leave behind a woman he cared deeply about, and there were no assurances he'd ever be free to return to her. Would the man ever be truly free in a world where injustice reigned?

Sympathy crept into Micah's thoughts. Had he faced leaving someone behind who he loved, could he have made such a choice? His boots clomped up the steps, and he knocked on the door.

Hannah answered and motioned him inside. "Have a seat in the dining room." Her face covered in tears, she could barely speak.

Micah removed his hat and set it on the coat rack. Following Hannah's directions, he entered the room. The table was set with exquisite china, covered with a cloth and the finest tableware he'd ever seen. He must have been too exhausted to notice it last night, but today, he felt out of place amid such finery.

"Good day, Sergeant Hughes." Mrs. Saunders's smile, although welcoming, was tinged with sadness.

"Good day, ma'am."

He sat, his movements awkward, and made every attempt not to disrupt the carefully set plates. More utensils were placed for one person than all the cups, trenchers, and spoons used by his entire family at a meal. Although awkward in his manners, his gracious hostess made him feel right at home.

"Please, help yourself," she said. "Miriam, could you pour the coffee this morning? Hannah is not feeling well."

A dark young woman poured a generous amount into his cup. "Thank you, Miss."

Her smile radiated at his gratitude. "You are welcome, sir."

Miriam had a different way of speaking with unfamiliar inflections to her words. Uncertain where she hailed from, Micah found her accent lilting and melodic. Although not refined, he knew better than to ask about her while she was present. He thought her speech lovely, just unfamiliar to his Yankee sensibilities.

After the servant left the room, Mrs. Saunders explained.

"Miriam came to live with us a few years ago. She was not born in this country." A disturbed expression of pain crept into her visage. "We are grateful we were able to ... rescue her."

"Well, she has a beautiful smile."

"Aye, she most certainly does." The darkness left Mrs. Saunders's face as she rested her hands on the edge of the table. "When must we leave for the county seat?"

He swallowed the coffee, then wiped his mouth with his napkin. "I'd say the sooner, the better. General Washington counts on us to glean recruits for this regiment forthwith. Colonel Greene needs time to muster then train them before they are ready for battle."

"Of course." She glanced upward. "Is that Colonel Nathanael Greene?"

"Nay, Col. Christopher Greene is his cousin. He'll be in charge of the regiment, under General Varnum."

"These names are so familiar to me from Jeremiah's letters. I almost feel like I know them."

He almost choked on his toast and drank cider to stop his cough. "I beg your pardon, Mrs. Saunders. I nearly forgot, and I regret I did not bring this up before." He met her surprised gaze. "I have your husband's personal effects for you, including several letters that never made it into a courier's hands. I must have been daft to forget."

Her eyes brimmed with tears, but she smiled. "I am beholden to you."

"Nay, Mrs. Saunders, 'tis I who am beholden to your husband's service in the cause for freedom. And to you as well, for your support of his endeavor. We will never forget him."

She stared at her hands. "Nay. Nor will I."

~

LYDIA COULD NOT BRING herself to delve into Jeremiah's letters that day, but it was all she could do to leave them in her bedchamber in a drawer. She must bid the words of her husband to wait one more day. Today, Ezekiel needed his freedom.

Riding in the carriage driven by Cuff, the young slave Jeremiah had purchased shortly after their marriage, Lydia's thoughts traveled over the rutted road of Ezekiel's life with them.

The first time she saw Ezekiel, he man's strength and quiet demeanor impressed her. He rarely spoke a harsh word to anyone, although she soon learned his calm spirit held a fierce loyalty to Jeremiah and then, to herself.

Jeremiah begged his father to allow Ezekiel to come to their Newport home when the couple married. Lydia's father-in-law had been in a generous mood. After all, his only son married the elder daughter of a wealthy shipowner. Why should he not reward his son's affections and commitment to such a prize catch?

Her father-in-law did not realize Jeremiah had an ulterior motive to his request. For some time, he'd known Lydia's maidservant, Hannah, had captured Ezekiel's affections. Jeremiah understood his own love for Lydia, and he could not imagine the thought his father might sell Ezekiel elsewhere. The couple might be separated forever.

Jeremiah's request to unite the two in the same household increased her love for the man she longed to wed. Longing for Jeremiah had turned into heated passion that found Lydia with child just two months after they wed. Her mother had spoken to her about the marriage bed obligation. But Lydia had discovered the "obligation" to be blissful.

The carriage jerked sideways on the dirt road, shaking her from her happy memories. She glanced at Ezekiel, astride the gelding. His loss would fill the household with grief.

Lydia would not contemplate the potential loss of the entire farm if she and the remaining servants could not keep it running well. She shuddered at the thought of being forced from her home and into the cold arms of her Tory mother. Lydia must make this work.

They drew close to the Bristol courthouse, and Sergeant Hughes, astride his mount, directed the carriage to the side of the road.

Cuff shouted, "Whoa," to the horses, and the carriage jerked to a stop.

Lydia waited for Cuff, who opened the door to the carriage. As she unfolded her legs from her cramped position, she wondered how long it would be before it would be impossible to climb into this transport—much less get out again. Cuff held out his cocoa-brown hand for her, and she gripped it with force while she held onto the window's rim with her other hand.

As she stepped down, she cringed. Voices shouted from the corner tavern. Those sounds metamorphosed in her mind to echoes from long ago.

The uproar grew, and her heart pounded faster. In her mind, she heard the auctioneer belting out words to incite a purchase.

'Gather round and see the finest flesh from Africa ye'll ever see. Limbs, strong as an ox. And the women, ready to satisfy your *deepest* desire.'

Lydia nearly lost the breakfast she'd struggled to ingest. Her stomach churned at comments about the slaves' anatomy pealing through the air as if it were the most natural marketplace conversation. Bids on human flesh. With each horrific comment about the women, exposed in vulnerable nakedness, Lydia swallowed back the bile and longed to spit the taste from her mouth.

She stood still, staring at the sky over the wharfs and envisioned the sounds of the slave trade that had been her father's livelihood for years. Today, there was no such auction. The slave ships had been stifled in their trade while the war raged on.

All she heard were the men who yelled in the tavern and the haunting calls of seagulls along the wharf. The sounds of the past, so vivid in her memory, refused to leave her mind at peace. The silence from the docks still echoed the horror.

"Mrs. Saunders?" Sergeant Hughes approached her, an image of concern crossing his expression. "Are you well, Mrs. Saunders? Perhaps we'd best hurry to the county magistrate's office."

He cupped his hand around her elbow, and his strength encouraged her to walk away from the horrific memories.

The sergeant rounded a bend and pointed toward the building where a sign recruiting "Negro, mulatto and Indian slaves" had been posted earlier by Private Bearslayer.

"Private Bearslayer arrived ahead and posted these. Come inside. I'll find you a chair."

The door opened with a high-pitched creak, and Lydia emerged into a crowded room that smelled of sweat and tobacco. Both white and colored men filled the room. A line in front of a wooden table stretched almost back to the door. At the table, men signed a parchment using a long quill pen.

"Well, well, good day, Lydia. And how does my sister-in-law fare?" Phineas examined her large belly with a smirk.

She swallowed with difficulty at the sight of her sister's husband.

His rancid breath wafted into her face. "I see your rebel husband being gone to war has not kept you from entertaining yourself in his absence."

Sudden heat coursed through Lydia at the vulgar insinuation.

Sergeant Hughes grabbed the man's cravat with such force, Phineas's face swelled and reddened.

"You will apologize to the lady this instant."

The sergeant's face, normally calm and kind, filled with the same fury she had experienced at Phineas's words.

"You will treat our hero's widow with respect, sir."

"I apologize."

For all his odious manner, her sister's husband was a coward to the core. Sergeant Hughes released Phineas and continued to glare at her brother-in-law.

Phineas readjusted his silk cravat. "So, Jeremiah is dead. I shall let your sister know." He pointed at Lydia's belly. "And does she know about this?"

"You know quite well that Phila and I rarely speak. I have nothing to say to her. Or you."

Lydia spun around so fast she grew dizzy.

A sturdy hand gripped her and guided her to a nearby chair. "Rest here, Mrs. Saunders."

How would she have endured this day without the sergeant's help? Lydia must remember to thank him.

She closed her eyes, only to reopen them when the grating voice of Phineas interrupted her short repose.

"You should be grateful I came today at all, Sergeant, especially since I'm freeing my best slave to join the 1st Rhode Island regiment."

Lydia turned her eyes toward Phineas's 'best slave.' The young man appeared to be no more than fifteen. *God help him.*

Sergeant Hughes ignored Phineas but focused his attention on her. "Mrs. Saunders, are you well enough to stand a moment and sign the papers to release Ezekiel?"

His compassion elicited her deep gratitude. In a world of ugliness, his kindness soothed like a healing balm.

"Aye." She pushed her awkward form up from the wooden chair and felt his hand on her back as he helped lift her weight upward. She clung with a weak grip to his arm and approached the table.

Lydia stood next to Ezekiel and bit her tongue to resist begging him to stay in Bristol. She needed him. How would the farm survive without him?

The recruiting soldier at the table glanced at her. "Do you own this slave?"

"Aye." Her voice quivered.

"And do ye agree to release this Negro to his freedom to fight in the Continental Army in Rhode Island's 1st Regiment?"

"Aye."

"Then sign here, ma'am."

She took the quill in her trembling hand, dipped it into the inkpot, and signed her name. Tears kept her from seeing if her signature was legible.

"Give the quill to the Negro and have him sign his *X* right here."

Outrage at the inference steeled Lydia's back upright. "His name is Ezekiel, and he can sign his name as well as you can, sir."

The soldier's eyes opened wide. "Beg yer pardon, ma'am."

Ezekiel took the pen from her, dipped it into the pot of ink, and signed his name with a flourish. He even made a definitive point of dotting the *i* in his name. He handed the pen back to the soldier and turned away when the discussion of a money exchange began.

"Certain sure this Negro should bring ye 120 shillings once he passes muster. The State of Rhode Island will pay ye handsomely for the sale."

Lydia shuddered. It took every ounce of her strength to refrain from screaming. Humans sold for blood money. She lowered her gaze and tried in vain to silence the voices in her head, accusing her, taunting her, calling her the Judas she knew she was.

Turning away, she hurried out the door.

3

Micah could barely keep from staring at Mrs. Saunders to be certain she fared well. He'd watched Cuff help her, awkward with child, as she struggled to climb into the carriage before the widow waved a final farewell to Ezekiel.

Had she waved to Micah as well? He probably imagined it. Although he reassured her Ezekiel would be watched over by him personally, Micah understood the ever-present dangers of war. There were no assurances Ezekiel would be protected from any and all harm.

Besides that, Micah, along with the other sergeants and officers, oversaw an entire regiment—200 men. They needed to muster these men into soldiers capable of surviving on a battlefield. As he scrutinized the undisciplined and stoop-shouldered men, Micah shook his head. Training these former slaves into battle-ready soldiers would require all their resources and patience.

His stomach roiled at the occasional revealing of a horribly scarred brand on the shoulder and chest of many of the slaves. "Branded like farm animals," he muttered under his breath.

Almost worse than the brands were the unseen scars that

kept the colored men from meeting the eyes of the officers and sergeants. Accustomed to submitting to their white masters, they'd been cowed into subservience.

This must change first. These men were military now. If they were to pass muster, they needed to learn drills and marches and how to handle their weapons. They needed to believe they were men with the confidence to stand off against another man of any shade of skin. They also must be free in their minds to proudly face off against any enemy. In their hearts, they must become free men.

～

AFTER SHE RETURNED HOME, Lydia slowly emerged from the carriage with Cuff's assistance. Hannah hurried out the front door to help her indoors. Her eyes held a thousand questions, but Hannah remained silent. Lydia was grateful she didn't have to fill in any details just now.

Comfort ran toward her mother.

"Dear, please go inside. 'tis still too cold to forget your cloak. I'll come with you indoors."

Her daughter's presence reminded her of the message she had yet to convey. The thought of telling Comfort her father would ne'er return tore at her soul. Would Comfort fully understand at this tender age? Death was so permanent, but her four-year-old lived in the day-to-day.

How would she understand what it meant that Papa would never come back to her? Never hold her or read a story to her again? For a moment, Lydia wished she were four again and did not understand the finality of death. But she remembered what she had discovered at the age of four. She breathed in deeply, then fought back the panic her haunting memory always elicited. Would that nightmare never cease?

Lydia forced her thoughts back to the present and put her

arm around her daughter's shoulder. Drawing the child indoors, she removed her cloak and hung it on the coat tree.

"Comfort, let us sit in the parlor together and talk."

Comfort's eyes danced with anticipation. "Can we read from a book together, Mama?"

"Of course, dear one." Lydia smiled, but her eyes were moist

They snuggled into the settee that Jeremiah had bought her for a wedding gift.

"I love this chair. Papa gave you this chair, did he not?"

"Aye, Comfort, he did."

Tears rolled down her cheeks, and Comfort's eyes narrowed when she stared at her mother.

"What is wrong, Mama?" Comfort placed her small hand on Lydia's face and smoothed away the moisture.

"Those soldiers who came here, Comfort. They came to tell us some news." Lydia sniffed sharply, and her lips contorted with the pain of revealing it. "Papa got very sick at the war camp. So sick, he died of a terrible fever."

"I had a fever once." Comfort cocked her head to the side. "What is died?"

"He ... cannot get better. God took him to heaven. We can't see him anymore. At least, not here on earth."

Tears emerged in Comfort's eyes. "He can't get better?"

"No, my dear love. Sometimes, our bodies are not strong, and we have to go to heaven instead of coming home to those we love."

"But I want Papa home."

"I know. I wish more than anything Papa could come home."

She held Comfort for a time while they both cried. When her daughter stopped, Lydia brushed the child's hair to the side. She picked up Comfort's small hand and placed it on her swollen belly. "Your Papa left us a gift, Comfort."

Comfort sniffed. "A gift?"

"Aye. Your father left us a wee baby to cherish. In a few

months, we shall get to love and hold a new little one. A gift from Papa."

The unborn child greeted Comfort with a healthy kick. She gasped. "Is that the wee baby?"

"Aye, Comfort." Lydia grinned. "That is exactly what you felt. Your new brother or sister was saying 'hello.'"

Comfort smiled, but her lips trembled. "I still want Papa to come home."

"Aye." She wrapped her arms around her daughter and hugged her. "Aye, Comfort. I truly wish that as well."

Lydia did not know how long they sat together, but Comfort fell asleep snuggled next to her. She refused to think about Jeremiah never coming home, nor how the farm would survive without Ezekiel, nor whether Ezekiel would return safely from the war.

All she wanted to think about at this moment was her children and the joy that stirred within her whenever she felt Jeremiah's child move within her womb. She would not allow the memories of the past, nor the worries of the present, to overcome the happiness this future gift birthed in her heart. She would cling to this hope in these desperate times, even if it seemed she clung to a rope on the verge of fraying.

As he'd promised, Micah started a letter to Lydia Saunders, for she'd begged him to let her know how Ezekiel fared. To keep her apprised of Ezekiel's well-being seemed simple enough. But penning a note to the winsome Mrs. Saunders stirred unfamiliar sensations in Micah—unbidden and pleasurable. He'd been able to keep this attraction hidden while he conducted business the last few days.

Yet now, as he sat by the campfire in the Massachusetts woods, he felt helpless to express ordinary sentiments that would hide the deeper excitement her presence elicited in his heart. When he thought about Lydia, he envisioned her glorious light-brown hair, the scent of lavender that emanated from her presence, and the soothing tone of her voice that enraptured him.

He'd become smitten with Lydia Saunders in a mere three-days' time. And this woman was with child and mother to a four-year-old. Not to mention, a widow—wife to a favorite officer, now deceased. An officer who'd provided a home for her that Micah could only dream about.

He shook his head in disgust, crumpled up the blank paper, and threw it into the fire.

"Can I join you?" Henry Bearslayer sat beside him on another rock.

"Sure." Micah raked tense fingers through his long hair.

"You are disturbed."

A man of few words, Henry rarely discussed feelings. His heritage as a Narragansett Indian exuded strength and bravery. It also discouraged most small talk with others. Micah had tried to involve him in conversation many a time, but Henry hesitated to engage in friendship. Yet this dependable and loyal soldier elicited deep trust in Micah.

While Henry's manner could be a conundrum, Micah would rather serve alongside him than many white soldiers. But, Henry's timing to visit irritated Micah. He'd rather be alone today and avoid small talk.

"It's the woman, isn't it?"

Henry's unexpected observation took Micah by surprise. He stared at the fire, then took a stick and drew lines in the dirt.

"When a woman captures a man's heart, the ropes she ties around his affections leave scars on a man's face." The Indian gave a rueful smile. "You may think you hide your feelings for her. But others can see your pain."

"Is it that obvious?" Micah wiped his palm across his face.

"Perhaps only to another who carries similar scars." Henry patted him on the arm. "I only know this because my heart was once imprisoned by one who was not free to love me. She belonged to a white man in New York."

Micah's mouth dropped open. "Why did you ne'er tell me before? We've served together these many months, and I ne'er knew."

"There is a time when one is wiser not to speak. At other times, one speaks when there is a wounded brother who needs help. You are wounded, but your situation is not without hope. Take comfort in that."

Without another word, Henry stood and returned to his tent.

Not without hope? Perhaps Henry did not understand the ways of the white man and their system of wealthy versus poor. But the man did understand the ways of a man and a woman. And in that, Micah found comfort.

4

The arrival of Lydia's Loyalist mother always sent her into a panic. Today's unexpected visit elicited even more distress. Lydia must face her, both newly widowed and very pregnant. She had not informed her mother of either situation.

Rarely did Octavia Warnock visit the Saunders's home without stirring anxiety in the entire household. Even the usually outgoing Comfort would sit quietly by Lydia's side. Instructed by Lydia, the child was polite, but the brash voice and stern manner of her grandmother frightened Comfort. Lydia understood. Octavia Warnock had never excelled in the ability to show affection, and her visit today filled Lydia with foreboding.

Likely, her brother-in-law had informed the family about Jeremiah's death as well as the upcoming birth.

So, when Lydia's mother arrived in a cloud of dirt stirred up by her carriage, Lydia had trouble re-focusing on spring planting.

"Well then, Miriam and Cuff. I had hoped to help you start planting corn and beans this warm day, but I suppose I must greet my mother."

"We can manage, Mrs. Saunders." Miriam glanced at Lydia with a sympathetic expression.

"Thank you." Lydia walked somberly toward the house, dreading this unexpected encounter.

Despite the day's brightness, Lydia's mother brought a shadow over the household that darkened every room she entered. Lydia braced herself for the storm clouds as she emerged from the back door into the parlor. She forced a smile. "Hello, Mother."

Octavia's eyes narrowed at her daughter's large belly. "So. I see you have been quite preoccupied, Lydia. Apparently, too preoccupied to let your mother know that, not only are you a widow, but you are carrying someone's child."

Fury seared through Lydia. "This is my husband's child. How dare you insinuate otherwise!" Her breathing quickened so fast, she plopped into a chair and concentrated on inhaling slowly lest she faint.

"Tsk. What else should I presume with your rebel husband far away?" Octavia brought out a Chinese fan and whisked it in front of her face.

Calm yourself. Lydia managed a strained smile. "Did it not occur to you that the Continental officers are given a furlough now and then? Jeremiah came home October last."

"What?" Her mother ceased moving the fan. "And you did not let me know he'd come home?"

"Truly, Mother?" Lydia narrowed her eyes. "You think I'd let your Tory-sympathizing friends know my husband was here? You know me better than that."

Octavia did not answer but glanced at her lap. Opening her silk reticule, her mother drew out a piece of jewelry. "Well, despite our differences in political matters, I am sorry your husband died." Her voice softened. "Here, I brought you a mourning ring to wear."

The chair legs creaked as Lydia stood then walked toward her mother. She didn't wish her mother to see her cry. But the gift of the mourning ring sealed Jeremiah's coffin in a new and gut-wrenching way. Her mouth contorted as she fought the eruption of emotions. Taking the silver ring from her mother's arthritic fingers, Lydia slipped it on her right hand. Mother still wore her own.

Sniffing sharply, Lydia composed herself. "It's been nearly five years since Father died. Yet, you still wear yours."

Her mother looked to the side and twisted the ring on her hand. "Aye. I find I cannot remove it."

You would if you knew.

Lydia shook the thought away and returned to her chair. Hannah came in and offered to bring coffee and biscuits.

"Yes, thank you, Hannah."

After she left, Octavia glared at her daughter. "Why do you do that?"

"Do what?"

"Treat your slaves with courtesy and pretend they are like us?"

Breathe easy, Lydia. "Because, Mother, they *are* like us. Their skin is merely darker."

Her mother thrust out of her chair, far faster than Lydia imagined she could. "They are slaves and should be treated as such. You act as if they are part of our family, and you must stop this at once."

Heat rose in Lydia's face. "You would treat them as less than human. I regard them as fellow humans made in the image of God! I have seen how you and father handled your slaves. You treat them far worse than animals. And father—" She stopped. Her heart pounded so quickly she feared she would be ill.

"And your father, what? You think I am not aware of your father's appetites for Negro women?"

Lydia's eyes widened in horror. "You knew?" She could barely get the words out. Her mouth dried, and she gripped the arms of the chair.

"I did not always know." Her mother looked down at her lap

33

then glanced up at Lydia. "Perhaps you did not remember when your father started sleeping in his own bedchamber. I told you 'twas because he snored."

Moisture rolled down Lydia's cheeks. "Mother, I am so sorry."

Octavia shrugged her shoulders. "'Twas neither here nor there to me. I already had you and Phila, and I experienced contentment. More contentment, truly, with your father in another chamber."

The baby turned in Lydia's belly, and she grabbed onto the moving child. Her stomach roiled from this conversation. How much did her mother know?

"I see your husband managed to serve his needs while home such a short time. And now you must bear the consequences of his lust."

"His lust?" Another wave of heat overcame her face. "'Twas our love that brought us together." She looked with sadness at her mother, who still mourned. And for an unfaithful husband? Lydia could not fathom this, nor would she ever understand her mother.

"So, tell me, Lydia. How did you know about your father?"

"Mother, please." Lydia's head swam. "I'm not feeling well." She grabbed the bell that would draw Hannah to the room and rang it.

Hannah rushed in. "Mrs. Saunders. Are you not well?"

"I fear my presence has once again upset my daughter." Octavia stood with her cane. "I shall see myself out."

"Please, Hannah." Lydia held onto her head, which throbbed an incessant beating. "Help me to my room."

Hannah wrapped her arms around her and guided her up the staircase. She brought Lydia to the bed and helped lift her legs.

"I'll send for the doctor, Mrs. Saunders." Hannah stroked her head with a tender touch before racing out the door.

Dear Hannah. A mulatto woman, more mother to me than my own.

She opened her eyes long enough to look at the image of a

weeping willow and an urn on the mourning ring. Her lips quivered, and she cried herself to sleep.

~

LYDIA AWOKE to the gentle pressure of Dr. Caldwell's hand on her face. His cool fingers soothed the flames of heat simmering on her head. Hannah brought a damp cloth and laid it on her forehead.

"Mrs. Saunders, I think it best you restrict your visitors to more ... congenial callers. Perhaps you might consider it orders from your physician." The doctor's wrinkled face broke into a grin, exposing well-worn teeth that befit his age.

Lydia knew Dr. Caldwell wished he could serve the soldiers in Washington's Army. But his age exempted her beloved physician from participating in the war camps. Although he expressed discontent with the situation, Lydia thanked God for his medical knowledge here in Bristol. She took comfort in his fatherly care.

"I understand, Dr. Caldwell." Lydia did not have the strength to argue. "I had not received any message from her stating her intent to visit. 'Twas unexpected."

Dr. Caldwell rolled his eyes. "I quite understand. But I insist you take care of yourself—and this wee one. Your husband would want it that way." He gave a sad smile. "I'm so sorry about his loss. Jeremiah was a good man."

"Aye." She glanced around the room. "Where is Comfort?"

Hannah grinned. "Soon as she saw her grandmother arrive, she high-tailed it to the barn to help Cuff and Miriam with the seeds. She and Rose have been playing in there ever since."

"Thank you, Hannah." Lydia exhaled and relaxed into the pillow. "And Dr. Caldwell."

He stood and gathered his haversack, filled to the brim with the tools of his trade and a few medicinals. "Hannah tells me you've been working way too hard since you freed Ezekiel. I

35

can't say I disagree with your decision, but I do fear you've taken on more than you can handle. You need to get more rest with Jeremiah's child on the way."

"I know. I'll try."

"I'll see if I can find some boys in town who can help you with the farm labor. Take some of the burden off you for a bit." He patted her arm.

"Thanks, Doctor Caldwell."

The elderly man hobbled out the door and slowly made his way down the stairs.

"See? I told you you was working too hard." Hannah grinned. "And now, I have the good doctor on my side." She turned to leave.

"Hannah, can you bring the box of letters to me that are in my top drawer?"

"They be letters from your husband, no doubt. If readin' 'em will keep you in bed, you can read them all day if you want." Hannah opened the drawer and located the stack tied together with a string. She carried them to Lydia then quietly left the room and closed the door.

Lydia stared at the folded parchment, still unopened after more than a month. Had she been too busy with work on the farm to open them? Or could it be fear of facing Jeremiah's final words that kept her from reading them?

Regardless of the reason, she untied the bundle and tenderly opened the first missive. Written in January, Jeremiah told of the numbers of soldiers smitten with illnesses of one sort or another. He spared her from the extent of the ailments plaguing the troops, although they were obviously serious. She dropped the letter to her lap and sighed, fighting yet another urge to cry.

Jeremiah's written words were fraught with concern for the state of the troops, despairing that many of the soldiers would end their commitment to the army come the turn of the New Year. Where would the new recruits be found, he wondered.

You did not know about the black regiment, dear husband. *And your friend, Ezekiel, who would offer to take your place.*

She sat and wiped her nose. The clean kerchief she found on her bedside table seemed unfamiliar. She looked at it more closely, realizing it belonged to Sergeant Hughes. Hannah must have laundered it and given it back to her.

Lydia lay back down and continued to read the letters, searching for words of intimacy she could cling to. But Jeremiah must have kept his thoughts to himself about his affections for her. Why did he not express it more?

She finally reached the letter he'd written shortly after his furlough of October last. More forthcoming about his love for her, he wrote that he wished they'd had more time together during his leave. He hoped they might resume their passions they'd known before he first left for Washington's Army in 1776. She sat up.

In 1776?

What about the passion they shared on their last night together? She knew Jeremiah had been somewhat drunk on wine that evening. But did he truly not remember the intensity of their love-making that night?

She read and re-read that letter, yet she could discover no recollections written of their ardor that night. Her heart sank. Had the wine diminished his memory of the bliss he experienced? Or was it merely one-sided, a thrilling memory for her alone?

Lydia lay down again and held the letter against her unborn child. She would never forget.

But what if she had told Jeremiah that she was with child and he did not recall their passion? Hot tears stung her eyes that he might think her unfaithful to him. She dabbed at them with Sergeant Hughes's handkerchief. If so, he might have accused her of the very betrayal her own mother had assumed.

For the first time since she'd heard of his death, gratitude for her decision to keep the child a secret filled her.

Jeremiah. Did you not remember?

5

M icah Hughes wondered which soldiers posed the greater difficulty—the new slave recruits or the common soldiers already a part of the 1st Rhode Island regiment? Tension between the groups could be sliced through with a bayonet. The black soldiers were separated from the whites by companies to decrease potential problems.

This assignment would be the greatest challenge of Micah's military career. Why was *he* chosen? He understood the general's choice of Corporal Bearslayer, recently promoted from Private, with his mixed heritage and understanding of racial tensions. But him?

Just a Yankee farmer from Connecticut, Micah's experience with a hunting musket and farm tools prepared him for hard work. What did he know about helping men of different colors get along? He was in over his head. The heated tempers that flared on more than one occasion were akin to working with a flame next to a barrel of gunpowder. Men could explode at any moment.

"So, when do we go back to marchin', Sergeant? Iffin' you don't mind me askin'?"

The weary eyes of Private Ralston entreated him for a break from the constant drills each day.

"Tomorrow, we march to Quidnesset and do a bit of buildin.' From there, we go to a remote place where we'll stay a week or two. Maybe three."

Private Ralston's face broke into a smile. "True enough? Time for furlough?"

"Hardly. How long you been in, Private?"

"Near three weeks now, sir."

"Three weeks?" Micah shook his head slowly. This new recruit tried his patience. "Ralston, I've been in two years and have *never* had furlough." Disgust seethed through his teeth.

The young private's Adam's apple bobbed, and his eyes widened. His skin turned paler than his own.

He was just a boy—a boy whose owner held his indenture. He'd been sent off to war, so the landowner didn't have to join up.

Micah cleared his throat. "Never mind. Go get some rest. You'll be up before dawn."

Ralston narrowed his eyes. "Aye, sir." He spun around and returned to his tent.

The young soldier had it tougher than many. His white skin didn't fit in with the black recruits, but neither did the seasoned soldiers accept him. Micah would have to watch out for him 'til he found his way. He covered his eyes and rubbed his aching head. What prickled at his spirit so much? What was wrong with him?

Usually calmer and level-headed, Micah wasn't annoyed so easily, especially by a new recruit who needed encouragement. He'd best get his feelings in check before he faced the dreaded orders of General Washington. The general required all new recruits in the Continentals to be immunized against smallpox— a sickening mess of an order.

After the regiment built a guardhouse in Quidnesset tomorrow, leaving sentinels behind to guard against the enemy, they'd search deep into the woods to find a hidden location where they could build some cabins. Once there, the camp physician would begin the tedious and painful process of inoculating the new men against smallpox.

It would take many days before the men would recover enough to no longer be contagious. These would be days of fever and vomiting, along with eruptions of ugly pustules on the skin. Remembering the stench of the pus during his own inoculation gripped Micah with nausea.

The worst of the variolation would be the almost certain loss of one or more men. And no wonder. After the physician cut through the skin on the recruit's arm, he forced the putrid substance gleaned from a suffering victim's pox under the healthy person's skin. A few soldiers would succumb to the whole process, while others were assured of immunity for life.

Although Micah knew the process ensured the army's overall health, it seemed a terrible price to be paid by the few. He hoped Ezekiel would not be counted in that number. How could he ever inform Lydia Saunders of yet another loss? He'd rather die than hurt her again.

MICAH TRIED HARD NOT to hover over Ezekiel, but the sergeant cringed at the site of the man. For one so muscular and healthy, the smallpox vaccination assaulted Ezekiel in a most cruel manner. All of the men bore eruptions of pustules on their skin, some more than others. All had some fever. But Ezekiel had more pox than most, and his fever was relentless.

Local women who'd already had the pox, or who had been immunized, tended the very ill. One nurse refused to touch the black men. Micah glared at her, grabbed the linen cloth and basin of water from her hand, and applied the cool compresses to the feverish foreheads.

One Negro patient opened his eyes and stared at Micah in surprise. "No need to tend me, Sergeant."

Micah grinned through the exasperation elicited in him by the nurse. "Always wanted to be a physician. Guess I missed my calling." He winked.

"Grateful, sir." The man closed his eyes again.

Days turned into a week, then two. Most of the men were back on their feet, playing card games to while away the time. Only a handful of the recruits still suffered, and the physician did his best to stave off the fever with medicinals.

Micah approached the doctor and spoke in a low voice. "Is there nothing more to be done for these men?"

Weariness etched itself in the man's countenance. He sighed. "I've already done all I can. We need the Great Physician to do the rest."

Micah held back his frustration. He walked outside, folded his arms, and stared at the trees overhead. They were just beginning to emerge with green buds. April had arrived, a time to celebrate new life. Yet he feared the life of some of these men would soon end. He didn't know whether to be exasperated with God or plead with Him for healing. Especially for Ezekiel.

The cabin door opened, and the physician walked up behind him. "I noticed you seemed concerned about that large black man. Ezekiel?"

"Aye?" Micah unfolded his arms and put his hands on his hips, expecting the worst.

He gave a relieved smile. "I think he'll recover. He made a turn." "Wish I could say that about the other three." The doctor turned around, sighed with exhaustion, and limped back to the cabin.

For the first time in many days, Micah inhaled a deep breath. *Thank You.*

∽

MICAH HELD the spoon in front of Ezekiel, who remained as weak as a child. "Come on. Eat."

Ezekiel grabbed the spoon from him and sat up slowly. "I can do this myself."

"Good. Then I needn't nursemaid you." He sat back in the chair by Ezekiel's cot and folded his arms, grinning.

Ezekiel's eyes narrowed. "What are you grinning about?" He sipped the soup.

"Allow me a moment to feel superior in strength to you." He put his hands in his lap. "I know it won't last for long, but I'm enjoying it while it's true. Until you're back to your normal weight, that is."

"It'll be quicker than you think, Sergeant."

"I've no doubt." Micah rubbed his hands together then leaned forward. "Soon as the doctor says it's safe, you can write a letter to Hannah. Don't want to send any contagion her way. But I'm sure she'll want to know you're well."

"Thank you, Sergeant. I'm beholden to you." Ezekiel met his eyes. "Maybe you could write to Mrs. Saunders and let her know I'm well. And that you're well too."

Micah paused. "I'm certain Hannah will pass along the message to her."

"Maybe. But maybe she'd want to hear from you too."

"Why?" He harrumphed. "I've nothing special to add to the message."

Ezekiel's eyes darkened. "She be needin' friends. I know you think she's just some wealthy lady who has everything she needs. But you're wrong. She has a heart to love people, but she has ghosts from her past that haunt her. You don't know."

Micah swallowed past the lump in his throat. "What do *I* have to offer her?"

"Hope." Ezekiel's eyes bore into Micah's. "She needs to know those nightmares of her past don't have to live in her mind forever. She needs to be free—to love again. Mr. Saunders is gone now. He was a fine man who loved her. But she needs

43

someone to protect her. Protect her children. And tell her—tell her those nightmares weren't her fault."

"Her fault?" Micah's brows furrowed. "Why are you telling me this, Ezekiel?"

"Because, Sergeant Hughes, I saw the way you looked at Mrs. Saunders. And I sensed how you was feeling for her whenever she be near you. Like she was some rare jewel you wanted to treasure, even though she seemed out of your reach. But even jewels can have scars. And scarred treasures can easily break, even when they look to be strong."

"I'll think about your words, Ezekiel." He turned to the side. "I need to get back to work." He stood.

Ezekiel grasped his arm. "Please, think about what I said."

"I shall."

As he left the cabin to get fresh air and sit by the campfire, Micah contemplated Ezekiel's confusing words. What ghosts from her past plagued Lydia Saunders? She seemed capable and kind, and even a knowledgeable manager in control of her family farm. How could fears beset such a lovely vessel?

Yet, Ezekiel knew her well. A 'scarred treasure,' he'd called her. Micah shivered from the cold and pulled his woolen coat tighter around his torso. The thought of Lydia being a vessel in danger of shattering didn't seem to fit. At the same time, it sent a wave of fear through his heart. He desperately wished he could shelter her from whatever fears threatened to break her. If only he knew how.

6

E zekiel's words lingered more deeply in Micah's mind
than he wanted. He'd finally reached an agreement with
his heart to stop dwelling on Lydia Saunders and the
feelings she evoked in him. But he could not forget Ezekiel's
troubling phrases. 'She needs friends. Ghosts from her past
haunt her.'

Micah could not understand how a woman of such means
could be without friends and on the verge of breaking. What
mystery lay behind the nightmares that filled her with guilt?

The campfire had nearly extinguished. He'd best stop
thinking about writing and actually write the letter. After
grabbing a stick, he stirred the glowing coals, then added more
wood. Inhaling deeply, Micah straightened out the parchment
that had wrinkled in his tightened fingers and dipped the quill in
a small pot of ink he'd set on the ground.

How should he address her? My dear Mrs. Saunders? Too
personal. Mrs. Saunders? That sounded too curt. How about
simply, Dear Mrs. Saunders? That sounded better. Not too
abrupt yet not overly personal.

He had to think through this letter before actually writing
the missive, lest he crumple away his remaining supply of paper.

Exhaling forcefully, he put quill to paper. Once he'd decided on the salutation, the rest seemed less difficult.

Micah first inquired about her health and told her he prayed she and her children were well. He started to ask if the unborn child continued to kick in a lively manner, but he realized that might be too personal a question.

You are so daft, Micah Hughes.

Next, he told her that Ezekiel fared well and appeared to be immunized against the smallpox. He explained that all the new recruits must be inoculated and that, while Ezekiel had been quite ill for a time, he had fully recovered and now ate hearty meals.

The troops were getting on better after the many days of isolation and illness, he wrote. Sickness from the pox inoculation seemed to draw the men into a spirit of camaraderie. He was grateful for it.

Micah paused in his writing. Now what? Just be friendly, Sergeant.

Here goes.

I pray all is well in Bristol and that you are not working too hard on the farm. I'm certain Cuff and the women should be able to manage the heavier chores. Please be kind to yourself as you have been so kind to others. And please thank your daughter, Comfort, for tending my scar whilst I visited your home. Tell her it still feels better.

Your humble servant,
Sergeant Micah Hughes

~

LYDIA WIPED the moisture from her forehead as she strode back into the cool barn. Unsure how long she'd been in the field, bending over and planting seeds, her back told her it was likely longer than she should have been.

"Mrs. Saunders!" Hannah entered the barn, hands on hips.

"Why you be working so hard outdoors? Dr. Caldwell would be scolding you for certain sure. Go back in the house, please, ma'am. You have this baby to think about."

Too weary to argue, Lydia knew the truth of Hannah's words. But she somehow needed to keep this farm going and grow enough food for winter. All of them depended on it. She grasped the water dipper from the edge of the rain barrel and swallowed a generous portion of the cool liquid.

She stared outdoors at Cuff and Miriam in the fields. They already worked long hours each day, except Sabbath. Someone had to help them. Though Dr. Caldwell tried to get help from the families in town, there weren't many boys available for fieldwork. The war still raged on, and planting season would not wait.

Dust arose down at the end of the road. Lydia paused to look, shielding her eyes from the bright sun with her hands.

"Is that Miz Phila's carriage, ma'am?"

All of Lydia's muscles tensed at once. "I'm afraid so, Hannah."

Hannah shook her head and walked back to the house, mumbling under her breath.

Lydia's younger sister, Phila, decimated the joy from every person she pretended to like. While some people had a gift to make others welcome in their presence, Phila used her web of deceit to draw in the naïve with pleasantries, and then impale them with her prickled tongue.

While Lydia considered Phila the comelier of the two sisters, her loveliness reached merely skin-deep—a ruse, as it were, to entrap others to her beauty, devour them, then spit out the victims who were too stunned to know what happened. Lydia knew all too well that Phila only kept around those who served her purposes. Until she tired of them, that is. The only one who'd survived Phila's predatory jaws was Phineas.

But even her husband appeared scarred and consumed from sharing a home with her. Lydia supposed the only reason her sister had remained with him all this time was because Phila would never leave the second-wealthiest owner of slave ships in the county. Selling humans had filled Phineas's coffers with enough gold to satisfy even Phila's appetite. And she devoured the blood money with relish.

As the carriage approached in a swirl of dust, her sister frowned at the work clothes Lydia wore. The carriage stopped so close to Lydia, she didn't have to move to have a conversation with her sister.

"You look a disgrace. Why are you not allowing the slaves to do this labor? Have you forgotten yourself?" Phila's perfect features grew uglier with each word she spoke.

Lydia smiled pleasantly. "And good day to you, as well, sister. Would you like some coffee in the parlor?"

Phila scrunched her nose in distaste. "I will take tea, thank you kindly."

"Well then, Phila, you will have to visit our mother to find East India tea to quench your thirst. Here we have coffee, and you are welcome to it. Do come inside, if you like."

She covered her nose with her kerchief. "And suffer your fetid clothing from working in the fields? You must think me mad."

Lydia wanted to agree but held her tongue.

"I see that what Phineas told me is true." Phila looked around at the fields where Cuff and Miriam worked. "You no longer own that large slave, do you? If Father were still alive, he would take back this farm from you and give it to me so it would be run properly."

Her eyes darkened as her teeth threatened like a rabid dog's. "But no. Father always gave you everything you wanted. You were his prize daughter, while he all but ignored my wants. You, the *favored* daughter. I wonder what he would say to your farming abilities if he were here. Mother has already spoken to her lawyer, you know."

A chill swept over Lydia. "Her lawyer? Pray tell, about what?"

Her sister sniffed in disgust. "What do you think? About the wretched management of this property by an inept widow who manages to find herself with child the moment she finds a man to her liking."

She slapped Phila across her cheek so hard that redness emerged before Lydia realized what she'd done. But she didn't care.

"How dare you? You of all women, would accuse me of this barbarism? Of adultery? This is Jeremiah's child! Now get out!" She pointed a shaky hand toward the road from which Phila had come.

Hannah hurried from the house toward Lydia, glared at Phila, and put her arm around Lydia's shoulder.

Phila tapped the roof of the carriage, sat back in a huff, and rubbed at her cheek.

Once the wagon disappeared, Lydia burst into tears.

"Come inside, Mrs. Saunders. I'll get you some cider."

Lydia would not have had the strength to walk the few rods back to the house without Hannah's support. Tears blinded her as she followed Hannah's prompts to take each step.

"Come into the parlor, Mrs. Saunders. You can put your feet up on the settee and rest."

She allowed Hannah to lift her legs onto the furniture. She closed her eyes and slept for a few moments. When she stirred, the servant handed her a glass of cider.

Lydia sipped the sweet liquid and closed her eyes with pleasure. "Thank you, dear Hannah."

"You are welcome. I—I thought this might cheer you up." She handed Lydia a letter. "This arrived from a post rider this morning while you worked in the field. Maybe a nice letter from Sergeant Hughes will help you forget your troubles. Iffin' it be no trouble for you, I'd like to hear news of Ezekiel." Hannah's eyes widened with anticipation.

Lydia smiled as she took the folded parchment. "Let me glance through it and see how he is." Lydia skimmed across the message from Sergeant Hughes to glean any information about

49

Hannah's beloved. She grinned and looked at Hannah. "Ezekiel is well. And, I am certain, missing you. He will write when he is no longer contagious from the pox inoculation."

Hannah's expression of joy morphed into fear. "Pox inoculation?"

"Aye. All of Washington's recruits are required to be immunized, lest an outbreak of smallpox decimate the regiments."

Hannah's lips quivered.

Lydia reached out to squeeze her hand. "He is well, Hannah."

"Oh. I am so grateful he's all right." Hannah looked down, and large tears dripped onto her apron. She swiped them away angrily. "Look at me cryin' like a baby while you be grievin' your husband. Please forgive me."

"Nothing to forgive, Hannah."

The servant hurried back to the kitchen.

Lydia inhaled a deep breath and slowly rubbed her firm belly. Feeling her unborn child reminded her of her sister's visit. She struggled to calm herself as she remembered Phila's horrid accusation. Of all the women to accuse her of such a sin.

She nearly laughed at Phila's insinuations that Father had loved Lydia more, giving her anything she wanted, even bequeathing the inheritance of the family farm to her. The irony sickened Lydia. Her father had not favored her—he'd tried to buy her off so she would not inform her mother of what she'd seen, of what he'd done.

'Now, you just did not understand what I was doing, did you, Lydia? I tried to help that slave. Let us stop by the sweet shop and get some biscuits to go with your tea, shall we?'

As if biscuits could remove the rancid taste that scene elicited. She remembered everything. The unkempt clothing. The saliva dripping from her father's lips. And that smell.

She shook her head as if to erase the memory. But she had learned through the years that finding a pleasant diversion from the horrid memory helped the most.

The letter from Sergeant Hughes.

Picking it up again, she could now indulge in its contents at leisure. She read: "Dear Mrs. Saunders ..."

Sergeant Hughes must have had a well-trained instructor at his school in Connecticut. Lydia marveled at the flourish he used to create the penmanship. Strong strokes with a quill had written this letter. Not unlike the strength she'd noticed in the man himself. She struggled to recall what the sergeant looked like. She remembered he had long brown hair, usually pulled back in a queue.

Except when he slept in the barn. His looks were not extraordinary, and he had that dreadful scar across his forehead. But his eyes—those were his strongest feature. They were hazel and seemed to change color with his expressions. If eyes were a reflection of the soul, as some said, then Sergeant Hughes must be a trustworthy man. He had the kindest eyes she'd ever seen.

Lydia stared at the fire. She shook herself from her sleepy trance and returned to the letter.

Reading about the smallpox event was difficult. *The poor men.* Then she realized Sergeant Hughes had been through the very same earlier in his enlistment. Her husband had, as well. The military life seemed fitting for the strong in spirit but not the faint of heart. Lydia admired more than ever the soldiers serving America.

While she read, unexpected questions regarding her and her children and their welfare surprised her, though she did not know why. Lydia supposed she'd not expected him to be concerned about her. She just thought he wrote to tell her about Ezekiel.

Then he expressed unease about her working too hard on the farm.

'Twas good he'd not seen me today, or I would have had both him and Hannah scolding me. She giggled. But when she read, 'Be kind to yourself as you have been kind to others,' she nearly laughed at the irony. *I was not particularly kind to my sister today.* But her

laughter quickly morphed into an intense emotion she found difficult to describe.

Her face contorted with his concern. Why did he care? She had so few people in her life who cared about her. Hannah cared, and Jeremiah had cared. Or had he? Even her husband had often seemed more preoccupied with the affairs of war more than the affairs of her heart. She shifted on the settee with embarrassment as she recalled a memory from their last evening together.

Jeremiah had spent so much time speaking with fellow Patriots until the wee hours, Lydia feared he would not spend any time with her in their bedchamber before returning to his regiment the following morning. She gave Jeremiah extra wine and flirted with him as she prepared for bed. It only took a few glasses of the fermented nectar—along with her request that he help her undress—to bring *her* to the forefront of his thoughts.

She'd convinced herself Jeremiah had seduced her. In truth, it had been her ploy. Perhaps that was the real reason she'd not told Jeremiah about the baby. Although nothing to be ashamed of, she'd hoped that Jeremiah cared enough to express his love for her without having to be convinced. Had he cared about her after all?

7

Although tensions in the camp had improved since the smallpox inoculation, Micah watched for any signs of animosity between the black free men in his company and the former slaves. At least they'd separated the white recruits into different companies to keep the strain manageable.

He had already seen the hostility between the companies with white soldiers and black units. But when Corporal Bearslayer approached him with news that a white corporal from another company had struck one of Micah's soldiers, heat arose under his already sweltering uniform. This had to stop. The former slave, not yet eighteen-years-old, had not provoked the assault, according to Henry.

Micah stomped toward the colonel's tent, paused while he inhaled deeply, went through the tent flap, and saluted his superior. "Colonel, sir. We have a problem with one of the corporals."

"At ease, Sergeant." The weary officer paused in his reading. "What seems to be the concern?"

"Corporal Beamon of Company C struck one of my soldiers, Private Wiles. He is a freed slave, sir."

"I wish I could say I was surprised." The colonel exhaled

slowly. "But this animosity must stop, here and now." He stared at the sentinel, who stood at the tent door. "Sergeant Baker, arrest Corporal Beamon, immediately. And place him under guard."

Micah kept his eyes straight ahead, but inside, his pulse raced with relief. Finally, the situation would be dealt with.

"Is that all, Sergeant Hughes?"

"Aye, sir. Thank you, sir." Micah saluted the colonel and left the tent.

Word of this disciplinary action spread through the camp, and the outrage of many men was evident. Some of the soldiers refused the guard to arrest Beamon. Curses erupted from Colonel Daggett. This sedition did the Negro-hating rebellious no favors, as Beamon and the others were confined under guard and put in irons. Within days, under orders from their general, the agitators were discharged from the military.

This action quelled further incidents between the white soldiers and blacks, but an unsteady peace prevailed. Micah wished the hatred in men's hearts could be as easily removed as army members. One could expel the perpetrators, but ill feelings were stubborn residents in the minds of those who refused to believe men of a darker skin color were equal.

At least the general's stance made his point.

HINTS OF SPRING appeared in the woods on this late April day. Otherwise, the day was like all the rest in East Greenwich. The regiment marched. They drilled. They practiced skills that mostly white men had done in the army before. Already impressed with his company's achievements, Micah appreciated their dedication to learning. They were men on a mission to be free.

He was always on the lookout for Ezekiel, who'd been placed in another company. Whenever he saw the man doing maneuvers with a musket, Micah admired his astute abilities. And whenever he saw Ezekiel, he thought of Lydia Saunders. How did she fare? Was she safe? He struggled with regret that his recruitment of her best slave might have put her in danger.

Yet the tide of circumstances that drew Ezekiel into the military felt like an ocean swell no man could have fought against. Try as he might, he wondered how he might have stopped the wave that prodded both Lydia and Ezekiel to make such a choice. The regiment would soon leave Rhode Island. Their upcoming march to Valley Forge would separate Ezekiel from Mrs. Saunders by hundreds of miles.

Deep in thought, Micah barely heard the private running after him.

"Sergeant, sir, a post for you."

He stopped, removed his tricorne hat, and wiped his sleeve across his sweat-covered forehead. He took the folded letter and stared at the sender's address. It stirred his heart to skip a beat. *Lydia.*

"Thank you, Private." He kept his voice steady, but his breathing sped up.

Searching for a place to be alone—a challenge amongst hundreds of soldiers—Micah found a fallen tree not far into the woods and sat. Why were his hands so unsteady? He needed to calm himself.

Opening the carefully folded parchment, he took in the feminine handwriting of its author. So delicate were the strokes of her hand, he imagined her small fingers lightly dipping the long quill into the inkpot and the fragile strokes dancing the ink across the paper. He closed his eyes to imagine it.

"Sergeant?"

He opened his eyes wide and stared at the private.

"Is all well, sir?"

The question from one of his men surprised him. "Well? Aye. I—I believe so. Just resting my eyes a bit, that's all."

The soldier saluted him and strode back to camp.

He must look pathetic. He certainly felt pathetic—like a man living in a dream world. He cleared his throat and held the letter open to read.

Dear Sergeant Hughes,

I am so grateful for you taking the time to apprise me of Ezekiel's situation. I often wonder how he fares and pray for his safety every day. I am most reassured that he survived the application of the smallpox. Hannah was greatly relieved, as well.

We are busy here on the plantation with planting. Hannah scolds me daily if I spend too much time helping Cuff and Miriam. But I am well, as is the child who is expected this summer.

Comfort asks about you and wonders how your scar is doing. I tell her repeatedly that it is healed, and she needn't worry. She has such a tender heart.

Miriam's daughter, Rose, who is also four years of age, keeps Comfort busy with games and dolls and such. The girls get on so well.

I have had visits from both my mother and sister. They both live in the center of Bristol. They did not stay for long.

I fear I am boring you with my tattle, so I must conclude this missive. I pray for you and Ezekiel and all the brave soldiers defending our land. May God watch over you.

Your humble servant,
Lydia Saunders

Micah stared at the open sheet of paper for a long while. He sensed Mrs. Saunders had so much more to say, yet something held her back. Her unspoken words struggled to escape her pen.

Did she work too hard? Could she manage her farm? And why did she say her mother and sister did not stay long?

He remembered the bad blood between Mrs. Saunders and her brother-in-law at the county seat office. With much animosity, she must feel so alone. And now she carried another child. Micah could not imagine her loneliness, especially knowing Jeremiah would not return.

Grateful that Hannah took care of her, he closed his eyes to contemplate the widow's situation. The little that he knew about Lydia Saunders, the more vivid her vulnerability revealed itself. Yet, he felt helpless to do anything about it. One thing he determined to do, however, was write to her more often.

He could interpret what she did not say with her words, but Ezekiel had opened his mind to understand. Lydia Saunders needed friends. Whether or not their relationship ever became more than that, Micah would remain a faithful friend to her. He told himself that, by doing so, he honored the memory of Lieutenant Saunders. If he said it to himself often enough, he might even believe it.

～

LYDIA LAY IN BED, unable to sleep. She was exhausted after working the fields, but her sister's words repeated themselves in her mind.

'Mother has called her lawyer. You are inept at keeping this farm going.'

She sat up in bed. The unborn child's kicks added to her discomfort and restlessness. Lydia stroked her child with soothing fingers as if the babe needed reassurance. *She* did.

What if her mother found legal means to remove her from this plantation? What would she and her children do? Where would Hannah and the other slaves go? They were like family to her—more than her own blood relations. She could never return to her mother's home. Far too many painful memories dwelled there. Not to mention the pain she and her children would endure living with the cold heart of Octavia Warnock.

Had Phila told the truth? Deceitful and untrustworthy, her sister might have made up this story just to upset her. Lydia would never put that past her. Phila thrived on others' turmoil.

There were no answers to be discovered tonight. Lydia would find out soon enough. She wished sleep would take away the throbbing inside her temples.

Lydia focused on the Sabbath, just hours away. It was the one day she could put aside fears about her future and listen to the minister's words. Words of life and encouragement amid the revolution. Where else could one find peace when war surrounded them?

"Mama?" Comfort rolled over and faced her in the bed.

"Yes, my sweet?"

"Are you not well, Mama? Hannah always says you work too hard."

Lydia attempted a smile, although the effort seemed weak. "Hannah just worries too much, that is all."

Her daughter crawled across the bed and snuggled against Lydia. Despite the warm evening, the child's presence brought a sense of well-being. Comfort was appropriately named.

"Can you read me the letter again?"

She grinned. "I've already read Sergeant Hughes's letter to you three times, my dearest." Lydia combed her daughter's hair with her fingers.

"I know. But hearing it makes me feel like my Papa is talking to me."

Lydia's lips contorted, and she sniffed sharply. "Very well. I shall read it. But only once. Then promise me you will go back to sleep."

"I promise, Mama."

"Very well, then."

She reached for the letter she'd kept on the nightstand. The full moon shone through the twelve-paned window, offering sufficient reading light. Lydia took note of the date Sergeant Hughes posted the letter, written on May 2. Lydia read it out loud.

Dear Mrs. Saunders,

I pray all is well with you and your children. It sounds like Hannah is seeing to your needs and ensuring you do not overtax yourself. Do please take care.

By the time you receive this letter, our regiment will have left Rhode Island. I cannot tell you our exact destination since the enemy can intercept missives. Suffice it to say, we will be farther away.

Please let Hannah know that Ezekiel is well, no longer wasted in sinew as he was during his smallpox difficulties. I am certain he could now easily beat me in a wrestling match. But I am too wise to engage him in such. I am certainly glad he is on our side in this war.

The recruits, including Ezekiel, are becoming true soldiers in every way. I am relieved that most have learned their new skills well and should prove themselves proficient in battle.

Please tell Comfort that I think she may be a fine nurse someday. Her skills in tending wounds are exemplary. I've seen many a nurse in camp here who could learn the compassion that she provides so naturally.

I pray all is well with you and the baby. Forgive me if this is too unseemly to discuss with you in a letter. I pray for your well-being.

Your humble servant,
Sergeant Micah Hughes

"Where does he write my name?"

"Right here. See?" Lydia took Comfort's small finger and traced it around the

outline of Sergeant Hughes's script.

"Could I learn to write my name?"

"Aye, and soon I suppose. But right now, dear one, back to bed as you promised."

She hugged her daughter, who grinned and scooted back under the covers. Lydia snuggled her and kissed her cheek.

"Mama?"

"Comfort, only one more question."

"I know. 'Tis not truly a question. I think Sergeant Hughes likes you."

59

Lydia's cheeks burned with heat. "Well, of course, I think he likes me. He is a friend. He was Papa's friend."

"Do you like him?"

Lydia stuttered. "Now, I told you only one question allowed."

Comfort grinned. "'Twas only one question, truly."

Do I like him?

She cleared her throat. "Of course, I like the sergeant. He is a very kind man. Now go to sleep."

Lydia crawled back under the covers and lay on her side. Why did Comfort's questions cause her such unease? And why did she anticipate the sergeant's letters with such earnestness?

She punched at her pillow as if fighting off the tender sentiments that grew in her heart toward Micah. Comfort was just a child, putting ideas in her mother's head. Lydia flopped onto her other side, facing the open window. An owl hooted outside. She'd always loved the sounds the night birds made. Somehow it made her feel less alone.

Could her loneliness lead her into feelings she found difficult to face? How did she truly feel about Sergeant Hughes? She barely knew the man. Then she remembered she'd only met Jeremiah twice before he'd asked her father for her hand. Somehow, they both just knew they had found their mate.

But now, she was older and wiser. And much in life had left her scarred. She would not succumb to her feelings quite so easily. She needed to keep her hedges of self-protection at the ready.

Yet in all of her attempts to reason away any feelings, she could not understand why the thought of Sergeant Hughes leaving Rhode Island left her so bereft of joy. He would be farther away than ever, perhaps in danger.

She closed her eyes and prayed for her family. For Ezekiel and Hannah. For Cuff and Miriam and little Rose.

Most of all, she prayed for Sergeant Micah Hughes, hot tears accompanying her entreaties to heaven.

8

As May grew warmer, Lydia grew more uncomfortable. She couldn't remember being so large at this point in her pregnancy with Comfort. She must send Cuff to fetch the midwife soon to see if all was well.

She ceased working in the fields as the laborious tasks sapped her strength and made her feel ill. Lydia felt frustrated and helpless when Cuff and the two women carried on the work. At least she could watch Comfort and Rose while the others worked outdoors.

Comfort persisted in her desire to learn her letters so she could spell her own name. Rose caught the enthusiasm for schooling, and Lydia enjoyed watching the two girls hold their smaller quills and dip them into the inkwell. Every time they did, Lydia held her breath, lest the inkwell tip over. But the girls had been cautioned, and they were careful.

Pride filled her heart as she watched both Comfort and Rose work hard to perfect their skills. She shivered at the thought Rose might have been sold into slavery had Miriam been bought by anyone else. Her mind transported her to a time four years before—a time she'd rather forget.

Father had wanted to buy Miriam after his last voyage on his slave ship, but Lydia saw something in the young woman's eyes that haunted her. She'd seen that look of fear and pain before. And she saw how her father stared at Miriam and made a large bid to the auctioneer. Horror gripped Lydia at the public scenario taking place. No one else saw it—but she did.

Only this time, Lydia was old enough to do something.

'Jeremiah, please bid on that slave!'

He'd been shocked and looked troubled at her request. 'But your father—'tis obvious he means to purchase her. How can I bid against my own father-in-law?'

'Please, Jeremiah, I beg you. Please trust me. This is most important.'

'But Lydia, it would publicly humiliate him were I to forcefully outbid him!'

'Jeremiah, I'd ne'er ask this of you if I did not know how important this is. Please!' Her eyes pled with him.

'Very well, Lydia. I'd do anything for you. Even if it angers your father.'

After the sale at the wharf, her father glared at her. His fear of public humiliation forced him to appear generous toward his new son-in-law by backing down on the bid. He was livid, but she did not care. He rarely spoke to her after that.

Not long after, someone found him floating in the filthy water near his slave ship. The exact cause of his death was never discovered.

"How does this look, ma'am?" Rose held up her handwriting for Lydia's inspection.

"Well done, Rose."

The child's bright smile shone on her lovely dark skin like sunlight in a storm.

Lydia stroked Rose's cheek with her hand that wore her mourning ring. *Thank you, Jeremiah.*

She leaned her head against the settee's back and nearly fell asleep until a disturbance outside startled her. Comfort and Rose had already run to the window.

"Mama, there is a man outside speaking with Cuff. He's upset. Come see."

Lydia maneuvered her large belly off the settee and sat up. She took in a deep breath and stood. Waddling toward the window, she hurried as quickly as she could. The man speaking with Cuff was certainly upset. He waved his hands and pointed toward the center of Bristol. Lydia recognized her mother's servant, Caesar.

Cuff ran toward the house and opened the front door wide. "Mrs. Saunders. There be trouble in Warren. Caesar says the King's Army may be heading toward Bristol. He fears your mother in danger, but she will not leave. She thinks she is safe from soldiers because she is Loyalist." Cuff struggled to keep up with the message in his broken English.

Mother! How would the king's soldiers know her loyalty to their side? She could be plundered the same as the Patriots.

"Cuff, prepare the carriage."

He ran to the barn.

"Caesar, where did you hear this? About Warren?"

"Some men arrived in Bristol with the warning. Soldiers be burning ships there, even a bridge. Houses plundered, women screaming and running for their lives." Caesar's eyes were wide with fear, and sweat dripped off his face.

"Caesar, get yourself some water and grab the gelding. You can ride with us back to Bristol."

"Mama!" Lydia's daughter clung to her skirts and cried. "Mama, please don't go! The bad men might hurt you." Tears poured down her pale cheeks.

Lydia hugged her tightly. "I'll be fine, Comfort. You stay here and keep Rose company."

"Mrs. Saunders, let me go instead." Hannah hurried toward her from the field. "You are too close to your confinement, Mrs. Saunders. Please, you must take care of yourself and this baby." The look in her eyes pled with her to change her mind.

"I must go, Hannah. She is my mother and ... she may not

know I care about her. I must tell her I do love her and want her to be safe. Perhaps—" She swallowed back tears. "Perhaps she will listen to me."

Cuff brought the carriage around to the steps. He jumped down from the driver's seat and flung open the door.

Lydia tilted Comfort's face to look at her. "Comfort, I promise you, I'll come back as soon as I look after grandmother." She kissed the top of her daughter's russet hair and squeezed her with a trembling grip. "Hannah, please take care of her." She whispered closer to Hannah's ear. "If you see any soldiers, hide in the woods."

Without another word, she stepped into the carriage, praying she would be able to maneuver her legs and belly inside. It seemed a miracle, but she managed to get every bit of her dress and body within the confines of the chaise. Cuff closed the door and jumped back onto the driver's seat as Caesar came astride, bareback on the gelding. The carriage lurched forward, and Lydia grabbed onto her belly.

Her breathing came so rapidly, she prayed she'd not faint. Had the king's soldiers made their way to Bristol? What did they want, save to terrorize the mostly patriot town? She knew full well her mother would not leave. Her naiveté that the king's soldiers would spare her home frustrated Lydia. Did her mother understand so little of the war and the ways of soldiers? Lydia had her fill of their cruelty when in Newport.

Lydia's baby was especially active with the carriage's movement. At times, her belly grew so taut she wondered if she were preparing for birth. But her midwife had assured her this was normal with second or third pregnancies. Still, she prayed she'd not give birth too early. She'd known of women whose infants arrived too soon. She could not lose this last child of Jeremiah's.

Please, God!

The closer they got to the Bristol wharf, the louder the sounds of turmoil arose through the streets. Some people had packed all their goods into wagons and drove by Lydia's carriage as they escaped the city.

The militia gathered, and their captain called out orders before they headed toward the north edge of town. She heard musket fire in the distance. And toward Warren, black smoke rose like a huge funeral pyre. Lydia's heart skipped a beat.

"Hurry, Cuff, hurry!" she yelled out the carriage window.

He flapped the reins faster.

When they arrived at her mother's two-story home with the gambrel roof, Lydia wrestled with the door latch, but it wouldn't budge. Cuff grabbed it and twisted hard.

He used both hands to help Lydia step out. "Please, watch your step, ma'am."

Lydia landed on the ground out of breath and gripped Cuff's arm. "Please take the carriage out back where it will not be visible from the street."

"Yes, ma'am."

Lifting her gown, she waddled toward the steps leading to her mother's mansion.

The door opened, and her mother emerged. "Lydia, what, pray tell, are you thinking? You should not be here. And in your condition!" She walked carefully down the steps to help Lydia climb them. "You did not need to come. I am fine. Even if the troops come here, they'll know I am loyal to the crown. See?" She pointed to the Union Jack flag she'd hung out her upstairs window.

"Mother, that will not protect you." Lydia stared at the Tory flag then looked at her mother, gently gripping her arm. "When the troops come through in a frenzy with the smoke of battle obscuring their vision, one house will seem as mutinous as the next. They will assume we are all insurgents."

Mother stared at Lydia's swollen belly. "Come inside." She helped her daughter into the house. "Please sit here, Lydia."

She did not argue, grateful for the comfort of a chair.

Her mother rang a bell for tea.

"Please, come with me to the farm." Lydia couldn't believe her mother—so calm, as though her world were not about to be shattered. "You will be safe there."

The report of musket shots sounded in the distance, but her mother appeared not to notice.

Lydia gripped the arms on the chair with tense fingers. "Mother, I know we have not been close. But I do care about you and do not wish any harm to befall you. Please."

Octavia Warnock poured Lydia a cup of tea, as though she'd not heard a word.

"Mother!" Lydia pushed herself out of the chair and moved toward the window.

"Really, Lydia, you should be abed in your confinement. Let me have my servant take you to one of the rooms."

"No, Mother! Do you not understand? Soldiers are coming!"

More shots and men shouting could be heard in the distance. A woman screamed.

"Please, my dear." Octavia strode toward Lydia. "I can see you are not comfortable. I want to help you."

"And I wish to help you!" Tears flowed down Lydia's cheeks as she swept her hand toward the door. "You must see and hear that danger is coming. Please leave with me and come to the farm!"

A cannon shot pierced the air. The concussion of the blast forced both Lydia and her mother to cover their ears. For the first time since she'd arrived, Lydia saw concern in her mother's eyes.

Her mother's voice shook. "That was certainly ... close."

"Come with me. Cuff awaits in the carriage out back. I beg you."

The sound of marching feet grew louder, accompanied by drums that shifted the beat of Lydia's heart, forcing it to keep pace. Lydia feared not just for her mother but for her unborn child.

"Let's go out the back." Her mother grabbed her arm.

Between the terror stiffening her legs and the awkward weight of her child, Lydia had difficulty moving forward. Her mother drew her toward the back door, but something shattered a window to the rear of the house. The smell of smoke drifted toward the parlor, and the women's eyes met, dread etched in her mother's expression.

"Mrs. Warnock!" One of the servants entered the parlor, her eyes wide. She breathed far too fast. "The soldiers!" She ran out the front door.

"Come, Lydia."

Her mother pulled her with a stronger force than Lydia could have imagined. She gripped her daughter's arms so tightly, Lydia cringed from the discomfort. But she didn't cry out. She just wanted to escape.

When they neared the front door, their escape to freedom, the portal burst open. The two women screamed. They faced not a soldier in the King's Army, but a German Hessian, one of the dreaded Goliaths of terror, standing before them with squinted eyes. These mercenaries were well-known for their strength and brutality.

He apprised both women clinging to each other. Walking toward Lydia, he stroked his large finger through her hair.

Octavia slapped the man's arm and screamed, "Stay away from my daughter!"

The soldier acted as if her powerful punch were no more than a soft pat. But his whack across Octavia's face sent her tumbling to the floor.

"Mother!" Lydia knelt on the floor and wrapped her arms around her weeping parent and held her close.

Dear God, help us.

9

For a moment, the Hessian ignored the women and looked around the room. Two other German soldiers arrived and spoke with the first man. Lydia couldn't understand one word.

She clung to her mother until one of the men lifted her by one arm, forcing her to stand, and pointed to a large cabinet. He said something in German.

Heart pounding, Lydia tried to show by her outstretched hands that she didn't understand.

He grabbed her arm and squeezed it until she cried out. Speaking through clenched teeth and staring directly into her eyes, he pointed to the top of the china closet.

Lydia stared at the doors of the closet. Since the cabinet was too high for her to reach, she stood on her tiptoes to show them. But the foul-smelling Hessian dragged a wooden chair across the floor and indicated she should climb on it. She attempted but kept losing her balance.

He picked her up and placed her on the chair, his repulsive hands stroking her legs when he did so. Lydia squelched back a sob as the man laughed and made disgusting motions with his hands to his fellow soldiers. Lydia wished with all her might she had a loaded musket in her hands.

Angry words came from the man, and he pointed firmly toward the door of the closet.

She opened her mother's china cabinet then stared at the exquisite dinnerware.

He directed her to hand him the plates and cups. One by one, she carefully handed him each plate. And one by one, the three Hessians took turns smashing the china plates on the floor.

"Do what they say, Lydia. Keep yourself safe." Her mother's weak voice melted into a sob.

Lydia continued to hand the plates to the soldiers. If she slowed, they grew angrier. As the supply dwindled, Lydia feared what might come next. After she handed him the last cup, which they smashed with glee, one of the soldiers peered through the cabinet and grunted. He turned his attention toward her.

Gripping the edge of the cabinet door to keep from falling, she closed her eyes until she felt herself lifted down, again with directed molestation along her legs. Terrorized, she could barely breathe.

More German words, then she felt the man force her rings off her hands. Her wedding ring. Then her mourning ring. Lydia opened her eyes as the soldiers slipped the jewelry inside wide openings at the tops of their boots. Next, they took off her mother's rings, but her wedding band was stuck behind her thickened joints. Her mother cried when they drew out their bayonets.

"Wait!" Lydia ran toward her mother and met her terrified eyes. "This may hurt, but I'll do it as gently as I can." The debilitation in her aging fingers prevented her mother from removing her wedding band for years. Lydia carefully twisted and turned the jewelry, spitting saliva onto her mother's fingers to provide lubrication.

Octavia closed her eyes tightly and moaned.

Finally, the ring slipped free. Lydia held it up to the soldier, who grabbed it from her.

"Thank you, dear." Her mother whispered. Pain reflected in each word.

Lydia gripped her mother's fingers and stroked them.

The soldier pulled Lydia upright again and stared at her décolletage. She squeezed her eyes shut.

A voice and the crack of a whip were so close to her own face that the rush of air swept against her own skin.

The Hessian fell to the floor, his cheek sliced open. He grabbed his face and looked with terror at a British officer, who yelled orders in German to the three men. They ran outside.

The officer walked to her mother and helped the middle-aged woman to her feet. Then, he led her to a chair, where she collapsed.

He stared at Lydia's belly, turned red in the face, and assisted her to a settee.

"I must express my regrets, dear ladies." Tipping his tricorne hat, he turned and left.

Lydia shivered and could not stop.

Her mother walked to the tea tray and added sugar and a dollop of cream to the cup that still stood, undisturbed. She carried it to Lydia and encouraged her to drink.

Lydia could not recall the last time she'd tasted tea, but she needed sustenance, and she would not refuse it now. After she guzzled the lukewarm liquid, she looked around the room.

"Mother, let's get out of here."

She heard no objections this time, and they headed out the front door.

The smoke from whatever had burned in back of the house had diminished. Lydia's mother helped her down the steps, and they headed for the side drive. Lydia expected to find Cuff. No carriage or servant could be seen.

"Cuff." She whispered his name, praying he'd been safe. How could they possibly escape?

"Come, Lydia." Her mother hurried her along the street darkened by spent gunpowder and the burning building across the way. The women covered their faces with kerchiefs and looked for a safe place to run. The home of Colonel Simeon Potter burned, but the women did not stop. Lydia barely had the energy to keep moving.

Suddenly, her mother stopped and covered her mouth with her other hand. "St. Michael's!" She pointed in the distance, where the Church of England was engulfed in fire.

Lydia's mother and sister were members, but the building hadn't been used since the war began. The women both stared at the flames licking around the tall steeple that held the church bell and a clock.

The image filled Lydia with both fascination and horror. She all but dragged her mother toward the Congregational meetinghouse where she worshiped, struggling to see through the haze. Relief flooded Lydia as two men ran toward the women and assisted them indoors. Several militia defended the church. Once inside, Lydia and her mother held onto each other and sobbed.

"I'm so sorry I did not listen to you, Lydia. To think what might have happened."

Lydia knew all too well what could have happened. Her recollections of the attack on Newport years ago had permanently marked her memory.

"Lydia, you must rest, my dear."

Turning toward the voice, Lydia was relieved to see her midwife, Deborah. The two women embraced.

Deborah laughed when the infant kicked at her. "Someone appears to be anxious to enter the world."

Lydia stroked her firm belly. "I am more than anxious to birth this little one."

Deborah led her to a church pew and opened the door to the bench row. "Lydia, please lie down and rest. You've had a terrible shock."

Lydia barely heard Deborah but closed her eyes, knowing they were safe at last.

~

LYDIA SAT UPRIGHT at the sound of Cuff's voice. She must have fallen asleep on the hard bench. She grabbed her cap, which threatened to come off, yawned, and looked around.

Why am I in the meetinghouse? The smell of smoke lingering in the air refreshed her memory.

Deborah came to her, leaned over the back of the pew, and touched her shoulder. "Lydia, you must put yerself in confinement, and soon."

"But, I've two months to go before this babe comes." Lydia rubbed her aching head.

"Are ya certain sure you know when yer time is comin'?"

"Aye, Deborah. 'Twas the only time I lay with my husband before he went back to camp."

"I need to examine ya soon in your home." Deborah shook her head slowly and kept her voice low. "Got to make sure there's only one wee one in the hearth." Deborah patted her arm and walked toward Cuff, who chatted with the clergyman.

More than one? This could not be. The thought of raising one more child without Jeremiah overwhelmed her. The possibility of giving birth to two more babies paralyzed her with fear.

She searched the meetinghouse for her mother, who sat in a pew visiting with one of the ladies from town. At one point, her mother cried, and the woman comforted her.

What would have happened to her mother had Lydia not come? The thought renewed the tension she'd just conquered with the nap. She pushed away these thoughts lest they cripple her mind.

Comfort. Was her daughter safe? Lydia forced herself to stand. "Cuff. Are you well?"

"I be fine, Mrs. Saunders." Her slave met her eyes. "I be worried about you."

She smiled to reassure him but hoped he didn't see the fear that still overshadowed her. "I am well. Let's go home if it's safe."

"Aye, ma'am." He strode toward her. "Soldiers have gone back to Newport."

Newport. Her first home with Jeremiah.

"I'm ready, then." She inched her way out of the pew, trying not to notice her belly hanging over the back of the pew in front. She remembered a neighbor from years before who'd birthed twins. The woman looked large to start with, so the presence of two babies seemed to just be added width. But Lydia's small frame seemed overburdened with the pregnancy. No wonder her back ached so.

After freeing herself from the confines of the row, Lydia breathed in and headed toward the door.

"Do you need my help, Mrs. Saunders?" Cuff looked at the ground.

Deborah must have told him to help her, but taking her arm without permission would embarrass him.

"No, Cuff, I'm fine. But thank you for offering."

Deborah caught her eye. "I'll see you on the morrow."

Lydia nodded and left the meetinghouse.

It amazed her that she could project such a peaceful image to others when, in her heart, she trembled with fear and uncertainty. And now that she might be having twins, she could only focus on her dread of the impending birth. That, and her daughter. If she did not survive this complicated childbirth, who would raise her precious child? Her mother? Phila? May that *never* be.

She didn't face such anxiety when she carried Comfort. Jeremiah had been there. Now, she had no one. The very ones who might give her child the best upbringing were her slaves. And would the law allow that, even if she freed them? And what would happen to Rose?

Cuff helped her into the carriage. It seemed impossible that just this morning, she'd set out to rescue her mother. Her intent had been carried out—but at such a cost to her peace of mind.

Lydia swiped at her legs whenever she envisioned the Hessian's hands stroking her. Wherever he'd touched her felt as if hot coals had singed her skin. Unseen scars of his molestation left her branded. She knew it could have been so much worse. While grateful it had not gone further, it still elicited tears during the carriage ride.

She pulled out her kerchief and dabbed at her eyes, peering out the window until Comfort rushed toward the carriage with her arms held out.

"Mama! Mama!" The poor child wailed for Lydia, and she grieved for her daughter's distress.

Her driver pulled up to the house, and Hannah opened the door. "Thank the good Lord, you're safe." She helped Lydia emerge from the carriage's tight quarters.

Lydia silently vowed not to ride it again until after the baby —or babies—arrived.

Comfort clung to Lydia's gown.

"Come inside, my little one." Lydia walked her up the steps and saw a smiling Miriam and Rose in the doorway.

"So good to have you back safe, ma'am."

"'Tis good to be home."

She squeezed Miriam's hand, smoothed Rose's tight curls, and lumbered into the house with Comfort still clinging to her. She sat on the settee, and Hannah helped her lift her legs onto the couch. Comfort curled into the crook of her arm and sucked her thumb.

"I thought you'd given that up, Comfort." She smiled and gently pulled her daughter's thumb from her mouth.

"It helps me not cry, Mama."

"I know. But I'm back now, so no more tears, all right?"

"All right."

Hannah brought her some cider and left the mother and daughter alone, wrapped in an embrace on the settee.

This is all I want. Peaceful quiet. My daughter and my babies. Nothing more.

Lydia wished she could hold this moment in time forever. With her daughter safely in her arms, her babies snug within her womb. Yet, something still seemed missing. Or could it be someone?

She'd long ago learned to survive without Jeremiah. They'd not been married long before he'd been given an army commission. While she missed him terribly, she often thought the military took first place in his affections. He'd supplied her every need but one: his presence. He'd shared sleeping quarters with troops far more than he'd shared their bed. She thought she'd become accustomed to being alone. She had not.

Weeping softly so as not to disturb Comfort, she took out her kerchief, wiped her eyes gently, then turned it over to use the other side. Her eyes focused on an embroidered letter *H* on the back, so old and frayed, the stitches were barely discernible.

She stroked her cheek with the soft, well-worn linen and inhaled its smell to see if a man's scent resided on the cloth. She didn't discern any. Hannah had laundered it at least twice since he gave it to her.

Yet, in her desperate search for a reminder of the man who'd gifted the kerchief to her, she wept again, for she knew who it was she missed. Micah Hughes.

And she realized that the whole time she faced danger this day, she'd longed for him, wished for his protection and kindness. She needed him. Fear flooded her heart that she desired him so deeply. He could not be here when she craved his presence the most, and that vulnerability overwhelmed her.

10

"Is this it, Sergeant Hughes?" The exhaustion in the young private's voice and the dried mud on his uniform testified to the weeks of slogging through muddy bogs in incessant rainfall.

Micah forced himself to remain upright and not collapse onto the ground after the weeks-long trek. "Aye, Private Barnes, we have reached camp."

While the regiment had looked forward to their arrival, they were not prepared for the stench of disease left from the numerous illnesses that had beset the troops at Valley Forge.

Micah's entire regiment covered their noses, infuriating him. "Men, you can thank Almighty God you were not here for the worst of the contagion. Next man who covers his nose gets two extra nights on guard duty. In the meantime, get some rest."

Rest, however, would not be for long, as the regiment was due to leave with Washington's main body of troops within a few days

Relief came when Micah realized military help had arrived during his absence. An officer in the Prussian Army named Baron von Steuben had astonishing influence on the rag-tag, filthy troops, who were now better disciplined.

Von Steuben's military training, along with a sense of humor, engaged and inspired the Americans. He, in turn, admired and respected these men who had so little, yet were willing to give their all to serve a fledgling country. The help from Von Steuben boosted morale after they suffered such a terrible winter at Valley Forge.

At the end of a long and arduous day spent learning new drills taught by the Baron, Micah watched as Ezekiel approached him.

The black soldier's brows wrinkled, and he rubbed his face frantically.

Micah stood. "What's wrong?"

Without answering, Ezekiel handed him a letter from Hannah.

"Are you certain you don't mind me reading this? It might get personal."

"Read it." Ezekiel nodded.

Micah's shoulders tightened, and he cleared his throat with a nervous cough. Sitting back down, he read.

My dearest Ezekiel,

Trouble came to Bristol in early May. We are all safe now, but the King's Army attacked first Warren, then the center of Bristol, where Mrs. Saunders's mother lives. We were fine here on the farm, but Mrs. Saunders insisted she go check on her mother. I begged her to stay home, but she would not listen.

Micah gripped the paper as Hannah described the ensuing events, including the attack on Lydia's mother's house, the destruction of their property, the plundering of the women's rings, and the burning of the church in town. But Micah had to stop reading for a moment and shut his eyes tightly after reading about the enemies' molestation of Lydia.

Dear God!

Then the news that Lydia expected twins who would likely birth in June. He handed the letter back to Ezekiel, covered his head with both hands, and stared at the ground for a moment. "I must go to her. Make sure she's well."

Ezekiel's eyes narrowed, and he slowly shook his head. "How?"

"I don't know. But I'll find a way." Micah pushed off from the rock he'd been sitting on and tromped with firm steps toward the colonel's tent.

Please God, give me favor.

Opening the tent flap, he walked into the darkened marquee and stood at attention. Could his superior see how much he trembled? "Colonel Daggett, sir."

The colonel looked up from writing a note. "Yes, Sergeant?"

"May I beg leave for a furlough, sir? There has been an emergency in Bristol."

Colonel Daggett sat back in his chair. "I'm well aware of what ensued there, sergeant. What is your business there?"

"It's —" He swallowed with difficulty. "It's personal, sir."

A pause before the colonel spoke again. "When's the last time you went on furlough, Hughes?"

"I've not been on furlough, sir, since signing on."

"And when was that?"

"Two years past."

Silence. "Well then, I believe it's time you went on leave. Perhaps we could also say you are going on a personal mission— to ascertain the well-being of General Varnum's wife, Martha. She happened to be in Warren that day, baking a wedding cake for a friend, when the scoundrels attacked. By all reports, it seems she is fine, but I know our general would like to know that firsthand, from one of his men."

Micah narrowed his gaze. "Aye, sir. Where is Mrs. Varnum now, sir?"

"I believe she's gone home to Bristol, staying with a friend due to the lobsterbacks burning down the Varnum's home there.

79

I assume you should be able to discover her whereabouts without difficulty?"

"Aye, sir."

"And I assume you will give my regards to Mrs. Saunders?"

Heat rose under Micah's tight cravat. "Of course, sir."

How did he know?

The colonel grinned. "Word gets around camp, you know, about letters that smell like lavender." He laughed. Pulling out another sheet of paper, he grabbed his quill and wrote. "Here are your furlough papers, Sergeant Hughes. Don't want our troops mistaking you for a deserter. And take that tracker fellow with you. Corporal Bearslayer? I'll write a note for him as well. Can't have you two picked off by enemy scouts along the way."

"No, sir. Thank you, sir."

The colonel handed Micah the papers, then grew more serious. "I do hope Mrs. Saunders fares well after that abominable raid in Bristol."

"I hope so as well, sir. Thank you, sir." Micah saluted his superior, turned, and left, breathing a sigh of relief. But he knew he'd only feel complete relief if Lydia were truly well. After what she'd been through, he could not be certain until he saw her with his own eyes.

Then he stopped short, fingering the papers that would be his key to furlough. Lydia would be bearing twins. He did not know if that put her in further danger, but he knew one thing. He wanted to be there for her, no matter what she endured. He never wanted her to face peril alone, ever again.

AFTER ASKING an armed sentinel near the Bristol wharf where General Varnum's wife could be found, Micah and Henry Bearslayer headed up Church Street and found the brick two-story with the iron fence in front.

"This looks like the place." Micah opened the walkway gate then looked down at his regimentals. "Aren't we a sight?"

His uniform was fairly clean when he left Valley Forge, but the spring mud had done its job by the time he'd reached Rhode Island. Looking at Henry's breeches & coat, his had fared no better.

They both walked up the front steps, and Micah knocked a few times. They waited just a moment before a Negro woman opened the door.

She stared at their uniforms a moment, then smiled. "You are welcome, so long as your uniform ain't a red color." Opening the door wide, she waved them in. "Wait here, sirs, and I'll get Mrs. Easton."

"Oh, but we're actually here to see General Varnum's wife. We're from his 1st Rhode Island Regiment, and he wished to commend his great concern for her. Due to the recent events here and in Warren, that is."

"Did someone say my husband's name?" A slightly graying woman with a silk dress whisked down the hallway toward Micah and Henry.

She appeared as gallant as her husband, but in a feminine manner. Micah stood still, enchanted by her smile.

"Mrs. Varnum." Micah bowed.

He then introduced Henry, who bowed in turn.

"Gentlemen, 'tis so kind of my dear consort to send you. But he needn't have feared, as I am quite well. Do come sit, and Mehitabel will bring us some coffee. If you please, Mehitabel."

"Of course, ma'am." The woman who had answered the door strode down the hall.

Micah and Henry each sat in tapestry-covered chairs. They stared around the room at the ornate furnishings. Micah felt out of place.

"So, tell me, gentlemen, does my husband fare well? I do so miss him."

"Aye, Mrs. Varnum, he is quite well. But he inquires as to

your safety and well-being after the recent attack here. He was greatly distressed and wished for us to make inquiries as to your health."

"Well, you can tell the general that I outmaneuvered those lobsterbacks into the field out back of my friend's house. I did hear those blaggards—excuse my language, sirs—I heard them say to 'shoot the women.' The gall of those scoundrels! None of the women were shot. The only casualty was the wedding cake I baked. It burned to a crisp whilst I hid in the tall grass." She grinned.

Both Micah and Henry smiled.

"I'm certain the general will be much pleased that 'twas only the cake that suffered injury." Micah tipped his head at her.

"Gentlemen, you must be exhausted and in need of washing up. Please say you'll spend a few nights here. I know my friends will welcome two of our brave Continental soldiers."

"Thank you so much, Mrs. Varnum, but we're actually on our way to the Saunders plantation. She is a friend, and we are checking on her as well."

"Please give her my regards. I understand both she and her mother were terrorized that day—and she with child! There is no end of the Hessians' despicable behavior."

Micah's eyes opened wide, and his pulse quickened. "'Twas Hessians? I thought 'twas just the King's Army that attacked."

"No, indeed." Mrs. Varnum narrowed her glare. "That wretched group of barbarians should be shot without mercy. They have utterly no conscience, in my opinion."

Reeling from this latest detail about the attack, Micah rubbed his throbbing forehead.

"Forgive me, gentleman. I can see you are tired. Let me offer you a room to freshen up. You can even shave before you visit your friends. Feel free to stay and rest if you like before riding to the plantation."

When Mehitabel came with the coffee, Mrs. Varnum

instructed her to place hot water and towels in the downstairs guest rooms so the men could clean up.

"Thank you, Mrs. Varnum. That is most generous of you." Micah forced thoughts of the attack to the back of his mind. He needed to get to Lydia. Soon.

"You are quite welcome. Your service to our country is a gift to all Americans. 'Tis the least we can do in return."

UNDER STRICT ORDERS from both Deborah and Dr. Caldwell, Lydia agreed to remain in bed for the duration of her confinement. She did not have the stamina to fight them both.

In truth, exhaustion from this pregnancy depleted her strength, and, aside from an early morning walk outdoors before the heat set in, she preferred staying on the settee in the parlor with a good book. *Aesop's Fables*, a favorite of her daughter, helped while away the hours each day.

Comfort and Rose entertained her with stories of discoveries found underneath rocks out in the garden. Lydia feigned interest in the insect descriptions the girls chattered about. Then, they scrambled to the nursery to find paper upon which they drew the bugs in detail and shared them with her.

Lydia attempted to be enthusiastic about the creatures, but she considered some of them to be quite grotesque. She'd never been a lover of insects. Her daughter took after Jeremiah in this. But she was grateful for these simple distractions because they took her mind off the ache in her back. They even relieved the difficulty of getting a short nap.

Deborah visited to check on her. "How do ye fare, on this beautiful summer morn, Lydia?"

Why did Deborah have to smile so much?

"In truth? My body no longer feels like my own. One twin or another begins frantic tumbling, waking me any time of day or night. They throttle my insides on their own schedule while sleeping eludes me." Tears pricked her eyes.

"Soon, these wee ones will be born, and you will love them as much as you love yer daughter." Deborah squeezed her hand. "Then all the discomfort will move to the back of your thoughts as the love ye have for them becomes foremost."

"I know what you say 'tis true. Yet the sooner these wee ones are birthed, the happier I will be.

"The later these wee ones are birthed, the *healthier* they will be. Ye are strong, my friend. God will strengthen ye when ye feel weak." Deborah patted her hand as she stood up. "I shall pray for ye."

"Thank you."

Yet carrying twins was only a part of the pain Lydia endured. She could not ignore the persistent pain that lived deep within her heart. It had become the greater challenge. It seemed obvious that, after weeks of no letters from Micah, he'd forgotten her. According to Hannah, Micah fared well, because she continued to hear from Ezekiel. Although grateful for that, the fact Micah had not written for so long added to her despair.

Since she'd allowed herself the luxury of needing Micah, a sea swell of emotion followed. Perhaps she should have left that hatch closed. Looking down at her enormous belly housing two babes, she understood how grotesque she must seem to a man. Why would any man desire to even look at her, much less care for her?

She'd chosen the most inopportune time in her life to open the keys to her heart that only trusted sparingly to start with. Would the part of her willing to place faith in a man become scarred like a long-dead tree in the woods? She sighed and lay her head back, fighting the sleep that sought her.

~

"Mrs. Saunders. Mrs. Saunders. You have a visitor." Hannah gently moved Lydia's arm to awaken her. Her friend grinned with her wide smile, looking for all the world like a naughty schoolgirl bent on some mischief.

"A visitor?" Lydia yawned and pushed herself upright on the settee. When she saw the man standing there, she gasped and felt her messy hair. It had completely come undone while she'd slept. *I am a sight!*

There he stood—Sergeant Hughes. He nodded to her. How had she not noticed how handsome his appearance was on his first visit? She must have been too consumed with Jeremiah to appreciate his strong, chiseled features that framed those deep-set, glorious eyes. His bright red face— either from sunburn or perhaps, embarrassment—surrounded an almost boyish grin.

"Sergeant Hughes. Please forgive my appearance." Now her face must match his in its ruddiness.

"I'm so sorry if I disturbed you."

"Nay, you have not," Her heart had taken on an unnatural rhythm, and she placed her hand over her chest, thinking she might calm herself with the touch. "I am so ... grateful to see you."

"And I, you." He cleared his throat. "I was so very concerned when I heard about the events of last month. I wanted to—I *needed*—to see for myself that you were well."

Was that a tremor in his voice?

His presence brought such healing to her heart. Words escaped her. She had no idea what to say. So many words had gone unspoken for so long that to express her deepest thoughts to this man seemed like a foreign language. How would he respond? Perhaps his feelings were not as deep as hers.

"I'll go make some coffee for our visitors." Hannah smiled while she left the room.

Lydia's brows furrowed. "Visitors?"

"Aye, Corporal Bearslayer has accompanied me. Lest I lose

my way." Micah shifted his stance but did not take his eyes from her face.

She held out her hand to him. "Please, come tell me how you are."

He all but ran toward her, grabbed her hand, and held it with trembling fingers. "Once I am certain you fare well, I shall be a happy man."

"I am well, now that you are here."

He knelt on the floor beside her and kissed her fingers. She automatically reached up to touch his face. Despite her efforts to quell them, tears emerged.

"I regret the terrible events that happened to you. But I do not regret that these events have brought me to you." He touched her face with gentle fingers. "I wish—I wish I'd been here to protect you."

"But you are here now. That is what matters." Her lips quivered, and tears flowed.

Micah leaned in closer until their lips were just a breath apart. His kiss, both unexpected and so very desired, embraced hers as though they belonged together.

He sought her mouth time and again before he paused a moment, holding her face with both hands. "I should have asked your permission."

"You have my permission." Her heart thrummed with passion.

He drew her close again, the eagerness of his lips seeming to speak of kisses that had been only dreamt of, now finally fulfilled. His breathing became erratic.

"I know I have no right to say this but, I love you, Lydia Saunders. I don't know what I'd have done had any further harm befallen you. I'm so sorry I could not protect you on that horrible day."

"I love you, Micah Hughes." Her own breath struggled to keep up with her racing heart. "I'm not certain how long I've loved you, but I think perhaps the moment you gave me your kerchief."

She laughed as he stroked her long, unkempt hair.

"I've ne'er seen your locks undone. So beautiful." He drew her tresses to his lips and kissed them.

"Mama." Comfort stopped short. "Sergeant Hughes!" The small girl ran toward him and threw herself into his arms.

He hugged her, then put his arm around her as they sat on the floor by the settee. "I'm so happy you are back. Can you stay?"

"For a time. I'm on furlough."

"Did you hear? Mama is going to have two wee babes, not just one!"

"I heard. I think that is wonderful."

Lydia wove her fingers through his hair, and he closed his eyes. She continued to stroke his head, which elicited a smile.

A tightness unlike any other gripped her belly, and she gasped.

"Lydia, what is it? The babies?"

"Aye, please call Hannah. She'll know what to do." Lydia moaned from the discomfort.

A look of terror crossed Micah's face. He jumped to his feet and grasped her hands. "I'll not leave you to bear this alone."

His fingers gripped hers so tightly, yet they comforted her.

Hannah hurried into the parlor led by Comfort, who'd raced to fetch her.

Her eyes were wide as saucers. "Oh my. Don't you fear, Mrs. Saunders. I'll have Cuff fetch the midwife. And Dr. Caldwell. Comfort, go get Cuff whilst Sergeant Hughes and I help her to the birthing chamber."

The child ran outdoors, and Micah and Hannah, one on each side, helped Lydia stand. Hannah guided them toward the birthing room on the first floor.

"The room's all ready for you, ma'am. Don't you be worrin'

about a thing." Hannah's voice trembled even while she attempted to soothe Lydia's anxiety.

"I won't worry, Hannah."

On their way down the hall, Lydia's legs buckled from a contraction, and she groaned.

Micah's face paled. He swallowed hard. "Hang on, Lydia. I think we're nearly there."

"Just a few more steps, Mrs. Saunders." Sweat formed on Hannah's brow as she struggled to maneuver Lydia into the room and onto the bed.

Lydia plopped onto the mattress, the movement setting off yet another tightness across her whole belly. "Help me, Micah!" She squinted her eyes shut.

He gripped her hand, and his lips drew close to her ear. "I'll not leave you, Lydia." A gentle kiss followed his quiet message.

She opened her eyes and captured his gaze. "I love you, Micah Hughes." Shocked at seeing tears form in his eyes, she treasured the look of concern and love that emanated from them.

"I love you, Lydia. And I will be here for you."

She prayed his words would give her the strength to face whatever lay ahead. She prayed God would give her the strength to survive.

11

Micah stood outside the birthing chamber door until Cuff approached him. "Come with me, Sergeant Hughes. You can wait in the kitchen with us."

Another scream from Lydia tore at his gut. He could not begin to imagine her pain. As the youngest in his family, he'd ne'er had to do 'the wait,' as his father called it. A time of distress for entire households especially became the burden for fathers of the infants.

Micah felt drawn almost silently into this role. Neither husband nor father, he embraced this new life. Falling in love with Lydia was an unexpected delight. It happened so quickly and naturally, he wondered how such an important event had occurred without fanfare? And yet here he was. The very willing victim of new responsibilities.

He wondered how Lydia saw him. Did she believe him fit for the part? Did he? He did not know, yet he embraced these new roles with enthusiasm, much as he'd embraced Lydia earlier that day. Her kisses sealed his heart with hers.

Cuff led him down the hall and past the dining room toward the kitchen. He remembered eating a meal here with Lydia on his last visit. How different everything appeared then.

Discomfort still arose at the finery in that room, but Micah ignored the surface details to dwell on the heart issue. Lydia said she loved him, and he would dine on the pleasure of her affections.

He could not possibly provide such a home for Lydia if she agreed to marry him. Somehow, in his spirit, he knew it would work out, although he had no idea how.

When he entered the kitchen, he searched the faces of those at the table. Henry sat in the middle, silent and drinking his coffee. His face held little expression, although he stopped and inquired about Lydia. When Cuff told him nothing had changed, Henry nodded and held the cup back up to his lips.

Comfort barely touched her cheese and bread. "Will Mama be all right, Sergeant Hughes?" Her wide eyes held hope.

"I'm certain she will be." Micah forced a smile. If he could only convince himself of that.

Both Comfort and Rose ate very little.

Micah bantered with the girls. "Not hungry, lassies? Perhaps I might borrow some of your food from your plate." He reached toward Comfort's.

She giggled and pulled it away. "Nay, 'tis mine."

"I say, cannot a soldier get some victuals here?"

He pretended disappointment, then winked at Comfort, and she giggled again.

A plate appeared out of nowhere. He looked at the server and grieved at her expression. Her lips quivered, and he placed a hand on her arm.

"I'm certain Mrs. Saunders will be fine, Miriam."

She did not answer but attempted to smile as she left the portion of food for him along with a tankard of cider.

"Thank you for the victuals, ma'am."

He noted the downcast faces around the table and looked at the two children. "Comfort and Rose, why do you not play outside a bit? Perhaps you can look for rocks."

Comfort squealed at Rose and covered her mouth in glee. "Or bugs! Let's go, Rose."

The two girls scooted off the bench and ran outdoors.

"Thank you, Sergeant Hughes. Not good for little ones to feel our worry." Cuff swallowed a drink from his tankard.

"No. I'm certain you are all concerned. As am I."

He stared at the delicious-looking salt pork and vegetables, but the thought of eating while Lydia bore such pain took his appetite away. "I guess I'm not as hungry as I thought, either."

"I am sorry, Sergeant. Food not good?" Miriam tried so hard to please.

"The food looks and smells delicious. It's just—"

"We know." Cuff nodded his understanding.

Silence ensued, occasionally broken by a piercing scream from the back room. Micah clamped his hand over his mouth, leaned on the table, and looked out the window. Anything to interrupt the unease.

Miriam startled them all by saying something loudly in her native tongue. Then she cried tears it seemed she'd withheld for some time.

Micah and Henry stared at each other.

"She say, Mrs. Saunders there with her when she gave birth to Rose." Cuff translated. "Ma'am comforted her. Her rescuer is now in pain. Miriam wishes she could help her."

Micah's mouth opened. "Her rescuer?"

"Aye." Cuff looked upward. "Miriam came on a ship from Africa. Only her name not Miriam then. She was the favorite of the slaver who owned the ship."

A chill needled up Micah's spine. "The favorite?"

"Aye. The slaver would hang her up by chains often. He rape her—in front of everyone."

Micah's stomach roiled at the horrific thought. Speech escaped him. He knew these slave ships were bad, but he had no idea how bad.

"When the ship came to port, those who were still alive were marched outside, naked and in chains."

Miriam diverted her eyes.

"When the auctioneer began, the slaver bid on her. He wanted her for himself. But the daughter of the slaver asked her husband to bid higher. Her husband won the bid and saved Miriam from the slaver. But ... Miriam was with child."

Micah swallowed. "Rose?"

Cuff looked at his hands on the table. "Aye."

"And the father?"

"The slaver."

Realization dawned on Micah, and he felt as if someone had punched him in his gut. "And the slaver?" He gripped the edge of the table.

"Mrs. Saunders's father."

Micah peered at Cuff. "Why did Lydia—Mrs. Saunders— wish to purchase Miriam? I know she does not approve of buying slaves."

"She say, she look at Miriam and knew. Somehow, she knew Miriam feared her father. She say, she would do something about it this time. She talk her husband into buying Miriam. Her father was very angry."

She'd do something about it this time?

This story baffled Micah. Then realization struck. "So, Rose?"

"She be Mrs. Saunders's sister."

Micah covered his face, tortured by the pain one man's lust had inflicted on so many. He wished Lydia's father were here so he could strangle the Negro-hating life out of the man. Then he realized he hated the father of the woman he loved. How does one reconcile this conflict? Lydia had carried this burden for years, and he now ached for her pain.

"So, where is Mrs. Saunders's father now?"

"Dead."

"How?"

"Don't know. They find him in the water next to his slave ship. I hope he choked on the filthy water."

Micah had never heard such venom from a slave before, yet he could not judge the man for his feelings. He struggled with his own. The minister at church spoke of loving one's enemies. But how do you love a man like the slaver? Micah's head pounded louder, and he covered his eyes again.

Comfort and Rose, their faces bright red and sweaty, ran into the kitchen with a basin of bugs.

"Look at what we found! This one's my favorite." Rose picked up the most unusual looking of the creatures.

Micah admired it.

Rose placed her brown hand on Micah's arm. "It's fun finding them under the rocks." She giggled and covered her mouth before the two girls ran outside again.

Did he see a hint of Lydia's smile in her sister? It seemed plain as day once he realized they were related.

Micah would ask Lydia how she knew about Miriam and her father. But not today.

For today, he thought about the children Lydia labored to birth. He envisioned the terrible scene of Lydia standing up to her father's bid at the auction block. He pondered Lydia taking Miriam and the infant she knew to be her sister and raising them in her own home. And he realized something about this woman he loved. Bravery and strength filled her spirit, blended with a passion for love and justice.

The bond that tied his heart to hers bound even tighter—a chain stronger than iron, yet softer than Lydia's skin. He was profoundly blessed.

12

Lydia could not recall such intense pain with her first delivery. Of course, this birthing was different with two babes struggling to be born. She attempted to smother her groans, but they escaped despite her efforts. So did occasional screams.

She hoped Comfort didn't hear her cries. *My poor girl!*

Deborah, the midwife, came to deliver the babies, but Hannah held Lydia's hand, bringing her the reassurance she desperately craved. She knew Dr. Caldwell had arrived, but she prayed he'd not be needed. Both Deborah and Hannah insisted the doctor be there in case anything went amiss. Lydia would not even dwell on that possibility.

Hour after hour, she labored, one gut-wrenching contraction after another. Sweat poured from her brow, and the heat smothered her. Hannah whisked a Chinese fan across her face in a kind attempt to cool her. Nothing helped. The motion of Hannah's hand annoyed her to the degree that she screamed at her servant to stop.

Deborah came into her view. "Dear Lydia, let me examine you."

"Why?" Lydia barely recognized her own angry voice.

"I think it might be time."

Lydia twisted on the damp bed sheets. When Deborah checked for dilation, Lydia screamed.

"Ye are fully ready, my dear Lydia. Ye may push out yer first babe."

Hannah got behind her on the bed and held her at an angle.

"Now Lydia, when I tell ye to push, do so with all yer might."

"I can't."

"Aye, ye can, my friend. Hannah and I will help ye."

Exhaustion smothered Lydia. She breathed in deeply, and her belly tightened with another contraction.

"There now, push, Lydia, push!"

She groaned and grunted and pushed with all her might.

"Take a deep breath."

Lydia followed the midwife's directions, again with deep grunts and incredible pressure from below.

"We're nearly there, Lydia. One more push should do it."

"I can't. I can't push anymore." She breathed so heavily she thought she'd faint.

"Aye, ye can, dear friend. One more good one!"

Determination steeled Lydia, and she grabbed her legs and squeezed them with all her might while pushing her baby out. Warmth flooded the bed, and the infant cried.

"'Tis a wee lass, Lydia!"

"A sister for Comfort! Such a blessin' all is well!" Hannah's voice, filled with delight, expressed the relief they all felt.

Deborah wiped the moisture off the child, and she held the babe up for Lydia to see. "She looks like you!" Deborah wore a wide grin.

Lydia reached her hand to touch the newborn. "Another daughter. Thank you, God. Perhaps she has a brother waiting to be born next." She breathed in deeply and smiled.

"Here. Let the lass nurse to help with the afterbirth. And to speed up that next babe." Deborah winked as she handed her daughter over. Her demeanor was more relaxed than Lydia had seen all day. "Twins born a bit early may not eat with as much vigor as those born on time, so we may have to work with her a bit."

Lydia scooted to a sitting position and put the infant to breast. They needn't have worried about this little one's ability to suckle, as she seemed to know what to do right away. The three women giggled as the girl latched on to her mama without difficulty.

After a few minutes, another strong contraction came upon Lydia. "It may be time, Deborah."

The midwife placed her hand across Lydia's tight belly and nodded. "Aye. Let me hand the little lass to Dr. Caldwell. I believe he is outside the door."

She wrapped the child in a blanket and carried her to the door.

THE DOOR OPENED AT LAST, and the midwife held a small squirming bundle in a blanket. Micah held his breath when Deborah handed the babe to the doctor, who opened the blanket and did a brief inspection. The doctor covered the infant again.

"Everything seems in order." The doctor grinned at him. "Would you like to hold her?"

"Aye, I would." He'd held a few babies in the war camp to help out the camp followers, but never had he held one so small. "A lass." Awe captured his attention as the small infant moved her arms and legs and turned her head toward one side, moving her mouth.

"She's looking to suckle." The doctor slapped his arm gently.

"Well, I'm not much help there." Micah placed his small finger near her mouth, and she sucked his finger with unexpected enthusiasm. "She is quite strong."

"Most girl babies are stronger than boys. Guess that's because they may someday go through childbirth. I think most of us men wouldn't survive."

Although Micah heard him, he was too busy staring with wonder at the baby to respond. "She looks like Lydia."

He looked upward when he heard desperate moans from within the chamber. The door opened abruptly.

"Dr. Caldwell, please come quickly."

The doctor's face turned ashen. Without saying a word, he entered the room and slammed the door shut.

Micah swayed his torso to soothe the baby and softly sang a lullaby he'd heard in the camp. Tears emerged and drenched his face.

If Lydia died, how would he live?

MICAH LEFT the baby girl with Miriam, who rocked her and sang to her. He stood against the birthing room door, praying, desperate for someone to let him in. He had to know how Lydia fared.

Finally, it opened slowly, and the doctor emerged. His gait seemed stiff, and he gripped Micah's arm. "Be gentle with her."

Gentle with whom?

He rushed into the room where Lydia lay on her side, her eyes open. He stopped and breathed a sigh of relief. His hands trembled as he crossed the room and reached for hers.

Lydia stared, motionless.

"Lydia, are you well?"

Deborah touched his arm. "The second child was lost." Moisture rolled down her cheeks, and she resumed cleaning up linens and the forceps the doctor had apparently used.

Lydia remained quiet for a moment, and one tear rolled from her eye. Her lips contorted. "'Twas a boy."

Hannah carried a bundle and walked out the door, followed by Deborah.

Lydia gripped Micah's hand. "They would not let me see him."

Micah's heart ached for her. He assumed the infant might frighten Lydia if he died some time ago. He'd heard of such things.

"Perhaps 'tis best. Lydia."

"No, I need to see him!" She sobbed convulsive sobs.

Miriam walked in carrying the lass. "Your little one needs to eat, ma'am."

Lydia screamed at Miriam. "I want to see my son!"

Micah startled.

The servant hurried out the door, carrying the girl.

He gripped her fingers, then Micah looked up at the ceiling and inhaled deeply. "Let me go ask." He kissed her cheek and left the room.

"Miriam, where is Hannah?"

"She went outside with the doctor, sir."

Micah scrambled past her and ran out the door. Hannah gave the bundle she'd carried out of the room to the physician, who laid it on the seat of his carriage.

"Doctor, wait!"

Dr. Caldwell held his reins and sighed. "What is it, Sergeant Hughes?"

"Mrs. Saunders wants to see the child. She said you would not let her."

He gave Micah a patronizing smile. "In these instances, sir, 'tis best the mother not see the child."

Micah smothered his rising anger. It was Lydia's child—and her choice. "Why? Does the child look frightening?"

"Nay, sir, he looks perfect. He just died. We're not certain why. I'd like to do a post-mortem examination."

"Without the mother's permission? And without allowing her to see him? This seems cruel indeed, sir."

"'Twould be most cruel, sir, to let her see her deceased infant." Dr. Caldwell's face reddened. "I am the authority on these things. You stick to your military know-how." He grasped the reins to flick them.

Micah grabbed them. "'Tis her desire, sir, to see her son. And you will comply. Sir?" Micah awaited his acquiescence.

The doctor's eyes protruded. "I assume you will be responsible for comforting her from the nightmares she'll likely endure?" He picked up the bundle next to him and handed it to Micah. "I'll be back tomorrow to pick him up for the postmortem."

"*If* Mrs. Saunders agrees, sir."

Without a word, Dr. Caldwell urged the horses to leave at a faster than usual pace. Dust encircled the man's exit.

It took Micah a moment to realize he held a dead infant in his arms. Although the doctor said the boy appeared perfect, Micah wanted to be sure the sight of her son would not give Lydia nightmares.

Slowly unfolding the outer blanket, Micah removed the next layer and found the face of the child. He lay so very still, and his color seemed somewhat blue. His lips were perfectly formed, resembling Lydia's. His russet hair looked like Comfort's. A perfect baby indeed. Micah smiled despite the obvious sadness of the event. He carried the child into the house and walked past Miriam and Cuff.

Hannah placed her hand on his arm as he moved past her. "Are you certain, sir? Is this the right thing to do?"

Micah cradled the boy and rocked him with his arms. "My father told me once my mother birthed a child who died. She begged him to see the infant, and at first, he refused. The child was somewhat deformed. She told him she didn't care—she wanted to hold her son.

"Finally, my father relented. She held him for a time, rocked him, and sang to him. My father said she needed to say her goodbyes to her child." Micah's eyes welled. "I believe Mrs. Saunders needs to, as well."

He left Cuff and Miriam weeping together, and Hannah

followed him down the hall. Lydia wailed for her son through the door.

The door creaked when he opened it and walked inside. "I—I have your son, if you wish to see him."

She reached toward Micah with hungry arms. "My boy!" She sobbed as she laid the child across her lap. When she saw his face, she tenderly stroked his cheek and smiled sadly. "You look so much like your father." She opened the blanket all the way and counted his fingers and toes. "He is perfect and without flaw." Rewrapping him as though he were alive, Lydia cradled him and stared at her first son.

She sang him a lullaby and stroked his russet hair. "He is beautiful, is he not?"

Micah found it difficult to speak. "Aye."

The new baby girl cried pitifully from down the hall.

Lydia looked up. "I hear my daughter needs me. Farewell, my son, and Godspeed." She kissed the boy, and tears dropped onto his still face. "I'll ne'er forget you."

She handed the boy back to Micah. "Thank you, my love. I shall ne'er forget your kindness."

He turned to leave as Hannah came in carrying the newborn girl.

"Micah," Lydia said.

He paused and looked at her.

"Please do not let the doctor take him. I—I cannot bear the thought he will cut open my perfect son. Can you give him a proper burial in our family plot?" Tears flowed down her cheeks.

"Of course, Lydia." He went to her and kissed her cheek. "I love you."

She covered her mouth to squelch a sob and reached for the lass Hannah held nearby. Lydia covered herself with a blanket as she nursed her daughter. The fussy child grew quiet and content almost at once.

Micah smothered his own sobs as he carried her precious treasure out to the barn. Cuff followed him.

"Can you show me where some wood is?" Micah wiped off his face with his sleeve.

Miriam followed close behind. "Let me take the boy. I make him a shroud so we can bury him."

"Thank you, Miriam."

Cuff brought some wood from the corner where it was stored. "This will work, I think."

"Aye. Where are the tools?"

Cuff touched Micah's arm. "You need not do this. Go to her. She need you now. I can make this coffin."

"Thanks." He hugged his arms to his chest as he walked back to the house. He'd helped with many a body since he'd gone to war. But this burial would be the most painful of all. He prayed it would be the last small body he'd ever have to carry.

13

The lingering image of Micah holding the still form of her son reminded Lydia of another lifeless child carried by a grieving mother a few years before.

Jeremiah had left for Washington's Army, and Lydia still lived in Newport with the servants. The King's Army took over the city, and terror lived in the hearts of the remaining Patriots. They feared being discovered and worried about leaving their homes behind.

One of the little boys who lived nearby played ball near the wall of the British fort. The mother later told Lydia the boy had tossed the ball over the wall, into the fort. The sentinel on duty yelled at the boy and told him to never do that again or he'd be shot.

The child, being no more than six or seven, threw it again, and it landed over the wall of the fort.

Lydia would never forget the mother screaming as she hurried toward the child. As Lydia watched in horror from her Newport home, the British guard shot the child dead. The sobs of that woman haunted Lydia still. And she now understood the guttural pain of losing her own child. A part of her heart had been cut out by the blade of death, never to fully recover.

Would this pain ever leave her? She did not know how it could.

A knock on the door awoke Lydia from her musings. "Come in."

Hannah entered. "Mrs. Saunders, may I get you anything?"

"Perhaps some cider, Hannah. I've no appetite for coffee this morning."

"And how be your little one, ma'am? Did she eat well last night?"

"Aye, quite well." Lydia gazed at her sleeping daughter. How different she looked from Comfort. Micah said she looked like her, but Lydia did not see it. Perhaps she'd see the resemblance as the child grew older.

The boy twin, however, looked so much like Comfort. They both took after Jeremiah. Lydia struggled again to smother her tears.

Hannah left the room.

Another knock. "Come in."

Micah held the door ajar. "May I come in, Lydia?"

"Aye, please do."

He pulled up a chair next to the bed and sat before looking at the infant in her arms. "She is beautiful. Much like her mother." He reached over and touched the baby's face, then placed his hand back in his lap and cleared his throat. "Cuff and I buried your son. We'd like to place a marker, but we do not know his name."

"Jeremiah. Like his father."

"Of course."

Silence ensued while she stared at the infant.

"And what will you call your daughter, Lydia?"

Her brow furrowed. "I have not decided yet. I always had Jeremiah in mind but, I ne'er thought of a lass's name."

"You have time to think about it."

"Aye."

He took ahold of her hand and squeezed it. "Lydia, I'm certain it's too soon to discuss any plans for marriage—"

"Far too soon." Her abrupt reply even took her by surprise. "I need some time."

She cringed at the look of hurt that crossed Micah's eyes.

He released her hand. "I only thought since I'm here for so short a time, we might at least discuss the matter. But I apologize if I entertained the idea too quickly." He gripped his legs.

"I need time, Micah. Time to sort through my grief. Sort through everything."

He cleared his throat and stood. "I see."

"Please do not misunderstand, Micah. I care for you deeply."

"Care for me? I thought two days ago you loved me."

Her tears nearly choked her as she swallowed them back.

"I think God has punished me for my affections toward you." There, she'd said what her troubled mind screamed at her ever since baby Jeremiah birthed and never breathed.

"Punished you?" He sat again and picked up her hands. "Why do you say this? We've done nothing wrong."

"I kissed you—with pleasure—whilst I carried my dead husband's child in my womb. And now, little Jeremiah is gone. God is judging me. For my sin. For my family's sins. I am not worthy of your love." Tears rolled down her face.

The baby awoke and fussed. Lydia placed the baby on her shoulder and patted her back.

"Lydia."

So much passion infused Micah's voice, she dared not look at his eyes.

"Please, Micah. Do not make this more difficult for me. My heart breaks as I say this to you, but I cannot allow you to ruin your life with such a sinner as myself."

"Lydia—"

"Please, Micah."

He stood and walked toward the door, turning to face her as

he reached for the handle. "I'll always love you, Lydia." He opened the door and left.

Lydia convulsed with her sobs. But this time, she not only mourned her son, she lamented the loss of the man who held her heart. The wages of her sin were worse than death.

∽

MICAH LOOKED STRAIGHT AHEAD when he exited the house. Someone followed him, but he refused to stop walking as he headed toward the barn to find his horse.

"Sergeant Hughes. Please stop." Hannah grabbed his arm. "Where are you going? Mrs. Saunders needs you." When she saw the look on his face, she covered her mouth. "What has happened, Sergeant?"

He paused to get ahold of his emotions. "Perhaps you can tell me, Hannah. She wants me to leave." He picked up his saddle and swung it onto his horse's back.

Hannah pulled him toward her until he looked at her. "Please, sir. Mrs. Saunders be hurting something terrible. She just lost her son. She's not thinking clear. Please, wait for her to get better."

Micah looked up at the rafters and exhaled. "Hannah, she wants me to go. I cannot stay and wait for her to decide that she is more than worthy of any man's love. Of my love. She says she sinned by—" Heat rushed to his face. "By kissing me whilst carrying Jeremiah's child." He shook his head, not knowing what to believe. "She thinks that's why the baby died."

She stood in Micah's way of adjusting the saddle. "Please, listen to me. Mrs. Saunders be carryin' guilt her whole life, but it has nothin' to do with her sins. They be her father's sins she's taking on her own soul. She has suffered as long as I've known her. She did better after she met Jeremiah, but that burden of guilt just waits for any chance to shout back into her ears that she be bad—a sinner woman."

Hannah's eyes brimmed. "Please, Sergeant. I know she has feelings for you. And there be nothing wrong with kissing a widow woman, with child or not."

"I cannot convince her of this, Hannah. I don't know who can. But she knows I love her." He sniffed. "And she knows where to write to me."

Hannah stood aside while he tightened the saddle, adjusted the stirrup, and mounted his horse.

"Please tell Corporal Bearslayer I'll meet him at Mrs. Varnum's house in Bristol." He pulled out a folded letter from inside his jacket. "And Hannah, I nearly forgot. Here's a letter from Ezekiel."

She thanked him and stepped back. Micah kicked his gelding far harder than necessary, and the horse bolted out the barn door and down the road toward Bristol.

THROUGH THE OPEN WINDOW, Lydia heard a horse gallop down the road. She listened until the sound ceased. There was no rider turning back. No second attempts to persuade her to change her mind.

And with his riding away, her heart traveled with him, leaving her bereft of all hope for love again. For his love had cost her dearly, and she could not risk any more pain. Not for herself—or for him.

Miriam entered the room with a cup of cider. "Here you go, ma'am."

"Thank you, Miriam." She gulped the refreshment. "I craved drink more than I thought."

"Yes, ma'am. I remember how I felt when I just had Rose. So very ready to drink water. And lots of it."

"Aye." Lydia looked out the open door and into the hallway. It seemed quieter than usual. "Do you know where Hannah is?"

"I think I saw her with a letter. She said the sergeant gave it to her from Ezekiel."

Lydia's pulse lurched at the mention of Micah. "I see."

"Can I get you anything?"

"Would you be able to take the baby and change her? I'm suddenly so very tired."

"Of course." Miriam picked up the sleepy infant. "I can bring her back to you when she hungry."

"Thank you, Miriam."

She rolled onto her side and hugged a pillow. She still felt discomfort from the birthing the previous day, but she'd been in pain after Comfort's birth as well. If only she could sleep. If only she could forget about Micah Hughes. If only she did not love him.

Lydia stopped herself. It seemed pointless to imagine the "if onlies." She knew she'd never forget Micah.

14

Lydia sat on the settee and observed her mother trying to tolerate the coffee. It was a lost cause. "I'm so sorry the coffee does not agree with you, Mother."

Octavia winced. "I suppose I could get used to it, doctored a great deal with cream and sugar, perhaps." She set the cup onto the saucer and placed it on the side table. "But, that is neither here nor there." She took out a fan and waved it in a vain attempt to cool off. "This heat is monstrous. It must have been miserable for you, carrying twins."

Lydia looked at her thumbs and twiddled them. "Aye."

"I know I've said this before, but I'm so very saddened about the boy." Her mother stopped fanning.

"Little Jeremiah." Lydia stared into space then out the window at nothing in particular.

Conversation paused for a moment before Octavia spoke again.

"So, did you hear why they burned down St. Michael's? The King's Army apparently thought the Patriots stored gunpowder underneath the building. What they thought to be stores were actually tombs. Now the whole pile looks like one giant grave.

Despicable act." She resumed fanning herself with an angry flick to her wrist.

Lydia tried to think of something to say. "Is your home much damaged, Mother?"

"It could have been worse. 'Tis repairable but will have to wait. With so many in the army and so much destruction, it will take time. And then, of course, so many of the men have been taken prisoners."

Lydia narrowed her eyes. "Who did they take?"

"William Gladding. The African, Caesar Blagrave. Hezekiah Usher. Too many to name."

"I had no idea. Have the militia gone to rescue them?"

"I do not know. Oh, and I heard Colonel Barton received a musket ball in his hip. Now he suffers from fever. Poor man."

"Mother," Lydia rubbed her forehead, "this terrible news does not help with my melancholy."

Octavia covered her mouth with two fingers. "I'm sorry, dear. I did not mean to add to your sorrows." Her eyes flickered as if in thought. "Let me see. Oh, your sister is with child."

Is that good news? Lydia held her tongue.

Miriam walked into the parlor carrying the fussy baby. Her mother glanced at the servant then looked away as she shifted in her seat.

"I just change her, ma'am." She acted as if Octavia were not there. "She seems quite hungry."

Lydia smiled when she gazed at her daughter. She undid her top stays and put the child to breast. At two weeks of age, the baby already ate with a vigorous appetite. Lydia giggled at her daughter's enthusiasm.

"It's nice to see you smile, Lydia. You've been through so much this last year."

So much longer than a year, Mother. "Aye, it's been difficult. But this wee one is a source of much joy."

Mother shifted to the edge of her chair. "Have you decided on a name yet?"

Lydia shook her head. "Nay. I know she needs one and soon. It does not befit her to always call her 'the baby.'"

"Well, I'm certain you'll come up with one. There are many lovely names of your grandmothers that might be fitting for her. Sarah? Or Priscilla?"

"I don't know. I keep trying to think of different ones, but none seem right. I think when I hear it, 'twill be obvious. 'Twill just seem right."

Her mother pushed on her cane and stood. "Well, my dear, I must be headed back to Bristol proper."

"Wait. Before you go. I—I wanted to ask you about something Phila said to me a few weeks ago."

"Phila? Whatever comes from her lips can ne'er be taken too seriously. I'll truly believe she is with child when her belly stands out." Her mother chuckled.

"She said something about your lawyer and this plantation."

Octavia scowled. "What on earth?"

Lydia inhaled a deep breath for courage. "She said you did not believe I took proper care of this farm, and you might seek legal means—to take it away." She exhaled with force.

Her mother all but growled. "That girl! The devil himself rules her tongue! Not an ounce of truth can be pulled from her speech on any day. I have ne'er done any such thing, nor would I. Your father left this land to you and your family. And that is that." She turned pale, and sweat dripped from her forehead.

Alarmed, Lydia swallowed with difficulty and unlatched the infant from nursing. "Mother, are you well?"

"I am fine, Lydia. But the older your sister gets, the more she reminds me of your father." Her mother took a few deep breaths with her eyes closed.

Mother walked slowly toward the door where her servant stood. He accompanied her outside and led her down the stairs. Lydia heard the man call for the carriage driver. Then the wheels of the chaise grabbed the dirt road and proceeded back to Bristol proper.

She'd not meant to upset her mother. But she needed to know the truth, which obviously could not be gleaned from Phila. While relieved the story of the lawyer was false, Lydia now feared for her mother's health—and just when they were on better speaking terms. It seemed life conspired against her to disallow joy. She truly must carry a mark of Cain. She prayed the mark would not befall her daughters.

~

"ARAMINTA JOY. SUCH A LOVELY NAME." Octavia Warnock looked at her youngest granddaughter.

Lydia grinned with pride. "I know not where the idea came from, but it somehow seemed perfect. I'd like to call her Minta.'"

It was now the beginning of August, which signaled Minta's two-month birthday.

Octavia grinned at Comfort, who stared with pride at her sister.

"Of course, your sister's name is just as beautiful as yours, Comfort."

The older sister giggled.

"I think we must celebrate this occasion of baby Minta receiving her name. Let us visit the sweet shop." Octavia Warnock looked younger than she appeared in years.

"You spoil your granddaughters, Mother." But Lydia was more than pleased that her mother was becoming the grandmamma she'd longed for her daughters to have.

Comfort burst with excitement. "If you buy sweets for Minta, I can eat them for her. She has no teeth yet."

Lydia rolled her eyes. "I believe we shall refrain from buying Minta any sweets just yet."

The blazing August sunlight caused Minta to squint. Lydia covered her eyes with a thin blanket.

Comfort clapped her hands together and started toward the

sweet shop. Lydia stopped her. "Comfort, please hold your Grandmama's hand whilst walking along the street."

Lydia's mother cast her daughter a grateful smile, and Comfort complied.

"We must get to know one another a bit better, Comfort." Octavia's warm grin elicited a giggle from the child.

"Yes, Grandmama." Comfort gave her a shy grin and held onto her gnarled fingers. "Were your hands always like that?"

"Comfort!" Heat infused Lydia's cheeks.

Octavia glanced at her daughter before answering, "Why, that's a very smart question, Comfort. No, they were not. Perhaps I did too much knitting in the day."

"You know how to knit?" Comfort's wide eyes glistened with excitement. "Can you teach me?"

"I can get you started a bit. But my old hands don't work quite as well these days. Perhaps your mother can help us."

"I think that would be lovely." Lydia was amazed at this transformation. The thought of spending joy-filled moments with her mother had always seemed out of reach—a treasure she desperately craved. Now she needed her more than ever, and she cherished every moment.

As they neared the sweet shop, Comfort squealed with excitement. "Sergeant Hughes! Sergeant Hughes! Mama, our friend!"

Lydia froze, unable to move. Her throat dried so fast, she craved cool water. If only she could reach the sweet shop before she grew completely parched. And before her heart thrummed, so fast she might faint.

Micah. He'd never appeared more handsome despite the scar on his forehead—a reminder of his loyalty to the American cause. His regiment had been issued newer uniforms, and he stood tall in his blue woolen coat with the white facing. He seemed taller than she remembered and certainly not so thin as when she'd first met him winter last.

He stared at her, mouth agape. Lydia's hand went to her

throat. As she stood, unable to move, Comfort raced to him and hugged his legs.

"Lydia? Who is that soldier?" Her mother's mouth stood open as she stared at the scene.

"That is Sergeant Micah Hughes. He is with the 1st Rhode Island Regiment." Her heart raced even faster when Micah approached

Holding Comfort's hand, he doffed his hat. "Mrs. Saunders. You are looking well."

"Thank you, Sergeant Hughes."

Did he have as much difficulty speaking as she did? Her brain turned to thick gruel, making it difficult to sort through her thoughts and find intelligible words.

He turned toward her mother and tipped his hat to her. "Ma'am?"

"Oh! Forgive me, Mother. This is Sergeant Micah Hughes. Sergeant Hughes, this is my mother, Mrs. Octavia Warnock." Lydia refused to use her father's first name in her mother's title.

"Very pleased to meet you, Mrs. Warnock." He turned toward Lydia. "Your infant looks well. Growing quite vigorously, I see." He gave a nervous laugh.

"Mama, can Sergeant Hughes come for dinner at the manor? We've not seen him in so long. Can he come?" Comfort held onto his hand while jumping up and down.

"Comfort, please—" Heat crept up Lydia's neck. She rubbed the back of it in hopes that no one noticed.

Sergeant Hughes stooped down to Comfort's level. "That would be most appreciated, but I'm afraid the regiment is making preparations right now. I cannot leave the fort for long."

Lydia's hands gripped the baby blankets. "Preparations?" Her dry mouth, now totally parched, made speaking more difficult.

She tried to read his expression but staring at him proved too painful. Both hurt and affection filled his gaze. She glanced at Minta and pretended to adjust her blanket.

He cleared his throat. "Aye, we are gathering several regiments here in Rhode Island. We expect orders any day now."

"I see."

Comfort cried. "Why did you not say goodbye to us after Minta was born?"

His head jerked upward. "Minta?"

"Aye. I named her Araminta Joy. 'Minta' for short."

"It's a lovely name. I'm sure she will wear it well."

The silence grew heavy.

He stared briefly then looked at the ground, pretending to inspect something on his boot. "Well then." He took in a deep breath and smiled with his mouth closed. "I must return to my company, forthwith. Perhaps I shall see you at another time." He doffed his army hat and turned.

Comfort grabbed his legs. "Please come back and see us. We miss you."

He returned the hug and drew Comfort's face upward. "I miss you, as well." He spoke it quietly, likely thinking he could not be heard by anyone else.

But Lydia had heard. Obviously, by her mother's expression, she had also. Lydia braced herself for a parental interrogation of prime importance. Her mother's curiosity would not be assuaged with simple explanations from her. Now, her mother would know exactly what sins Lydia had committed.

15

Lydia's legs moved with unfamiliar stiffness as she ambled toward her mother's mansion. Her limbs seemed to beg to return to the side of Micah Hughes, but her mind forced her to stay on course. Ignoring her heart, she struggled the whole way.

By the time they reached her mother's steps, Lydia's inner battle had exhausted her. Nearly too fatigued and thirsty to cry, she held onto Minta with one hand while gripping the handrail with the other. She dragged herself up the five stairs. Entering the front door, Lydia searched for the nearest chair and collapsed.

Her mother removed her bonnet. "Comfort, you can follow Cecelia into the kitchen for fresh cider, if you like."

The child licked her lips and followed the servant to the back room.

She called after her. "And please bring us some as well, Cecelia."

"Yes, ma'am."

Lydia unwrapped Minta and stroked her daughter's chubby cheeks. She spoke baby talk to the infant, who responded with delightful smiles. She hoped her mother would forget the encounter with Micah.

"Look at her grin, Mother. She is such a happy child."

Octavia settled herself onto the chair next to Lydia and stared at her daughter. Her interrogation had already begun with her eyes. "So, Lydia—"

"Mother, I know what you are about to ask. But 'tis nothing, truly." She didn't look at her mother and instead continued to coo at the baby.

"If 'twas nothing, dear, then why did you grow pale at the sight of the man and blush like a schoolgirl when he approached you? I was not born yesterday, Lydia. My eyes may be dimming, but some things are obvious, even for the nearly blind."

Her emotions betrayed her when her eyes welled. "I—I barely know where to begin."

Octavia reached for her daughter's hand and squeezed it. "Try at the beginning. When did you meet this Sergeant Hughes?"

Lydia inhaled a shuddering breath for courage then told her mother about the arrival of the sergeant and Corporal Bearslayer the previous March when they brought the news of Jeremiah's death.

She explained about Ezekiel and his desire to join the army and, though it pained and worried her, she experienced an inner prompt to free the slave and allow him to join. Then she filled her mother in on the confrontation with Phineas at the county seat and how Micah had defended her honor.

"Phineas actually accused me of adultery, right in front of God and all mankind!" Lydia burst into tears.

"That son-in-law of mine—he deserves Phila!" Octavia grumbled under her breath, then stopped. She patted Lydia's hand. "Please, go on, dear."

"After they returned to the army, the sergeant and I corresponded. I wanted to be certain Ezekiel fared well." Lydia stopped, her forehead furrowed as she thought. "I really don't know when I began to anxiously await his next missive. It seemed that with every letter I received, I looked forward even more to the next one. He was always so kind and concerned for my well-being. I've never met anyone like him."

Her mother observed her before asking, "So, this all took place before the attack here in town?"

"Aye." Lydia closed her eyes. "The attack showed me how alone I felt—how vulnerable. How much I needed someone." She opened her eyes and gazed at her mother. "But the strange thing I realized, 'twas not Jeremiah I longed for. 'Twas Micah Hughes." Sobs wracked her body as great tears rolled down her cheeks. She pulled out a kerchief. *His* kerchief.

Not caring that her face likely appeared swollen and uncomely, she blew her nose. "Then, when I received no further letters from him, I despaired of ever seeing him again. Until—"

"Until he arrived near the time of your confinement, if I judge this rightly."

She dabbed under her eyes, trying to regain her composure, and nodded. "Aye. When Micah arrived, I could not contain my joy. He seemed just as pleased to see me. We kissed," she averted her eyes from her mother's, "with such passion." She couldn't contain the tears anymore and sobbed into the handkerchief with one hand while hugging Minta with the other.

Between her sobs, she sputtered, "And then, little Jeremiah died during the birthing. I knew 'twas my fault. If I'd not kissed him—" The tears flowed freely.

"If you'd not kissed the sergeant? You believe that is what killed your son?" Her mother's hand caressed her cheek. "Oh, dear Lydia, you carry such an unbearable burden."

She looked her mother in the eyes. "How could it be otherwise? A woman with child by her husband kisses another man whilst the infant is still in her womb? How sinful must that be seen by God? Such a betrayal to my husband, proven by my son's demise!" She sat, shaking her head.

"A betrayal to your dead husband? Lydia, dear, you are a

widow. Widows do not commit adultery by kissing another man." She turned Lydia's face toward hers. "Look at me."

Lydia gazed at her mother. She wished she could cover her face for the embarrassment permeating her spirit.

"You have long carried the guilt of your father's sins. I'm not certain when you became aware of his dark nature, but I've mourned for your beautiful spirit beset by the knowledge of evil far too young."

She stared down at her lap, her eyes too swollen to focus.

"Look at me, daughter." Octavia lifted Lydia's chin. "You are so filled with beauty in your heart. 'Tis easy to see why a man would love you. I was so pleased when Jeremiah came into your life and treasured your kindness and made you feel loved. But he is gone now." Tears dripped from her mother's eyes.

Mother sniffed back her sadness and went on. "I saw the look on your face when the sergeant came toward you. You love him. And if I read his expression correctly, he loves you as well. Do not take love for granted. 'Tis a gift, both fragile and easily shattered. I know this." Her face grew dark, and Lydia recognized anger there as well as pain.

Poor Mother.

"But Mother, the baby. He is dead, and I feel responsible—as if I killed him!"

Her mother sighed deeply. "You have not killed your child, Lydia. We don't know why these things happen. You are not the first woman to lose an infant during a birthing, and you won't be the last. We do not understand God's ways sometimes. Nor do we know His purposes in the darker things of this life."

Lydia met her mother's pale blue eyes. "I've never heard you speak of such things, Mother."

She harrumphed. "Perhaps because I've changed."

That appeared obvious to Lydia, but whatever change had occurred, she'd never felt such affection for her parent before. "I love you, Mother."

Octavia's eyes brimmed and overflowed. "I've waited so long to hear you say that, dear."

Her mother stood in front of Lydia's chair. She bent over, wrapped her arms around Lydia and the now-resting infant, and the women embraced with a long-overdue hug.

Cecelia brought the cider with glasses on a tray but did not speak. She left the room quietly, closing the door to the kitchen.

The women separated, and her mother sat with difficulty.

"I should have come to you with your sore leg." Lydia's eyes narrowed in concern.

"Well, you have precious cargo on your lap. 'Twould not do to have your little one disturbed." Mother smiled.

As if on cue, Minta awoke with a start and promptly voiced her displeasure that she'd not eaten for two hours. "There, there, dear Minta. I do not think you shall starve." The girl's mouth opened wide while she searched for her source of sustenance, then sighed with contentment as she gulped down her mother's milk.

The baby's grandmother stared at the child with a thoughtful smile. "She looks like you, Lydia."

Lydia smiled. "That's what Micah said." Heat flushed her cheeks, and she refused to peer at her mother's penetrating gaze. But she could feel every particle of revelation that now infused her mother's understanding.

"I see now. Minta. *Micah.*" Her mother would not release her stare.

Lydia refused to have her entertain a misunderstanding. "Minta is Jeremiah's child, Mother. I'll not have you believe otherwise."

"I know this, Lydia, because I know *you.* But your choice of names for your beloved daughter should tell you something. You've named her after the man who loves you—the man *you* love. That should tell you much. I know one thing for certain. It reveals your heart to your old mother."

She stared at her nursing baby. "'Tis too late."

"Why?"

"Because I've told him I could not live with the guilt."

"Well then, you must find a way to alleviate your soul's guilt and return to the man with open arms."

So much easier said than done.

～

LYDIA and all the servants dressed in clean clothes for the meetinghouse service the next Sabbath day. Comfort protested putting on her "itchy" dress, as she called it.

"'Tis not a play day, Comfort, but a day to go to church." Lydia insisted.

Comfort pouted but allowed Hannah to help her get dressed.

Hannah, Lydia, and Comfort squeezed into the one-horse chaise, with Lydia holding onto the baby. Now that she'd returned to her smaller form, getting in and out of the buggy caused far less distress. She recalled the days of carrying the twins and riding in this vehicle with dread.

As Cuff drove the chaise, Comfort waved at Miriam and Rose astride the mare beside them. "I wish I could ride the horse."

"Perhaps when you're older." Lydia's gaze swept along the acreage, and she focused on the family plot. In particular at the grave of baby Jeremiah. She regretted his father's body lay interred at Valley Forge. Somehow it would have comforted Lydia to know they were side by side.

She forced her eyes to focus on the travelers inside the carriage and smiled, grateful for the blessing of these three.

When they arrived at the meetinghouse, Cuff helped them out, and Lydia handed Minta to Hannah. As she emerged from the chaise, a uniformed soldier in the distance caught her eye. *Micah.* She followed him with her eyes, but she lost him in the throng of residents and the larger-than-usual numbers of military men who attended this morning. What was occurring?

"Come on, Mama." Comfort waved to her, and Lydia smiled, relieved her daughter had not spotted Micah and run over to him.

Lydia took the baby from Hannah and carried her into the murmuring crowd gathered in the wooden building. Cuff moved ahead of her, opening the latch on the pew door so she could go in first. She slid down the row, estimating the number of seats needed, then carefully sat. Minta fussed, and Lydia placed her on her shoulder, hoping the child wouldn't spit up onto her newly cleaned gown. It had been over two months since the birthing, and Lydia finally fit into this dress. The thought of a milk stain embarrassed her.

But then she thought of her son and wished with all her heart he had survived to stain all of her clothing. She would not focus on this frivolous concern. She would savor these moments with her surviving daughter, no matter how many messes the child created. She stroked Minta's back with a swirling sweep, and the infant fell asleep. Lydia closed her eyes for a moment.

She opened them when the minister spoke, knowing her closed eyes would lull her into a nap. Her heart beat more quickly when she noticed Micah two rows ahead with his company of soldiers. The man's intense gaze wasn't fixed on the pulpit but focused on her. Her heart lurched, skipping a beat altogether. Her breathing quickened when their eyes met. He turned to look at the front, but he had not smiled. Her heart sank.

The minister told of a man named John Newton. A fellow clergyman, who had heard Mr. Newton speak at a New Year's service five years prior, sent him a sermon. The message made such an impression, that clergyman sent it to his friend in Bristol.

He explained that Mr. Newton, now a man of the cloth himself, spoke of his past as a slaver on the ships to Africa.

Absolute silence filled the meetinghouse. The minister smiled at his congregation. "I knew that would draw your attention." He proceeded with the message, every ear listening to every word coming from the pulpit. "Mr. Newton humbly confessed his sins as a slaver—buying humans, trading them for rum, beating the men, and abusing the women."

Lydia cringed in her seat and shut her eyes in a vain attempt to erase horrifying images that hid in the darkest corners of her mind. Her breathing increased, and Hannah's hand gripped hers.

"John Newton continued many years in this life as a seaman, until one day a near-tragedy onboard his ship awoke his soul to his need for salvation. His need for grace, despite his wickedness. On one of his voyages, his ship sustained a deep hole that filled rapidly with the ocean's depths.

"Mr. Newton cried out for God to save him. In what some may ascribe as a miracle, some of the ship's cargo broke free, slid into the gaping hole, and plugged the source of certain ocean death.

"John Newton met grace that day when he confessed his sin as a slaver and turned his life over to the God who could save not just his body, but his soul as well. Thereafter, Mr. Newton campaigned for the abolition of slavery."

Lydia's eyes opened wide, and she stared at the minister. A slaver, forgiven by God? Fighting to abolish the very sin he'd so lustfully supported?

Even her father could have been forgiven if he'd asked God for mercy and changed his ways? It seemed impossible that such sins were within the realm of grace. Yet the nightmares of her past had blinded her to the fact that she served a God of mercy. A God of grace.

God did not hold her responsible for her father's sin of slavery. But she suddenly had a revelation. She *was* accountable for her sin of hatred toward her father.

Please forgive me.

Hot tears dripped onto her lap—tears of relief that washed the anger from her heart. Her refusal to forgive her father had so hardened her soul that she had been enslaved all these years, chained by the iron clasps of her own sin. Not her father's.

She looked upward and inhaled deeply. Hannah startled at the sound, but then she smiled at Lydia. The look of peace must be as evident on her face as it felt in her soul.

She could finally be free.

I must tell Micah.

After the service concluded and the troops exited the building, she handed Minta to Hannah. "Please hold her. I must find Micah."

The crowds thwarted her efforts at every turn. She stood on tiptoe and craned her neck but couldn't see him for the dozens of congregants standing around chatting. Usually, Lydia enjoyed seeing familiar faces on Sabbath day, but today, just one face became the focus of her search. And he was gone. Had she lost a final chance to tell him what had happened? Tell him she truly did love him?

Lydia raced outside past friends, her gaze craning for the one person she sought. Several people tried to speak with her. "Forgive me, please, I must find someone."

She approached one soldier in regimentals. "Please, sir, have you seen Sergeant Hughes? I can't seem to find him in this crowd."

"Sorry, Miss, I believe he has returned to the fort."

Hopelessness filled her heart as she thanked the kind corporal and turned to go back inside the meetinghouse. Looking for an empty chair, Lydia all but collapsed, discouraged and disheartened. Would she ever see him again?

16

Footsteps echoed in the nearly empty meetinghouse, and Lydia turned to see Hannah carrying her squirming bundle in her arms.

"I believe your little one be ready for her lunch, ma'am." Hannah handed the crying infant to her mother.

"Thank you, Hannah." She'd not found Micah, and she despaired of doing so. She did not know the army's plans, but it seemed as if the "preparations" Micah spoke of would soon be carried out.

"You look sad, ma'am." Hannah sat next to her on the bench.

"I am. I thought perhaps I'd find Micah, but he's left. And I don't know when they leave. Or where they're going."

"They be leavin' soon. That's why I want to talk with you."

Lydia furrowed her brow. "Of course, we can talk. But how do you know about the army leaving soon?"

"From Ezekiel." A smile bloomed on Hannah's face, and she blushed.

"He's here? Of course, he is. He's in the same regiment. I'd love to see him."

"He wants to see you too, Mrs. Saunders. But he's afraid to

ask you somethin' because he say you already do so much for him."

"Afraid? What would cause him to fear asking something of me?" Lydia used her free hand to place an encouraging touch on Hannah's arm.

"Ezekiel, he wish to marry me."

"That's wonderful! But I cannot say it surprises me."

Hannah giggled. "No, it should not be a surprise. But he be free, and I am not. He don't know what to do about that."

Lydia shut her eyes and pressed the side of her head. "I must be daft. I did not even think." Lydia reached toward Hannah and gripped her arm. "But, I'm not certain how to do that. Free you, that is."

Hannah's grin brought the sunlight indoors. "I told Ezekiel you would do this."

Lydia grew somber. "Does this mean you'll be leaving me?"

"No, ma'am. I want to stay with you for now while Ezekiel be away at the army. Maybe after the war be over, we can talk about leaving. But that not anytime soon. But to marry, I should be a free woman to marry a free man."

"Of course. When do you wish to marry?"

"We hope to today, if we can."

"Today? But what about a cake and a celebration?"

"Ma'am, it's war time. We be happy to have one or two nights together. The party does not matter."

"You're right. The war always puts our lives in perspective, does it not?" She squeezed Hannah's hand. "I am so happy for you. When do I get to see Ezekiel?"

"I be here, ma'am." Ezekiel's deep voice boomed from the back of the room.

Lydia placed her sleeping baby on her shoulder and re-adjusted her gown. Standing, she nearly grew dizzy to see not just Ezekiel but Micah with him.

"Oh–" She looked down, then back at the two, engaging them with a broad grin. "I'm so happy to see you both." She truly wished she did not cry so easily, but the good Lord must have handed out rivers full of tears to her on the day of her birth. Her eyes readily shared a few gills' worth.

Ezekiel walked up to her first. He looked different, somehow, in a very good way. He'd always seemed healthy, but, were it possible, he appeared even stronger. His demeanor bore the biggest change. He stood tall and looked straight into her eyes when he spoke. He smiled often.

Here stood a man who'd been subdued by his place in life but emerged like a butterfly from the chrysalis of slavery. He'd been released to become free in his heart. Lydia knew without a doubt, she'd done the right thing.

"So good to see you, ma'am. You seem to be well, and I am so pleased about your new daughter." He held his tricorne hat with a tight grip. "I am so sorry about your son."

"Thank you, Ezekiel. That is most kind. Micah helped me when that happened. He is a true friend." She hoped Micah heard her.

"Your daughter looks like you."

Lydia's face burned as she stared at her sleeping girl. "That's what Micah says as well." She paused. "Hannah tells me you have plans. I could not be more pleased. And Hannah is a free woman. When someone can tell me how to do this in legal terms, that is."

Micah stepped closer. "I can help with that."

Lydia's knees weakened when he drew close. "Good day, Micah." Her voice sounded breathless.

"Good day, Lydia." He reached for her hand as he bowed and kissed her fingers. The touch of his lips on her skin rippled through her with pleasure.

"I think we best leave these two alone. I believe they have some talkin' to do." Ezekiel placed his arm around Hannah's waist, and they left the meetinghouse, glancing over their shoulders, grinning as they went.

The couple stared at each other as though too afraid to speak. The silence grew awkward.

"Micah, I've made a terrible mistake." She looked at the floor and shifted her feet.

"And what mistake is that?" His low voice sent chills up her back as he fidgeted with the rim of his tricorne hat.

"I—I forgot to tell you that I was wrong." She bit her lip.

"Wrong about what?"

She mustered up her courage and looked him in the eyes. "I said that I made a mistake when I kissed you. That my boy's death served as punishment for my sin. I know now, 'twas not a sin to do so. I said many things that day I know hurt you. But the worst thing I did was I neglected to tell you ... that I love you."

Her tears flowed freely, and she did not have a kerchief. She picked up a corner of Minta's baby blanket and dapped at the moisture under her eyes.

He took out a clean kerchief and handed it to her. "I think I'd best get more of these since the woman I love seems to require them so often." He held it out to her.

"Thank you, Micah." She took it and held it close to her face, inhaling his scent. "Can you ever forgive me?"

"Forgive you for what? Grieving? Being confused and upset? Lydia, I acted like an absolute dunderhead for asking you about getting married at such a moment. What was I thinking?"

She laughed amidst her tears. "I know not. All I know is I am miserable without you, and so sad you will be leaving soon."

He wrapped his arms around her and Minta, holding them close. She relaxed into his embrace, afraid to move lest the moment be torn from her.

She inhaled the scent of woodsmoke, cider, and soap on his uniform then stroked the soft wool of his jacket and tried to memorize the pattern of the weave. Reaching up to touch his cheek that had not been shaved for a few days, she then searched for strands of his hair that had come undone from his queue. She did not want to forget anything about him when he went to battle. She suddenly longed for so much more.

"Micah." She spoke next to his ear. "I'd like to discuss something." She kissed his neck below his ear.

He pulled away, longing in his eyes. "Would that be about our future together?"

"Aye. I refused to speak of it with you in June. But would it be too forward of me to bring it up to you again? To tell you how much I long to marry you?"

"Nay, 'tis not too forward." He shook his head and smiled. "I would be the happiest of men to know you would wait for me so we could become man and wife." He kissed her forehead.

"But, I hoped we could marry right away—before you leave. I do not wish to wait." She stroked his face with her palm, and he kissed it as she drew it past his lips.

"Are you certain, Lydia? You've already been a war widow once. What if something happens to me? I cannot put you through that again."

She covered his lips with her fingers to shush him. "Were something to happen to you—and I pray with all my heart nothing shall—then I would want the army informing Mrs. Hughes, not Mrs. Saunders. I no longer wish to be known just as Jeremiah's widow. He was a wonderful man in so many ways. But I wish to be your wife. I long for you. Every part of you."

Micah took the baby and set her in a safe nook in the pew.

Then he took Lydia into his embrace, holding her out just far enough that he could make eye contact. "You are so lovely. I don't know how God saw fit to bless me with you, but I am grateful. I long for you as well. But I'll only agree to marry before I leave if you are certain beyond measure. I do not want you to have regrets."

"No regrets, Micah. Only love."

He tilted his head and drew near. His lips met hers slowly, passionately, and with a certainty that their marriage would be the fulfillment of so much.

She could feel his heartbeat beneath her fingertips. Breathless, she drew away. "Perhaps we'd best get ready for two weddings."

"Make ours first, then." Micah laughed and kissed her again.

~

MICAH HAD to settle for getting the second wedding ceremony, but he understood. The other couple had been officially engaged before they were, after all. Ezekiel had known Hannah far longer than he knew Lydia.

Although their courtship had been few in months, Micah's passion for Lydia made it seem they'd known one another their entire lifetime. When he focused on his future bride, it seemed easier to forget the coming battles. But the very knowledge that the upcoming campaign against the King's Army could take place at any time increased his passion for the one night they were assured of sharing their marriage bed.

Micah longed for it to begin, all the while dreading its ending.

He and Ezekiel arranged for the justice of the peace to arrive at Lydia's home at dusk. Both men jested about that evening, nervous and excited.

Ezekiel checked once again to be sure they had the documents that declared he and Hannah to be free. How foreign it would be for Micah to even consider the need for such a letter. To always have the threat of slavery hanging over one's head? Of not being believed they were free and equal with all men? Would this war for independence change that? He prayed it would.

Micah felt great pride in the commitment his company of black soldiers had made to the army. They were some of the best and the bravest. Some of them joined because their masters did not wish to. But Micah believed they were by far better soldiers than their masters would have been. These men knew what real freedom meant, and they determined to fight for it.

"Sergeant Hughes, sir, what do you think the women be doing right now?"

He buttoned his clean shirt and laughed. "I'm not yet privy to the ways of women in the bedchamber, Ezekiel, so I can only guess they are washing up and applying something to make themselves smell ..." He looked up, pretending to sniff the air. "Smell delicious."

They both laughed, then Ezekiel grew serious. "Sergeant Hughes, what happen to them if anything happen to us?"

It was a question Micah had asked himself over and over today. Who would watch out for them? What if one or both women were with child and the husbands never returned home? Lydia had already been through that once, and he hoped against hope she would not face that again. Despite his bride's strength, he now knew her vulnerabilities, and he feared for her and their family.

But he'd not dwell on that. Not tonight, at least. Tonight, he anticipated a celebration of love and later, more celebration to come in the bedchamber. He would focus on that far more pleasant thought.

LYDIA AND HANNAH took over an hour to decide which gowns they would wear for the ceremony. Lydia insisted Hannah wear one of her silk brocades, and she did not argue. Hannah's eyes glistened with excitement at the prospect.

Miriam helped Lydia with her stays and pulled them tight. "Not too snug, Miriam, or Minta will not get to eat."

Hannah laughed. "I be certain your new husband will help you loosen them, ma'am."

Lydia covered her mouth and laughed as heat rushed to her face. "Hannah, I am quite shocked."

"I don't know why, ma'am, since you know how babies get made."

She threw a bundle of ribbons at Hannah, and they both bent over laughing—as far as their corsets allowed.

Moments of laughter had been scarce during the war, and anticipating these weddings provided a reprieve from the fear that, at any moment, it might be time for battle again. That thought increased Lydia's desire to spend every moment possible with her new husband. She prayed it would turn into a long lifetime of love.

A knock sounded, and Miriam hurried to answer. She did not open the door but spoke through it. "Is that you, Cuff? They are almost ready."

"Aye. The justice of the peace be here, Miriam. Please tell them the men are ready."

"Well, ready or not, 'tis time." Lydia took in the image of Hannah in a crimson-red silk. "Oh, Hannah, you've never looked more beautiful. Ezekiel will be smitten by your loveliness."

"And you." Hannah pointed at Lydia. "I think the sergeant will take you to the bedchamber the moment those vows be spoken."

Lydia covered her mouth. "Shame on you!" She laughed. "We'll stay like respectable hostesses for a few moments—before both rushing off to our bedchambers!"

Miriam burst into giggles. Lydia could not remember her ever losing herself in a good, hearty laugh before. She hoped her servant could find more joy in America after such a cruel beginning to her life here.

Hannah took a deep breath. "Well, are we ready?"

Lydia inhaled, exhaled, and nodded. "Aye, I am more than ready."

LYDIA WORE her night shift and waited for her new husband to join her in bed, while Miriam brought Minta in for a feeding.

"You needn't come back for her, Miriam. She can sleep in the cradle in here."

"Very well, ma'am." Miriam grinned as she walked out.

After Minta had nursed herself to sleep, Lydia placed her gently in the cradle. Then Lydia waited. She wondered why she was so nervous until she realized her married life to Micah would be a totally new life. Her life with Jeremiah had ended. She was experiencing the fears of a new bride, and she rejoiced in the anticipation. She nearly jumped when Micah walked in.

"Were you not expecting me?" He grinned and walked toward her.

"I was hoping you would come, my love." She reached her arms out toward him.

"If one of my soldiers—or anyone—had said to me even yesterday that I'd be sharing this bedchamber with my wife tonight, I'd have called him a liar." He leaned toward her and caressed her face with his lips.

"When I saw you along the street last week, I feared I'd see animosity in your eyes. I thought you hated me. But when I drew closer, I saw something I'd not expected. I saw hope that we could be together again."

His soft kisses thrilled her sensibilities.

"What you saw was love. Love that never ceased for you. Love that would have waited a thousand years for you to come back to me, if that's what it took." Passion filled his eyes. "I am a most fortunate man."

She leaned over toward the nightstand, blew out the candle, then reached out for her husband's embrace. His warm hands drew her to himself and loved her. Excited her. With his kisses, she lost herself in his love.

17

Lydia awoke the next morning and turned to look at her new husband. The empty pillow and bed where he'd lain filled her with dread. "Micah?"

Perhaps he'd gone downstairs to eat breakfast, although she'd hoped they could eat together on their first morning as man and wife. She sat up, then closed her eyes, remembering the passion of the night before. The memory sent shivers through her, and a smile emerged onto her face.

Minta stirred in her cradle. Lydia stood and picked up her precious girl. While she prepared to feed her, out of the corner of her eye, she noticed a letter sitting on her dresser. Her heart lurched with fear. She grimaced at the familiar handwriting.

The baby cried, so she attached her to nurse while still standing, then picked up the letter with a shaking hand.

She sat on the edge of the bed then opened the note from her new husband with one hand. Her breathing quickened while she struggled to focus on the words.

My dearest Lydia,

Ezekiel and I were both called away to join the regiment in the middle of the night. I tried not to disturb you, but I kissed your cheek. One last memory for my heart until we are together again.

I'd hoped we would have at least one more night together, enveloped in the love that you so passionately shared with me. I truly understand now why God created woman for man, because I now feel complete. I'd no idea before just how much I needed you.

We've not been told where we're going, although I have my suspicions. Suffice it to say, it will be a difficult campaign, and I covet your prayers for your husband, who loves you with all his heart.

Forgive my hurried scrawl, but General Sullivan awaits.

Know that I love you every minute of every day.

Your loving husband,
Micah

Lydia stared at the letter. *He's gone?* With a sharp knock on the door, she looked up.

Hannah burst through the door, holding a letter, tears rolling freely down her face. "They be gone!" It sounded more like a wail than words.

She rushed toward Lydia, and the two women wept together as they sat side by side. Words escaped her. She'd gone from intense pleasure the night before to indescribable pain and loss this morning. How does one reconcile such a shift in one's heart?

The infant cooed, capturing her attention. Her innocence and sweetness drew Lydia to focus on her. Despite the numbness in Lydia's soul, Minta drew her back to life, rejoicing in this reminder that love surrounded her. She would dwell on that until the day she reunited with Micah. She would not even entertain the thought he might not return to her. She did not know how she could bear it if he did not.

~

10 August 1778

My Dearest Lydia,

YESTERDAY, our regiment was called from Fort Barton to inspect the British-held fort on Butts Hill. They ferried us across the inlet in a light rain. Upon arrival, we crept slowly toward the enemy soldiers we could see at a distance. We might as well have stood and walked the distance, for all the danger we were in.

The "soldiers" were nothing more than hay-filled red coats with branches for muskets. At least we confiscated the coats for some future purpose. Colonel Topham seemed disappointed, hoping to test our fighting skills. I was just as pleased none were required.

From the top of the hill, in the distance, we have a clear view of the waterways where, after the fog cleared this morning, Admiral Howe's fleet emerged like ghost ships. By their movements, I'm certain Admiral d'Estaing is readying for sea battle. Only God knows how this will play out.

I can see thick storm clouds to the south and east, and there's a chill in the air—so at odds with the heat of late. I'm certain we'll be fine.

How are you and the little ones? Please tell Comfort there are very interesting bugs here on Aquidneck Island. Perhaps, when the war is over, we can take a ferry here and find some together.

I pray we will soon be together again. Being with my new family is the most wonderful dream I can ponder. I miss you all. Especially my beautiful bride.

Your loving husband,
Micah

Lydia read the letter over and over, touching the paper that his hand had touched. The storm he'd written about now sent torrents of rain over her Bristol plantation, and the onslaught of wind, thunder, and lightning terrified her. She could not recall such a storm before.

And Micah was out in this storm, likely with no shelter.

She prayed as she'd never prayed before, asking God that he

and the troops would be spared from harm. She could not imagine what camp conditions they endured without proper shelter.

Another crackle of thunder brought a crying Comfort into her room. "Mama!"

Even Minta awoke, startled by the storm's ferocity, which resembled a cannon's blast in the way it rattled the house. Lydia cuddled both of her daughters close.

The storm did not ebb, and Lydia worried it would damage the house. Perhaps the barn. Would the horses be all right? She remembered Cuff said he would close the barn doors and latch them. What would she have done without Cuff's help? Ezekiel had taught him much about taking care of a farm.

Despite the loudness of this storm, exhaustion overwhelmed Lydia, and she prayed they all could sleep.

She nursed Minta, hoping the infant's eyes would close. Although she loved to feel the warmth of her baby, she feared falling asleep in bed with such a small one. Ever since she was young and had read the Old Testament story about Solomon and the woman who'd accidentally lain on her infant during the night and suffocated her, Lydia worried this could happen.

It broke Lydia's heart to imagine awakening to find her child gone to eternity. Minta went back to sleep, and Lydia carefully placed her back in the cradle.

Comfort, still wide-awake, curled close to Lydia. "Mama, will Papa be safe in this storm?"

Despite the raging weather, Lydia smiled at her daughter, already calling Micah *Papa*. "Your Papa is a very smart man and a very good soldier. I'm certain he'll be fine. He's been in very bad weather before."

"Yes, but this is a scary storm. Do you think he's afraid?"

"Did I forget to tell you how brave your Papa is? He is the bravest man I've ever known." Lydia kissed the top of her head just before a bright flash of light illuminated the atmosphere, followed by an ear-piercing crack of thunder. They both jumped, and Lydia forced a laugh. "Now that seemed to be quite a drumbeat, was it not?"

"I wish the drummer would go away."

She stroked Comfort's hair. "I know, my sweet. I'm tired, and I wish he'd go away as well." She kissed her daughter again and gave her a hug, then rocked her like she did long ago.

"I wish I were a baby again. Then you'd rock me like you rock Minta."

"Well, if you like, I can rock you for a few minutes each night before bed. And when you think you're too grown up for rocking, you can tell me to stop. What do you say?"

"I love you, Mama."

"I love you, too, Comfort."

And I love you, too, my husband. May God watch over you wherever you are.

THE STORM that threatened earlier in the day hit Aquidneck Island by late afternoon. The pelting rain drenched everything, leaving the soldiers soaked and their campsite filled with mud. Micah had never seen such a gale, and the thunder and lightning added to the atmospheric fray.

The rain did not relent but worsened through the night.

"Find anything to shelter yourselves!" Major Ward shouted above the storm.

Micah hid with his fellow soldiers in their tent. They took turns holding onto each corner in an attempt to keep it together.

Although still August, the month did not matter as cold air whistled with the wind. Men shivered while they lay in their drenched uniforms. Micah hoped thinking of Lydia and the warmth of their bed would lessen the cold, but it just made him miss her more.

Ammunition cartridges lay in puddles, and Micah held his musket up out of the rain as much as he could. No dry place could be found to protect firelocks. The only good thing about their wet weaponry was that the enemy troops were likely in the same situation.

Any fighting between them during that storm would have to be hand to hand, without a shot fired. Since both British and American soldiers were trained to shoot at their enemies, they'd likely have at least two days of peace.

Not a tent in camp withstood the wind and beating of the rain. A particularly strong blast of wind blew away the last of the tents, forcing Micah and his companions to run for a barn, where they shared the shelter with some pigs and horses.

After nearly two days of brutal weather, the storm ebbed, revealing the formerly organized campsite as the swamp it had become. Micah barely knew where to begin to clean up. All the men shivered while they searched for anything salvageable.

When General Sullivan heard about the condition of the camp, he ordered the commissary to issue one and a half gills of rum to each soldier. Micah didn't think the reward made up for the distress of the last two days. But perhaps it might warm up his troops.

Micah needn't have worried about getting warm since, right after the cold storm ceased, the intense August heat returned, bringing with it sunshine to dry their soggy clothes and weapons.

Now that Mother Nature had ceased her assault, everyone readied for the next conflict with the more dangerous enemy of the two. This battle would surely prove to be the more destructive.

He prayed the coming engagement would not destroy him— or the life of anyone in his regiment. He knew from experience the deadly side of war, and it seemed difficult to believe they would come away unscathed.

IT TOOK three days of dry weather after the storm before the roads were passable. Lydia prepared to leave for town to deliver clothing and household goods to the meetinghouse. Their congregation had been collecting much-needed items to help those displaced by the fires in Warren and Bristol the previous May. So many had suffered, and many were still in need.

After her mother had told her about several prisoners taken away by the King's Army, Lydia had been further horrified to hear about the arrest of the minister in Warren. The enemy assumed he had allegiance to the insurgents, since so many Patriots attended his church.

For this "crime," Minister Thompson was taken to New York and, for a short time, placed on board the dreaded prison ship, the *Jersey*. By some miracle, the clergyman was released by the enemy.

The *Jersey* was a retired ship in Wallabout Bay, notorious for prisoners never returning alive. It had been built to hold about 400 sailors. Reports from spies indicated it now housed over 1,000 men condemned to a life of starvation, filth, and certain death.

The fact that the minister had been released alive seemed nothing short of a miracle. He, like so many others who'd lost their homes in the attack, desperately needed clothing. Any former prisoners who were fortunate enough to return home were covered in lice and had to bury their clothes rather than infest their families.

Lydia had a storage-full left from Jeremiah, and they served no purpose sitting in a chest in her home. She knew her deceased husband would want them to help another in need. Micah could never wear them, since he was taller than her first husband.

She planned to go to the town center with Hannah and the baby. But when Miriam served breakfast that morning instead of Hannah, Lydia asked where she might be.

"Hannah be not feelin' well this mornin.'" Miriam poured her a cup of coffee.

"Oh dear, I hope the floodwaters did not cause her illness of any sort." Lydia sipped her coffee.

"No, I think not." Miriam raised an eyebrow at Lydia.

"Miriam, what are you getting at?" Lydia's eyes widened, and she placed her hands on both cheeks. "She isn't! Does she think she is?"

"She might could be." Miriam chuckled. "She does show signs. Maybe we know soon whether or not a new baby comes."

Lydia sat back in her chair and smiled. New life. Another baby to live in their home. There could be no greater gift, and she rejoiced in the thought.

"I'll tell Hannah she must rest more, especially in the mornings. Miriam, would you be able to fix breakfast, or do you want me to help cook?"

"No offense, ma'am, but I think we all be safer with me cookin' instead of you." Miriam winked.

Lydia faked insult, with her fists on her hips. "Well, I never! I'm so terribly offended!" She covered her mouth to keep from laughing. "Actually, you're correct, and I'm more than happy to leave you the honors of being cook." She pushed her chair back and rose. "I'll take Comfort and the baby with me to distribute the clothing. Perhaps I'll stop in and visit Mother whilst I'm there."

"Very well, ma'am."

Lydia walked to the barn to ask Cuff to get the chaise ready. "We'll leave just as soon as I can load up the clothes."

While she walked back to the house, a carriage came up the drive. *Phila.* Her heart sank. What did she want now?

Her sister's driver stopped in front of the house and helped Phila step out. She made a great show of her enlarging belly by walking with an exaggerated waddle.

"Good day, Phila. And what brings you here? I'm actually getting ready to head into town."

"Whatever for? It's such a mess, with vagabonds walking the streets looking for a free meal."

"Are you aware that many are homeless after the attack by the king's troops? And the Hessians?" Lydia still had difficulty even saying that word.

"Well, they likely were insurgents plotting against the government. Perhaps they should leave town rather than stay and disrupt the city." Phila opened her Chinese fan. "It's so warm today."

Phila could easily incite Lydia's anger. She prayed for self-restraint. "I really must be getting on with my day, Phila."

"Oh, I'd not planned on being here for long anyway, what with the baby and all." She slowly swirled her palm over the bulge.

"Yes, Mother told me. I'm sure you're delighted. And how does Phineas feel? He must be quite happy as well."

"Well, he keeps saying he does not recall when last we had—you know—marital relations, but I keep reminding him that surely it would have been right around the time I became with child. Phineas is so forgetful." Phila fanned herself.

"I see." Lydia inhaled a deep breath.

"So, how is your new little one? You had a boy, did you not?"

Lydia's cheeks grew so hot she felt she'd been in front of a hearth for hours. "Aye, Phila. I had a son. But he died. His twin, my daughter, is very much alive and doing well."

"Oh, I am so forgetful. Mother did tell me that, after all."

Lydia waited for an 'I'm so very sorry,' or 'It must be so painful when your newborn dies.' But there were no such sentiments. Only Phila, dwelling on herself. Barely tolerating the lowlier creatures around her.

"Good day, Phila." Lydia spun around and stomped toward her house.

"Well, can't I see your new baby first? Lydia?"

She slammed the door and leaned against it. As Phila

climbed back into her carriage, Lydia heard her complain to her driver about her sister's ill manners.

Hatred filtered through Lydia like cankerworm in fruit trees. She replayed the conversation with Phila in her mind. She would never forgive her sister for her wretched selfishness. Lydia hated it when she cried from anger. At least she hadn't cried in front of Phila. That would only encourage her evil nature.

Then she recalled the message about John Newton—a wretched slaver who did despicable things to people. Yet God gave him mercy, and he truly changed.

Was her hatred for Phila any less evil than the hatred for men of a different color? Hatred was evil, in any form.

Lydia could not change Phila. But Lydia could refuse to hate her. It might be a battle every day, but she determined to win it.

18

Micah's regiment had no sooner dried out from the storm when several boats arrived from Howland's Ferry, carrying more troops. Much to everyone's relief, the boats also delivered supplies of fresh cartridges and casks of gunpowder.

But the increased military activity portended battles soon to come. While the confrontation between American troops and the King's Army grew imminent, Micah felt a deepening sense of dread.

He'd hoped to have time to write another letter to Lydia, even asking someone if they knew the date that day. He made note that the 14th of August had arrived already, but with all the camp activity, he could set aside no time to write in private.

Occasionally he saw Ezekiel nearby, and they connected momentarily with a look. He read the same expression on Ezekiel's face that his own, no doubt, reflected. They'd had far too little time with their brides and worried there would be no more nights of such pleasure.

Love and war were a constant and agonizing conflict in a soldier's heart. Perhaps that's why the ancient Romans forbade their soldiers to marry. Despite the pain of it, Micah would not have missed the one night he and Lydia spent together, even if it turned out to be their last.

He slept fitfully that night, despite a long workday of war preparations. When the cannon sounded at the crack of dawn, Micah and his company dragged their weary bodies from their tents and assembled. The next two cannon blasts, thirty minutes later, brought them hustling into columns. Situated in full regimentals and armed with dry armaments, the men awaited the triple cannon blasts that thrust the troops forward toward Newport.

Micah pushed thoughts of Lydia to the back of his mind. If he and his regiment were to survive this battle, he needed to focus on one thing—killing the enemy.

~

LYDIA TRIED to forget her sister's visit, although that was akin to ignoring a cannon blast in one's house. Phila had a way of unnerving her peace of mind—she always had—but as the sisters grew up, the venom from Lydia's tongue became more brutal. More vindictive. Lydia had to pray away her hurt and anger, once again.

Cuff drove the carriage. It lurched a bit, shaking Lydia from her troubling thoughts. She took in the bundle of sweetness in her lap and watched the infant's closed eyes and mouth move in her restful state. *What do you dream of, my sweet?*

The baby had grown so much in the last couple of weeks, Lydia's arms ached. She shifted her hold to a more comfortable position. It didn't seem possible Minta could be two months old now. Her mother would enjoy seeing her and Comfort today.

She stared at the bundle of clothes Jeremiah once wore and smiled, remembering the fitting when Jeremiah objected to being measured. He loved to be active and not stand still for something so mundane as getting a new waistcoat.

Lydia hoped she could share many such happy memories

with Jeremiah's daughters while they grew. She wanted her girls to know their first Papa was a loving father and faithful soldier, very much like Micah.

She looked forward to seeing her mother again. Lydia had sent her a note to tell her she married Micah. Her mother sent a precious letter in return, which Lydia would treasure always.

Once a bustling hub of happy residents, Bristol was now a sad place to visit. Lydia noted its burned-out buildings and residents lined up for food at the meetinghouse. The chimney remnants of many charred homes stood like tombstones amidst the clutter of destruction. Would the town ever regain its former beauty?

In many ways, she thought its present condition an appropriate reflection of the horrid slave trade the town tolerated for so many years. The grotesque remnants of fiery destruction seemed a just recompense for the hideous reality of wealth gained from blood money.

"What happened to all the houses, Mama?" Comfort's eyes widened.

"Some bad people came here, but they are gone now." Lydia controlled the quivering in her voice, lest it frighten her daughter further.

"Will they come back?" The child's lips quivered.

"Nay, my dearest. They are gone. Never to return." Lydia prayed in her heart that was so.

Cuff drew the carriage to a halt, and Lydia climbed out.

"Cuff, can you hold the baby whilst I take these garments inside?"

"Nay, ma'am. I carry the clothes for you." He reached into the carriage and swept the large bundle into his arms.

"Thank you, Cuff."

Lydia noticed the minister waving at her. She returned his greeting and approached the clergyman, whose shoulders slumped in weariness. "Are you well? Do you need help?"

He placed his hand on her arm. "We can always use more

help, but a new mother does not need to stand in line, serving those without a home."

"But I want to do something."

"You already have by bringing these clothes. Many will be grateful for this contribution."

Lydia paused to think. "Mayhap I can bring some food from our garden. God has blessed us with an abundance of beans and corn this year."

The minister took the clothes from Cuff. "That would be most appreciated. Thank you again, Mrs. Sa—I mean, Mrs. Hughes. And might I congratulate you on your recent wedding?"

Heat infused Lydia's cheeks, and she grinned. "Thank you, Minister." She curtsied. "Now I'll be visiting my mother. But we'll deliver food in the next day or so."

He tipped his hat at her. "Thank you again."

She climbed back into the carriage, holding Minta, who stirred awake and looked around. "Welcome to Bristol, little one. Should we go visit your Grandmama, Comfort?"

"Aye, Mama." Comfort's cheeks dimpled.

Cuff guided the horse carefully around the numerous crowds in the street. Between people left without a residence and the carpenters doing repairs, Lydia had never seen the streets so busy.

When they arrived at Mother's house, Lydia stood a moment and stared. This was the home she'd grown up in. The house that held so many dreadful memories. Inhaling deeply, she hoped her better relationship with her mother would transform her dread at entering this place.

She gripped the railing and ascended the five steps with Minta and Comfort. After she knocked on the great wooden portal, Cecelia answered. The slave's brows furrowed.

"Is all well, Cecelia?"

"Nay, ma'am. Your mother be quite ill."

"What? Has the doctor been here?"

"Aye, ma'am. He give her medicine, but she still not well."

"I'll go see her." She turned toward Comfort and said, "You stay with Cecelia, dearest."

"But, Mama—"

"Nay, my love. I cannot risk you or your sister becoming ill. Besides, Cecelia might need your help to watch Minta. Do you think you could do that?"

Comfort stood taller. "Yes, Mama."

"There's my brave girl."

Lydia hugged Comfort, then handed the sleepy Minta to the servant. She started to climb the stairs to her mother's room, but Cecelia stepped in her path and shook her head.

"She be in the room over here." She pointed toward the downstairs bedchamber.

Lydia grew more concerned. Were the stairs too difficult for her mother to climb?

Her fears grew when she entered the darkened chamber and saw her mother propped up with pillows. She slept, but her breathing was shallow. When Lydia pulled one curtain aside so she could see better, alarm gripped her at her mother's pale countenance.

The noise awoke Mother. "Who's there?"

"It's me, Mother. I'm so sorry I disturbed you." Lydia took her hand and sat on the edge of the large bed.

Mother gave a weak smile, and it brought a hint of color to her cheeks. "How kind of you to visit, Lydia. So sorry I cannot serve you tea in the parlor."

"No matter, Mother. How long have you been ill? And why did you not send for me?" Lydia bit her lip and shifted on the bed.

"There's just not much to be done for me, Lydia. Cecelia takes care of me, and the doctor brings my medicinals."

"What does he say is wrong?"

"Oh, he says 'tis dropsy of my heart, but he frets without cause. 'Tis nothing to concern yourself with."

Even speaking just a few sentences labored her mother's breathing.

Lydia gripped her hand. "Mother, please listen to Dr. Caldwell. You mustn't over-exert yourself."

"You worry too much, Lydia. You always have." She reached up to touch Lydia's cheek. "Even when you were young, you carried the burden of the world on your shoulders. There were times," she paused to catch her breath, "I wished I could make you happy in your heart."

Lydia's eyes brimmed. "I am happy, Mama. Truly. I have two wonderful daughters. And a beloved husband."

Darkness swept across Mother's expression. "Aye, you do. So much more than I had."

Swallowing with difficulty past the growing lump in her throat, Lydia wished she could tell her mother she'd had a beloved husband as well, but they both knew it was not true.

"Is there anything I can do for you, Mama? I feel so helpless." The tears that had brimmed now flowed freely.

Mother attempted a weak smile. "You can come see me again. It seems there is much we need to discuss. But I am so very tired today."

Lydia leaned over and kissed her cheek. "I love you, Mama."

Her mother closed her eyes and smiled. "I love you so much as well, dear Lydia."

She forced herself to stand from her mother's bedside. Her knees weakened as she walked toward the open door. Looking back, she prayed it would not be her last visit with her mother. She craved more moments of tenderness with her and bemoaned the years of disharmony.

Lydia knew things had changed for the better ever since the attack on her mother's home. It seemed it took the threat of death to bring new life to their relationship.

Cecelia waited outside the door. "'Twas good you came to see her, ma'am. Doctor's not certain how long she has. I wanted to have Caesar send for you, but Mrs. Warnock would not have it. She said she not want to worry you."

"You can send Caesar for me anytime, Cecelia." Lydia touched her arm. "I'll be back very soon. Thank you for seeing to her needs."

As she left the house, her feet dragged with a weight of sadness. Many times, she'd left this house, anxious to escape this prison that sucked the joy from her spirit. Today, the necessity of leaving stole her joy once more. But she would return to share the remaining moments her mother had on this earth.

THE AMERICAN ARMY, with thousands of infantrymen and over a thousand on horseback, lined up in three columns and headed south toward Newport. Micah thought the sight of well-disciplined and organized troops, banners flying in the breeze and united with one purpose, would impress even the King's Army.

In just a few short years, the Americans proved they knew how to defend their country. Today they campaigned to free the city of Newport from British occupation.

Micah marched with his regiment and watched his company of black soldiers march in straight formation. Pride surged in his heart at the hard-working group of ex-slaves. They proved their loyalty to the cause of freedom and were worthy fellow soldiers.

Artillery units transported heavy cannons on wagons down both the east and west roads. Militia covered their flanks. General Sullivan, astride his mount, led 200 horsemen as they paraded across the frontlines from the east column of troops to the west. The soldiers marched as one, in time with the music that inspired their steps.

With so many American warriors encompassing the island, how could they not defeat the British Army? Just before five in the evening, the general halted the impressive army. They were on high ground, facing the enemy. Micah wondered which side would fire first.

When neither side raised a weapon, the Americans were ordered to pitch camp. Their work had just begun that evening. General Sullivan ordered the militia to dig trenches on the western edge of Honeyman Hill, the highest ground in the area and the perfect location to place artillery. While the soldiers worked the trenches, Continental troops provided cover for them from enemy fire.

Victory appeared assured, until word filtered through to Micah that hundreds of troops who'd signed on for a limited period of time deserted their units. One group of Massachusetts militia had signed on for a mere fifteen days of service. When their commitment finished, they returned home to harvest their crops.

It troubled Micah that, on the eve of this important battle, men would put their own needs ahead of their country's future. He'd already served over two years. Could these men not have stayed for two more weeks?

Yet other recruits joined the cause, and on the evening of August 16, Micah and his company welcomed a thick fog. The vapor obscured the work of the militia units digging trenches and creating earthen redoubts to provide protection from the enemy.

Come the light of day, the enemy would see the American bulwarks, and the long-anticipated confrontation would begin.

Micah fought to smother thoughts of Lydia. But that was a battle he could not win.

19

When the fog cleared the next morning, the alarmed British troops fired. Despite the mile-long distance between the opposing armies, the American troops who worked on the entrenchment ceased their efforts during the daytime in order to avoid becoming targets. Several shots actually reached them. Micah heard a British cannonball barely missed the Marquis de Lafayette.

Even at night, British guns continued to fire at the workers, who dropped to the ground with each musket flash. Most of the men stood again, brushed off their uniforms, and continued with their work. Three of the brave men were wounded, and some cannons were rendered useless.

Micah and a few of his company took their turn digging, hauling dirt, and building. Doing anything was better than sitting—and waiting.

He returned to his company at dawn, covered with dirt and sweat, craving something to drink. Someone handed him a canteen, and he guzzled the contents down. As he lowered the flask, Ezekiel emerged from where his company awaited further orders. The former slave walked tall and with determination.

"Sergeant Hughes, may I ask a favor of you, sir?" His words carried fear, despite the calm appearance on his face.

"I will if I can, Ezekiel."

"Please ... promise me you will deliver this letter to Hannah. In case anything goes wrong."

Micah took the folded parchment from Ezekiel's trembling fingers. His face might not reflect his concern, but his grip betrayed his true feelings.

"I will." Then he remembered he needed to do the same. "And I'll write one for Lydia. If you'd be so kind as to deliver. Just in case." Micah struggled to smile.

The men stared at one another with many thoughts unspoken yet communicated silently.

"Thank you, sir." Ezekiel saluted the sergeant.

Micah saluted in return. He watched the man with the broad shoulders stride back to his company. Would both letters need to be delivered? He prayed neither would be necessary.

Before Micah washed up in his tent, he determined that he'd write this missive to his wife. This could be the last moment he'd have the opportunity.

Fumbling through his haversack, he found what he needed. Grabbing a thick book to support his pen, he covered the quill's end with the ink, took a deep breath, and wrote.

18 August 1788
My dearest Lydia,

I pray this letter finds you well. In truth, I pray this missive need never be delivered to you, my beautiful wife. If you receive this, then something has happened to me.

Should I not be able to return to you, I want you to know that our one night together wrapped in your arms was the most treasured day of my life. Even thinking about it now nearly takes my breath away. Although I wish our love could be enjoyed every day on this earth, please know that I'd rather have that one night in my thoughts than never to have known your love. You have made me a happy husband.

I have written to my brother at East Haddam to apprise him of our marriage. Should you need to leave Rhode Island, or should you merely wish to, my brother will welcome you and our daughters into his home. 'Tis not a prosperous farm, but our children would never be in need. My brother is a kind man. He's never married, so our family home is large enough to accommodate everyone. Including your servants, should you wish to bring them.

Please know how dear you are to me. I pray you are well and do not grieve for me. Please look to your future. And tell Comfort and Minta that I love them both.

My love for you is boundless and lives in my heart forever.

With all my love,
Micah

As he put his bottle of ink and goose quill away, he noticed droplets of moisture on the page. He blotted the paper with his kerchief, careful not to smear the ink. After sprinkling talc over the words, he blew away the excess, closed his eyes, and prayed this letter would never need be delivered.

LYDIA PLANNED to visit her mother again, but before she could leave, Caesar arrived with a message.

"Mrs. Hughes, your mother. She not well."

"I'll be there forthwith. And please send for the doctor, Caesar."

"He already there, ma'am." Caesar turned and hurried back to his gelding.

Although she knew things were not going well, Lydia did not feel ready for this. How unfair it seemed that, just when things from the past were beginning to heal between them, her mother would not be long for this world. Why could not this have been mended long ago?

At least it has been mended. The sudden thought prompted Lydia to put aside her regrets and focus on getting to her mother —before it was too late.

Miriam served breakfast to Comfort and Rose, who giggled together at the table.

When Lydia entered the room, her daughter stopped laughing. "What is wrong, Mama?"

She took in a slow, deep breath. "Comfort, I must go to see your grandmama in town. She is quite ill." Lydia met Miriam's gaze and nodded. "I need you to stay with Miriam and Rose." She turned her attention back to the girls. "So be on your best behavior."

"I will." Comfort slid off the chair and ran to her mother, hugging her tightly. "Please tell Grandmama I hope she feels well very soon."

Lydia held back a sob. "I shall, Comfort." How she wished she could bring her older daughter with her, but Lydia feared it might be too distressing for the four-year-old. "I shall."

She kissed the top of Comfort's head and held her for a moment. With regret, she released her daughter and thanked Miriam for her care.

Lydia picked up Minta from her downstairs cradle and headed for the front door.

Hannah stopped her. "Ma'am, everything not all right?"

Hannah's paler-than-usual brown complexion reminded Lydia of happier news for their future with a babe on the way. Today's news was far more troubling.

"My mother is quite ill, so I must go to her."

"I will say a prayer for her, Mrs. Hughes."

"Thank you, dear Hannah. Please stay abed if you are not well today." She gripped the doorknob and paused. *Please, God, make me strong.*

After thrusting the door open, she found Cuff working in the garden. "Please bring the carriage round, Cuff."

He dropped the hoe, noticed her tear-covered face, and ran for the barn.

Minta fussed, and Lydia bounced the infant in her arms as she awaited the arrival of the chaise. Cuff pulled the carriage to the bottom of the front steps within moments. Moments that seemed like hours to Lydia. *Please don't let me be too late.*

By the time she'd climbed into the chaise, Minta screamed for her food. Lydia undid her top stays with trembling fingers and put the baby to breast. As she felt her milk let down, Lydia ceased holding back her tears.

Had her mother fed her like she now fed her daughter? While some slave owners found wet nurses to feed their infants, Lydia remembered once when nursing Comfort that her mother mentioned how much she loved feeding Lydia herself rather than giving her to someone else. How had that detail escaped her memory so easily?

Perhaps she'd focused so long on her mother's faults, she'd neglected to recall the special moments of love they had shared together.

Minta needed to be burped, and Lydia laughed when she belched loudly. "I'm glad you relieved your tummy here rather than in your grandmama's house." The infant smiled at Lydia, and, despite her sadness, she grinned and nuzzled her daughter's cheek. "You are a treasure, dear one."

The carriage came to a stop, and Lydia quickly re-tied her stays. Cuff opened the door and helped her exit. "Thank you, Cuff."

Her heart grew as heavy as her legs when she ascended the stone steps. Minta wiggled in her arms, so she held her tightly to her chest.

Before she could knock on the door, Cecelia opened it. "Please come in, ma'am. The doctor just be leavin'."

One look at Dr. Caldwell's face informed her things were not going well.

He looked more weary than usual, his wrinkles deepening with his frown. "I'm afraid she does not have long, Mrs. Hughes."

"So, 'tis her heart then. And there's nothing more you can do for her?"

"I'm afraid not. She has had some hints of this before, but I fear 'tis past the point where she might recover. 'Twill be difficult for her to talk, but she will be relieved to see you."

"Shall I send for my sister, then?" She swallowed back the bad taste that emerged in her throat.

He paused before answering her. "Your mother specifically asked me *not* to send for your sister."

"I see."

"'Tis most unusual, I must say, but your mother knows her own mind." He patted her hand. "I know she's happy you are here." He peeked at Minta, who cooed and grinned at him. "She's a lovely little one. Such a joy to have new life in the midst of sadness. Fare thee well, Mrs. Hughes."

"Good day, doctor." As he exited the door, she wondered how physicians tolerated so much illness and tragedy every day of their lives. Loss seemed difficult enough when it happened to one's own family. Doctors were forced to share in everyone's grief. How did they manage the burden of it?

Turning toward the bedchamber, Lydia trudged down the hallway. Both anxious to see her mother yet dreading the death-bed conversation, Lydia prayed for strength before approaching her mother's bedside.

"Mother, I've brought Minta to see you." Lydia forced a smile.

With weighted lids, Mother battled to open her eyes then finally won the struggle. Minta rewarded her with a big grin.

"Precious little one." Her mother barely whispered. Lydia leaned closer so she could discern her words.

The baby suddenly grew serious and her mouth contorted.

"Oh dear, I know that face. We're about to have a happier infant but a foul-smelling room." Lydia giggled.

Mother started to laugh then coughed instead. Cecelia came in to offer her some water.

"I'm fine." Mother's voice betrayed her words. "Can you take the baby a moment? I believe she needs to be cleaned."

Lydia started to object, but Cecelia grinned when she took Minta.

"I take good care of your baby, ma'am." Cecelia spoke to the infant the whole way out of the room.

Lydia turned her attention back to her mother. "She loves little ones, does she not?"

Mother's eyes watered.

"I'm sorry, Mama. I did not mean to upset you." Lydia grabbed her arm with tenderness.

"'Tis not your fault, but my own. I made Cecelia give up her baby. 'Twas so very evil of me. Cecelia cried so when they took her son." Tears flowed down her mother's cheeks and dripped onto her linen pillowcase. "I have so many sins to confess."

Shocked at this revelation, Lydia wondered why she had not remembered Cecelia having a baby. But then, she likely lived in Newport with Jeremiah at the time of the child's birth.

Forcing the horror from her thoughts at this confession, Lydia squeezed her hand. "God can forgive anything, if you ask Him."

Mother's expression softened as she managed a weak smile. "Aye. I have kept God busy lately telling Him my many sins."

She held her mother's thin, gnarled hand and lifted it to her lips. "Remember what the minister said that day at the meetinghouse? God even forgave the slaver named John Newton."

Mother's face paled as she clung to Lydia's fingers. "I never gave him a chance to confess his sins, did I?"

Confusion filled Lydia's thoughts. "You never gave who a chance?"

Her mother squeezed her eyes shut and grew breathless.

"Can I get you some water, Mama?" Lydia propped her pillows higher to make her mother more comfortable.

After a moment, Octavia opened her eyes again and captured Lydia's gaze. "I must confess something to you, Lydia. I did a terrible thing."

Lydia's eyes narrowed, and she shook her head slowly. "What must you confess?"

Mother pulled her down toward her, then whispered near Lydia's ear. "I killed your father."

Her breath caught, then she gasped. "Killed him? Whatever do you mean?" Lydia kept her voice low.

She coughed, and Lydia held her up to sip more liquid. Mother raised up her palm. "That's enough. Let me finish."

Lydia could barely look at her mother, yet she took in every word. She had to know what happened.

"'Twas right after you moved to Newport. I saw your father in the barn with one of the slaves. Again." She took a breath. "I did not confront him, but something inside my soul said, 'Enough!'"

"That night, when he came inside for his rum, I put poison in his drink. He was too drunk to notice anything unusual. As soon as he lost consciousness, I called two of the slaves in and told them if they wanted their freedom, I would grant it. But they must dispose of my husband down at the wharf."

Mother wheezed, and Lydia gave her more of the medicinal. She did not know whether she should be horrified at her mother's actions or sympathetic to her plight of living with a cruel and adulterous husband. But to kill him? Lydia rubbed her forehead to ease a growing headache.

Her mother continued. "I wrote out the papers to free the men, then watched outside in the dark to be certain no one saw what we did. When the alley was empty, they took your father away." She clutched her hands together and held them to her mouth. "But to think I took away his chance of being forgiven." She tried to shake her head.

Lydia wanted to speak, but words escaped her. She knew she must say something. But how could she respond? How *should* she respond?

Forgiveness. The word echoed in her mind over and over. It may have been too late for her father. But her mother could still repent.

"Mama, I love you so. God will forgive you, if you ask Him."

Her mother's tears flowed throughout her wrinkles. "He would forgive a woman who murdered her husband?"

Lydia held her hand with a reassuring grip. "Remember John Newton? He murdered countless Africans. If not directly, he was still responsible for the deaths of many men and women. God forgave him because he asked to be forgiven. And he truly repented."

"Then I will ask God to forgive me of my most terrible sin. Pray with me, Lydia."

The two women bowed their heads. While her mother gasped for air and prayed in between breaths, Lydia wept tears of hope and joy, sadness and horror—the many facets of life here on earth. When Mother finished, Lydia looked up, amazed at the peaceful expression on her dying mother's face.

"Lydia, one more thing." She pointed weakly to the dresser. "In the bottom drawer on the left is a leather folder. Inside is my will. Please go get it and take it to my lawyer after I'm gone. He'll take care of everything."

"Very well."

Lydia held onto her mother's hand. She only let go when Cecelia brought Minta in to be fed.

"Thank you, dear Cecelia." Lydia looked into Cecelia's sad eyes when she handed the baby back to her.

Lydia sat in the bedside chair and fed Minta. As her daughter nursed, she grew drowsy and could no longer keep her eyes open.

When Lydia startled awake, daylight had passed. Darkness had overtaken the room, along with silence.

"Mother?"

Lydia felt for the quilts on the bed and set the sleeping baby on it. She lit a candle and held it near her mother's still face. Although she no longer breathed, a look of peace covered her countenance. Lydia sat by her sleeping baby and wept.

~

"THANK YOU FOR SEEING ME, Mr. Popkins." Lydia wore another mourning ring on her hand, a new one in memory of her mother.

"I'm so very sorry about the passing of your sole surviving parent, Mrs. Hughes. I'm certain this is made more difficult with your new husband being away at battle. It seems most of the town has left to help the troops on Aquidneck."

Lydia's hopes rose. "Have you any news, Mr. Popkins? About the Rhode Island regiments, sir?"

"Only that the French ships suffered serious damage in that terrible storm. They were forced to limp toward Boston for repairs. It did not sit well with General Sullivan, of course."

Her heart lurched as she feared to question him further. "Does that put the troops in more danger?"

"I'm not certain, Mrs. Hughes, although I know the call went out for reinforcements, and many answered the request." He smiled and raked his hand through his unkempt, long hair.

In her childhood, Lydia always thought her parents' lawyer had peculiar habits. Mainly, not pulling his hair back with a ribbon. He seemed to not mind when it looked askew. The older Lydia became, the less she focused on such trivial matters.

"Thank you for your encouragement, Mr. Popkins." She waited while he read through the document.

"Yes, now I remember the terms of her will. She changed it within the last few years. Said she'd had a change of heart about how she wanted the estate to be divided." He glanced upward, past his spectacles. "In fact, 'tis not to be divided at all, but the entire estate goes to you."

She wrinkled her brow. "The entire estate to me? What about Phila?"

"It seems after your sister married, your mother decided she did not need anything left to her." He handed Lydia the will. "So, Mrs. Hughes. The estate is yours to dispose of as you please. I'm certain the addition of several slaves will help you on the farm." He grinned.

Lydia took a deep breath. "Thank you, Mr. Popkins." She stood to leave.

"Again, I am so saddened about your mother. I'm certain you miss her greatly."

"I do, Mr. Popkins. So very much. And I thank you."

She curtsied, and he bowed to her before she walked out the door.

In the foyer of his office, Hannah awaited, holding Minta, who fussed.

"I hope she did not cause you too much trouble." She took the squirming baby from Hannah's arms.

"Nay, never, ma'am. It's good practice for me, besides."

Lydia stared into the rich brown eyes of her dear friend and servant and made a resolution.

The first thing she intended to do with her mother's slaves was free them. In truth, she needed to free them all, Cuff and Miriam included. They could stay with her in the household if they chose. But they would no longer be bound by the invisible chains of being owned. She may be the daughter of a slaver. But she would no longer be an owner of slaves.

20

The home she grew up in drew her into its every room, like some dark spirit forcing her to relive her past. It both fascinated and horrified Lydia.

She'd not been through the inner chambers on the second floor since she'd married Jeremiah. She remembered gladly accepting his proposal of marriage since it meant she could escape this house. While she loved Jeremiah when they made their marriage vows, Lydia now wondered if her wedding proved to be more a celebration of rescue from this prison of haunting memories.

When she opened the door to her mother's room, she inhaled lavender and roses. They were her mother's favorites, and Lydia would always think of her whenever the aromas wafted her way.

Mother's room looked like it always had. The high ceilings gave the impression of a place of worship, but little prayer occurred here, from what Lydia observed. The lush maroon draperies had a thin coating of dust in the creases, as did the windowsills.

Lydia stared out the window at the street below, where workers hustled, beggars begged, and vendors plied their goods.

Just an ordinary day in Bristol. And yet it wasn't. At least, not for her. Nothing was ordinary when a loved one died.

She turned toward her mother's dresser and spotted the jewelry box Father had given to her one Christmas. Her mother had effused over the scrollwork in the wood. Then, upon opening the lid, Mother had gushed over the necklace he'd purchased for her.

With blood money from his slave ships.

If she thought deeply enough, she could remember when her parents shared this bedroom together. Those were the days when her mother laughed more. Then, when Father moved into his own room, Mother's laughter ceased. She had discovered the truth about him—the truth Lydia herself had witnessed. She shivered.

When she dropped the scrolled jewelry box onto the dresser, it sounded harsh and hollow in this empty chamber. Ready to leave it all behind, she hurried out of the room.

As Lydia closed the door, she looked down the hall toward her own bedchamber. She'd grown up sleeping in there, crying into her pillow most nights while wishing her life could be different.

She straightened her back and forced brave steps toward her old room. Gripping the door handle, she turned it and peeked inside. It looked as if she'd just left. Nothing had been touched or moved. All had been left the same, merely dusted so it would be ready for her in case she decided to return.

Her mother had no idea that Lydia would never think of coming back.

Stepping into her past, as if the clock of time had rewound six years, she imagined herself a young woman of eighteen. But she did not feel young. She knew too much about life already, and she often wondered if she'd ever felt like a child.

Looking around at the large chamber, Lydia was amazed at the assortment of dolls everywhere. Did she ever play with them? She could barely remember.

She did recollect one cloth doll that someone had given her so long ago, but she could not recall who gave it to her. Picking it up, Lydia smiled at the faded-wool-yarn hair and the linen dress that Lydia enjoyed stroking when the doll kept her company in bed. *I wonder if Comfort would like this.* She held it snug in her arm and searched for two more dolls, one for Rose and one for Minta. She laid them on the bed, then moved to the dresser.

Its drawers pulled with difficulty being a bit sticky from the moisture in the ocean air. When Lydia finally got the top one open, she grew excited to see clothes of all sizes from her childhood. Her mother must have saved them.

Comfort and Rose did not need them, but Lydia could donate them at the meetinghouse to help the families who'd lost so much in the attack. She made a mental note to arrange for these to be delivered there, along with her mother's clothing. Lydia closed the dresser drawer, gathered the three dolls, and hurried out of the room.

Father's room down the hall held dark remembrances of an evil man. Even thinking about approaching that chamber, where she might catch a whiff of his pipe tobacco, brought bile to her throat. Perhaps her father's clothing might still be in his room, but she immediately dismissed the idea of searching his dresser. She'd never so much as enter his chamber, much less touch the clothing that had covered his body.

She'd had more than enough of revisiting this house and her past. Time to return to the present.

Lydia descended the stairs and found the four slaves she'd inherited waiting for her in the hallway. *I inherited them as the property they'd been deemed.* Lydia felt nauseated at the thought but forced herself to move on to this next step. It was the only way she could think of to try to make amends for the sins of her father.

She faced the two women and two men, the remnants of the staff that had served her parents throughout the years. She read fear in their eyes, as she imagined their uncertainty about their future filled them with consternation.

"Thank you for coming, all of you. And please let me assure you that you will be well cared for. I do not wish you to be concerned about your safety in any way." Lydia took in a deep breath. "I have visited Mr. Popkins, my mother's lawyer, and asked him to draw up the legal documents that are necessary in order to give all of you your freedom. You will be slaves no more."

Absolute silence filled the hallway. Mouths dropped agape, and four sets of wide eyes stared at her. Lydia couldn't tell if they were happy about this announcement or terrified. Finally, Caesar spoke.

"Ma'am? You're sayin' we be free?" He looked over his shoulder and pointed. "Free to walk out that door? Anytime we want?" He looked back at her with the same hope she'd seen in Hannah's eyes when she'd asked for Lydia's blessing to marry Ezekiel.

Tears filled Lydia's eyes. "Aye, Caesar. But you must always be ready to show these papers. They will prove you are free so that no one will try to arrest you for being a runaway."

The reality of the danger these faithful servants might face instilled new fear in her spirit. Could they now be in more peril than ever?

"Of course, I could use your help on my farm out in the country. You'd still be free in every sense of the word. But you would be paid in food, clean rooms to stay in, and a small wage. I'm not certain what I can afford right now. But, when my husband returns, we can arrange a fair sum to give to you. If that is acceptable to you."

Lydia bit her lip as she awaited their responses. The four stood speechless. What were they thinking? They reminded Lydia of a bird she'd found when she was a child. It had broken its wing, and Lydia and one of her mother's servants helped the bird mend. But even when it healed and could fly away, the bird refused to do so. It had the choice to be free yet remained trapped in a cage whose door lay wide open.

She looked from one to the next, waiting for some response.

Caesar stepped forward. "Ma'am, forgive our silence. We be most heartened by your words. They just be so— unexpected." He shrugged.

"Perhaps the four of you would like to meet together in the parlor and discuss what you'd like to do." She motioned her hand toward the room with the finely upholstered furniture.

"Meet in the parlor? You mean, sit in those chairs and talk?" Cecelia narrowed her eyes, but Lydia saw a glimmer of joy in them.

"Aye, Cecelia. That's exactly what I mean. Caesar, perhaps you can drive out to the farm after everyone has had a chance to make a decision. I must be going back to my home since I'm certain my baby needs me about now."

"Thank you, ma'am." Caesar's eyes were moist as he bowed.

"I look forward to hearing from you all." Smiling, Lydia spun around and returned to the carriage awaiting her out front.

MICAH and his regiment readied themselves for the upcoming battle to regain Newport. It had been just two days past that Micah had written the letter to Lydia, in case he should not return from war. His heart thrummed with fervor as they awaited the orders to form battle lines. But when news that Admiral d'Estaing had decided to withdraw his French troops back to the port in Boston, anger rippled through Micah's veins.

Audible curses became common in camp as the men vented their displeasure. The foulest obscenities spewed from General Sullivan, whose booming voice carried across the encampment.

Everyone knew the success of this military campaign depended on the assault by the French battleships, who were to work in conjunction with the American ground attack. Without the French assistance, the Continental forces would be as weakened as a man who'd just lost a leg.

Micah tried to smother his anger. But the thought that the French deserted them in the army's time of need rankled at his spirit. He'd given up so much to be here, like all the other men who'd signed on.

The greatest source of his discontent was missing Lydia. Perhaps the older men who'd been married many years did not experience the hunger he felt. He craved time with Lydia, her warmth and love. D'Estaing's decision affected so many in this campaign, and Micah attempted not to loathe the man.

Major Ward reassured the 1st Regiment that emissaries, including General Nathanael Greene and the Frenchman, Marquis de Lafayette, were on their way to attempt to reason with the admiral. They even proposed that delaying the French fleet's withdrawal by just two days would be a sufficient help to win a successful retaking of the city of Newport.

But their efforts failed, and D'Estaing's decision infuriated the American officers. Anti-French sentiment filtered throughout the American troops like an infestation of *la grippe*.

This time of animosity festered nearly a week. Councils of war were held, but few productive decisions were made. Micah heard that the Frenchman, Lafayette, often became the target of Sullivan's anger, to the point rumors suggested the two might call a dual.

Things calmed as letters from General Washington encouraged harmony with the French, who so often had supported the American cause.

Finally, a voice of reason. But it had been a week of wasted effort, in Micah's view. One more week he could not be with Lydia. And while the battle of the officers took place within tents, most of the infantry dealt with the physical assault from the enemy. The near-constant cannon and mortar fire from the King's Army kept the regiments on alert and responding in kind.

The next day, the officers held another war council, this time to determine what to do now that the French had deserted the fight. Major Ward informed Micah and the other sergeants that some of their leaders proposed they evacuate the island, while others suggested a bold attack on the British frontlines.

"What do you think, Major?" Micah stood with the others who nodded their heads, wondering the same.

"With two companies of Massachusetts volunteers leaving, not to mention the scores of others who've returned to their businesses, it would seem foolishness to attack. There is much concern about our shrinking numbers." Major Ward put his hands on his hips and shook his head slowly. "I'm certain our general will choose the proper course. For now, you're dismissed, gentlemen."

Micah and the others returned to their companies. No one knew what to say. Fear about the success of any American assault had grown. This concern served to further incite more desertions of volunteers, including hundreds from New Hampshire and Rhode Island.

Micah wondered just how many American soldiers would be left to fight. One thing seemed certain—the fewer troops there were, the greater the chances of being injured—or killed. *Dear God, keep us safe.*

To add to the misery, the heat and squalid camp conditions brewed illnesses, especially amongst the volunteers. Seasoned Continentals like himself had grown immune to many of the camp diseases, but the newer recruits fell victim. Just one more reason to incite discontent.

While most of the army deserters were volunteers who could not be forced to remain, one drum major attempted to desert to the enemy. This made Micah ill. It was one thing to leave your post for being homesick. To leave as a traitor incurred everyone's anger, and General Sullivan did not take it lightly, especially on the eve of pending war. They sentenced the man to hang, and the officers carried out the order for all the troops to see.

Micah understood the punishment, but he vowed in his mind

to never tell Lydia about it. He did not wish to think about the execution again, much less describe it to her.

When the officers held another council of war the following day, they encouraged General Sullivan to retreat immediately. He finally agreed to at least withdraw cannons and begin the process, but he would not yet order a full retreat. Sullivan delayed one more day.

Frustration seethed through Micah. He just wanted this war to be over. He wanted to go home as much as all the others, and the inactivity made the wait much harder to bear.

To add to his concerns, he'd not received any communication from Lydia for two weeks. Was she well? Were the children ill? Being isolated from his new family took a toll on his spirit, which struggled to find hope in these surroundings.

With reports of sentries being kidnapped by the enemy, Micah's options for finding a place to be alone were limited. He'd always been refreshed at his Connecticut home by walking through the woods. While growing up on the farm, he often ran among the trees, creating new diversions, pretending downed tree trunks were a tent in the forest.

Books were his companion in his woodland hideaways, along with his dog, Hero. His older brother had named the pet for saving Micah from a rain-swollen river one spring. Hero had become Micah's dog until, old and gray-muzzled, the faithful dog took his last breath one day. By then, Micah was in his teens, yet he cried like a small child when his canine friend died.

"Sergeant Hughes, are you all right, sir?"

"What?" Micah realized he had tears running down his face and sniffed sharply.

He stared up at the young private, whose eyes were filled with concern.

"I'm all right, thanks."

The young soldier moved on. Micah stood and brushed off his dusty coat. He'd not thought of that dog in years. And in all the years he'd been at war, he'd never cried like that until now.

Lydia had opened Micah's heart, and the tender feelings he'd protected for so long were left exposed by his love for her. It was glorious, and at times, so very painful.

~

THE NEXT DAY, when Major Ward called together his sergeants from the 1st Rhode Island, the firmness in his jaw told Micah a decision had been reached.

"Men, with our numbers of troops ready for duty now greatly depleted, General Sullivan and his officers made a unanimous decision to withdraw our army back to Butts Hill, where we started when we first arrived on the island. We'll set up defenses there.

"Should we find we are reinforced by the return of Admiral d'Estaing, we will continue with our original plan to attack the British fort at Newport. Otherwise, we'll be in a position to evacuate back to the mainland. So, gentlemen, get your companies ready and await the call to arms. You are dismissed."

The thought of returning to the mainland instilled fresh hope in Micah. Much danger awaited the army between here and home, however, so he forced himself to focus. He needed to concentrate on fighting to his best ability and try to stay alive in the process.

21

In the silence of darkness that evening of August 28, the American troops marched north. With stealth, they dismantled their tents, gathered their haversacks and arms, and headed toward their escape route.

Exhausted from the heat and frustrated by the long wait, Micah marched with as much enthusiasm as he could muster.

Some of the men in his regiment wore grins, while others yawned. Relieved to be on their way to Howland's ferry—their access off the island—Micah battled the trepidation nudging against the forefront of his thoughts.

The five-mile distance would not be traversed with ease. At any moment, the enemy might discover their plans and come after them. That concern made him edgy, and he shushed his men at the slightest cough.

By early morning, the main body of the army reached Butts Hill. Micah and his company collapsed near the earthen works made by the British Army sometime before. There was justice in the Americans enjoying the fruits of the enemy's labors.

At dawn, Micah awoke. He peered over the edge of Butts Hill and looked out over the meadow, where the army of militia and Continentals spread nearly two miles wide. The regiments were situated according to plan to defray any attack from the south. He knew it would not be long before enemy troops approached.

He tensed at the sound of gunfire nearby, to the west. The shouts of battle elicited fire in his veins.

Major Ward ordered the regiment to form a line behind the thick earthen walls, strengthened by a buttress of sharpened trees pointing outward. As the men crouched there, Micah felt the intensity of the day's heat increasing through his woolen coat.

"Sergeant, sir. Can we take these coats off? The heat be unbearable." Ezekiel's request seemed understandable.

Micah peeked up and caught the eye of Major Ward, who nodded his approval. Micah looked back at Ezekiel and nodded. Keeping low, the companies of the 1st Rhode Island tore off their sweat-covered coats, exposing black skin beneath their linen shirts.

The sergeant wished he could do the same. Continentals, however, had to maintain stricter dress code, no matter the discomfort.

Sounds of fighting in the distance ensued for at least an hour before he heard the major ready their troops for an attack. Every muscle in Micah's body tensed as musket barrels lined the top of the earthen fortress.

When Micah peered over the top, sweat dripped past his ears. He tightened his grip on his firelock. *Hessians.* He gritted his teeth as he remembered the mercenaries and their treatment of Lydia in Bristol the previous May. Micah's anger sharpened his focus.

"Fire!"

Gladly.

A deafening roar of muskets exploded everywhere, and choking gunpowder clouded the humid atmosphere. Numerous Hessians fell.

Their commanding officer veered the frontal assault toward

their right, where they were met with more shots fired from behind stone walls. The enemy pulled back in retreat.

Only then did Micah realize how fast his heart beat. He breathed in deeply, coughing when he inhaled the spent gunpowder. He hoped he'd killed the man responsible for hurting Lydia. He knew the likelihood to be doubtful, but the thought pleased him none the less.

"How'd we do, Sergeant?" The private next to him looked at him with wide eyes. This was the man's first taste of war. Likely his first time killing.

Micah wiped the sweat from his brow and nodded. "You fought like a true soldier, Private."

The young man grinned proudly and reloaded his musket.

Major Wade searched the horizon with squinted eyes. "Well done, lads. But don't get too comfortable. This battle's not over yet."

Micah reloaded his musket and tugged at his bayonet. Fixed and ready. He planned on killing as many Hessians as he could.

It seemed just a few moments before the same Hessian officer attacked again, this time with the support of a line of ships in the harbor firing grapeshot. The American troops spread out, some venturing into the surrounding woods to return fire.

At home running through thickets and woods, Micah joined them and slipped carefully through copse of trees. Time after time, he positioned himself then aimed carefully at his targets. *Just like hunting in Connecticut.* Only instead of deer and bear, the King's Army received his lead balls.

Micah slipped back up Butts Hill toward the fort, and he noticed the number of American troops covering the area had increased. Other brigades had joined the 1st Rhode Island to assist the persistent attack of the Hessians. Although uncertain how many regiments were present, Micah was grateful for the added support. He grew confident they could stop them.

The Americans now faced the heaviest assault of all. Micah tore off a paper cartridge and loaded his musket.

Ezekiel approached him behind the redoubt. "Sergeant, can you cover me while I move down to that bush? I can be sittin' pretty and take 'em down as they come by, but I need cover to get there."

"You're quite the Yankee soldier. Tell me when you're ready, and I'll give you cover." Micah propped his rifle over the earthen mound. "Ready when you are."

Ezekiel poised like a bobcat. "Now!"

Micah half stood and shot a Hessian who pointed his rifle at Ezekiel.

The black man ran in a zig-zag pattern while Micah reloaded, fired, then loaded again, each time hitting his mark as Hessians pointed at the Yankee. When Ezekiel reached the large group of bushes, Micah sighed in relief.

He occasionally heard shots coming from the bush as the Hessians crept up the hill.

American cannon fire came into constant play as it pummeled the growing numbers of enemy troops that covered the lower edge of the hill. The enemy moved like a swarm of ants approaching a sugar cone.

General Greene sent another regiment down the left flank to meet the Hessians. Bodies of German and British soldiers fell one after another.

So many American troops joined the counterassault against the King's Army that firepower rained from both muskets and cannons, filling the atmosphere. The final blow to the Hessians became an aggressive bayonet attack by one of the American regiments. The enemy finally retreated.

Micah leaped over the embankment, intent on following the Hessians as they fled. He fired one shot, which made its mark. Then he reloaded and poised to fire again when everything shattered in front of him.

He stared at his musket, now split in half. When he

reached for the broken barrel, he was missing part of his left hand. He glared in horror at the bloodied appendage, then felt a searing slice in his right leg as a Hessian lying on the ground slashed his calf with a bayonet. Falling down the uneven slope, Micah rolled past the Hessian, who stood and followed after him, holding his bayonet over Micah's chest. Before he could impale him, a large black figure lunged at the Hessian with a fixed bayonet and stabbed him repeatedly until he moved no longer.

Pain gripped Micah with such intensity he cried out. Ezekiel appeared over him. Warmth flooded Micah's sleeve and his breeches. His body was on fire, and he couldn't speak.

"Hold on, Sergeant, sir."

Ezekiel tried to lift him, but Micah screamed for him to stop. Another private from the regiment came and helped Ezekiel hoist Micah over his shoulder and carry him to safety. Shots continued to fire, and Micah knew he was going to die.

Take care of Lydia.

Everything went black.

LYDIA PACKED up the dresses from the house in Bristol and called for Hannah to help her carry them downstairs. The carriage waited out front. But before Lydia picked up the first pile, a strange sensation forced her to pause mid-step. She nearly cried out with the sudden fear that rippled through her.

"Ma'am, is somethin' wrong? You have such a look on your face. Like you seen a ghost or somethin'."

Forcing a deep breath, Lydia told herself to stop being foolish. "'Tis nothing, Hannah. Let's get these downstairs so Cuff can take them to the meetinghouse. And please, take care of yourself going down those steps."

They each carried a bundle as they descended.

Comfort and Rose played on the first floor. They giggled and ran from room to room, chatting about this and that and playing with the dolls Lydia had given them.

Cecelia cooed at Minta and sang her a song in her African language that sounded both melodic and sad. The woman had a sweet voice, and Lydia forced herself to focus on the lullaby rather than the feeling of fright she'd experienced a few minutes before.

Cuff met the women on the porch and carried the clothes down the front stoop to the awaiting carriage. As he loaded them, a commotion stirred in the streets. More than usual numbers of people ran toward homes while shouting an alarm.

Lydia held her hands to shield her eyes from the sun as she observed the scene from the porch. One older gentleman hobbled with speed toward the doctor's home across the street. The man pounded on the door, which was answered by a maid who disappeared in an instant. Within a moment, Dr. Caldwell burst through the open portal, carrying his haversack, and ran, limping, toward the wharf.

Unaware she'd even moved, Lydia numbly followed the doctor and then ran faster and faster until she'd reached him.

She pulled on his arm to stop him. "Dr. Caldwell, what has occurred?"

The older man struggled to catch his breath as he licked his lips. "Fighting. There's been fighting on Aquidneck, and they're bringing the wounded here and to Tiverton. We'll have to set up an infirmary."

Lydia's heart skipped a beat, and her knees weakened, quite certain the fear she'd experienced had something to do with the injured men. "Use my mother's home. I'll ready the beds." She spun back around, nearly running into a boy playing with a stick he pretended was a musket.

"Bam. Bam!" The boy pretended he shot his friend.

"Please stop!" She screamed at the child.

The child blinked at her and dropped his stick.

Hysteria threatened her sensibilities. She could not even

think about who the wounded might be. With so many troops on the island, surely Micah and Ezekiel were unharmed. She kept telling herself that. Lydia hurried back to her mother's house and ran up the stone steps.

Hannah's eyes widened. "What happened?"

Lydia gasped for air and started to cry. "There's been fighting. On the island. They're bringing the wounded here, and I told them to use this home as a hospital." She covered her mouth with both hands. "What if it's our husbands?"

"Now let us not give in to this fear, ma'am. We must believe they be all right." Hannah squeezed Lydia's arms, then lowered her voice. "And we don't want the little girls to be worried now, do we?"

Lydia wiped away her tears. "You're right. But I think it might be difficult for Comfort and Rose to be here when the soldiers are brought in." She turned toward Cecelia.

Lydia was grateful Cecelia and Caesar decided to stay with her family. The other two freed slaves had chosen to leave. Lydia wished them well and told them she'd be praying for their safety.

"Can you go back to the farm with Rose and Comfort, Cecelia? Hannah can help me with the baby." She whispered closer to Cecelia. "Soldiers have been wounded on the island, and they'll be bringing them here for care. Please leave the lassies with Miriam and return forthwith."

Cecelia's eyes narrowed. "I hope all be well with your husband and Ezekiel."

"Thank you. We pray so."

Lydia called the two girls over. "Young ladies, 'tis time to return to the farm. Cecelia will go with you in the carriage."

Comfort pouted. "But Mama, Rose and I were good like you asked."

"I know, my sweet. But 'tis going to get busy here with some visitors, and we must give them enough room to be comfortable, mustn't we?"

"All right." Comfort's eyes brightened with mischief. "Since we've been so good, might we have a piece of cake?"

Despite her fears, Lydia giggled. "Aye, you may. Now get on with you both." She took the baby from Cecelia's arms, and the servant herded the two girls out to the carriage.

"Hannah, could you go ask Cuff to put the clothes to the side for now and take the three of them back to the farm? I've no idea how soon the soldiers may arrive, and I want the little ones gone before they might see something ... difficult."

"Aye, Mrs. Hughes."

She reached out to squeeze her friend's hand. "I've no idea what I would do without you, Hannah."

"I feel the same way about you, ma'am."

They'd started their relationship years ago as servant and mistress, but the events of their lives had forged a friendship between the two that sealed a mutual affection and faithfulness. They would always be there to support one another through both joy-filled events and the painful times. Lydia was grateful—especially today, when their futures might be turned upside down by a war they both hated.

22

Lydia steeled herself for the arrival of the wounded. She and Hannah prepared each room in her mother's house —she'd asked Hannah to prepare Father's chamber— and beds were turned down and ready. She would never be certain her heart was ready, however. It trembled with fear that loved ones might be among the wounded.

What if Micah or Ezekiel had been wounded and sent to Tiverton instead? She prayed not, but if so, she hoped someone would send word to her. Surely they would send for her, would they not? She forced her mind to focus on what she could do at this moment.

She checked to be certain basins of water and linens were in each room at the bedside. Lydia shuddered at the thought of war wounds. Her upbringing had exposed her to other horrors, but she'd been spared from seeing serious sickness and injury. This would be a challenge she'd never imagined. She wasn't very good with blood. How would she bear the sight? *God, give me strength.*

Lydia heard someone arrive nearby in the street and hurried downstairs. She flung the door open and inhaled sharply. Soldiers carried a man through her front door. His eyes were closed, and she nearly gasped when she looked at him. He had no arm.

Forcing herself to be stronger, she directed the men upstairs. "The maid will show you to a bedchamber." She wondered why the patient had been silent. Perhaps they'd given him strong medicinal? Or had he lost consciousness from pain? *Please, God, help him.*

In a few moments, the next patient arrived. This man moaned loudly, and his cries tore at Lydia's heart.

"Please take him to a bed upstairs. There's a basin of water nearby and linens."

One of the four men carrying the patient glanced at her. "Thank you, ma'am."

Cuff came through the door. "The doctor wants to know how many more we can take."

Lydia calculated the number in her head. "Five more. Six, if one of them is Micah or Ezekiel." She bit her bottom lip. She'd finally voiced her worry to someone besides Hannah.

His fear-filled eyes met hers. "Aye, ma'am." He spun around to search for Dr. Caldwell.

She could hear Hannah upstairs bustling around, giving directions to the men who'd brought the wounded.

One of the Continental soldiers came downstairs and approached her. "Excuse me, ma'am. Be you Mrs. Micah Hughes?" His dirt and sweat-covered face glistened in the late-afternoon sun that shone through the front door.

Lydia's breath caught. Her heart raced so fast she felt ill. "Aye."

His gaze narrowed as he stared at her. "Perhaps you best sit down, ma'am. In the parlor."

"Nay." She grabbed both of his arms. "Please tell me if my husband is wounded."

He looked down, then met her eyes. "Aye, he is. They are bringing him here forthwith. I wanted to prepare you –"

Before he could say anymore, she ran down the front steps toward the wharf. She paid no attention to the men walking but stopped to look at each wounded man carried on a stretcher or blanket. When she approached one of the groups carrying a patient with dark hair, she stopped and forced herself to look closely at the man they transported.

"Micah!" A sob burst from her throat, and she covered her mouth as she took in the unmoving, blood-covered form of the man she loved.

Someone took her arm and led her back to the house. She turned and, through her tears, saw Dr. Caldwell.

"Lydia, we need to get your husband to the camp surgeon with haste. He is on his way in the flatboat and knows he is needed forthwith. He and I will attend Sergeant Hughes. Show me what room you want him in." Dr. Caldwell held her arm securely, otherwise, she'd have fallen as she stumbled her way back to her mother's house. He helped her up the stairs.

Hannah met her at the top, concern etched in her countenance. "I just heard, ma'am." She hugged Lydia, who shook and could not speak.

Lydia turned and saw the men carrying Micah arrive. They carefully stepped up the five stairs and carried him into the foyer.

"Over in this room." She barely recognized her own voice, strained with terror. She shut her eyes a moment when they walked past her, but she prayed for strength as she helped them get Micah onto her mother's bed.

When they moved him, her husband cried out in pain. His garbled words made no sense.

"They gave him laudanum, Mrs. Hughes." One of the soldiers, just a young lad, looked at her with concern.

"Thank you. You've helped him, and I am grateful."

After the young man looked at Micah once more, he walked quietly away with the rest of the men.

Lydia leaned over her husband, avoiding the images of the bloodied bandages on his hand and leg. "Micah, I love you." She stroked his disheveled hair and kissed the scar on his forehead. "The doctor is coming to help you and will take care of your wounds. Please, Micah. Be strong. I need you. We all need you." Hot tears dripped onto his shirt and unbuttoned waistcoat.

Dr. Caldwell and another man hurried in. "Mrs. Hughes, this is the camp surgeon, Mr. Bell. He is familiar with the wounds your husband sustained and needs to operate on them forthwith. Your husband has already lost much blood."

"What ..." Lydia swallowed past a dry lump in her throat. "What are his wounds?"

"From what the men informed me, your husband lost some fingers on his left hand. He also has a serious bayonet wound to the back of his right leg. They wrapped both wounds, but the bleeding has been profuse. I must remove the bandages and sew the lacerations in his leg and do what I can for his hand."

His words sounded far away. Lights flashed in front of her eyes, and saltiness bathed her tongue. "Micah—"

WHEN SHE AWOKE, a strange woman held a cool cloth on her forehead.

Lydia tried to focus her eyes on her surroundings, but even when she could see clearly, she did not recognize where she was. "Who—?"

"I am Martha Varnum, Mrs. Hughes. You are in my home."

She pushed herself to sit up with arms like heavy weights. "How did I get here?"

"Some kindly soldiers carried you here. They said you were not feeling well, and Dr. Caldwell asked them to bring you. You are more than welcome to stay until you are feeling better."

Lydia felt a sore spot on her head and winced. "Did I fall?"

"Aye, you lost consciousness, poor dear. Before the doctor or Mr. Bell could catch you, you'd fallen to the floor." Mrs. Varnum rang a bell. When her maid entered, she asked her to bring some tea and sugar.

"Shhh." Mrs. Varnum giggled and held her finger to her mouth. "I won't tell we're drinking tea if you won't." She grew serious. "I think, considering your shock today, you might need some tea to sustain you. I keep a secret container for just such emergencies. And I believe seeing your wounded husband return from war is just such an emergency."

Lydia's mouth trembled. "My poor husband." Tears poured down her face.

Mrs. Varnum handed her a handkerchief.

"Thank you." Lydia dabbed at her eyes and cheeks then wept even more. "Micah gave me his kerchief the first day we met."

"Oh, dear." Mrs. Varnum bit her lip. "I did not mean to stir a sad memory."

Minta cried from down the hall. "Minta! Where is she?"

Cecelia walked into the room with the screaming baby and handed her to Lydia.

She stroked her daughter's cheek. "My poor little one."

Cecelia curtsied and went back to the kitchen.

"You feel free to nurse your baby, Mrs. Hughes. She looks hungry, and that will comfort you, as well."

Lydia had never thought about it before, yet she realized now that Mrs. Varnum was right. Whenever she could relax and nurse, a calmness filled her.

The baby latched right on, and her flailing arms quieted as she became satisfied.

Mrs. Varnum smiled. "I do so miss nursing my little ones. But they are grown now and will soon be nursing their own babies."

"I am so grateful for your kindness, Mrs. Varnum."

"Please, call me Martha. We are neighbors, after all."

"Then you must call me Lydia." She looked down at Minta and tried not to imagine what Micah endured at the moment. "Have you heard how my husband is doing?"

"Nay, but your servant—Hannah, I believe—said she'd come to get you as soon as the surgeon finished."

"I'm not a very good wife, am I? Fainting when my husband needs me the most." She sobbed as quietly as she could so as not to distress Minta.

Martha sat next to her on the settee and squeezed her arm. "Nonsense, Lydia. You could not help your husband while the surgeon worked on him. He might not even be aware you were there, as I'm quite certain the laudanum would cloud his mind."

She looked intently at Lydia. "You will be there with him as he heals. He will be in a great deal of pain. You will comfort him and tend him in so many ways. You will love him and soothe him. No one else can do that for him like you can."

"I do not feel very strong, Martha. What if I cannot even bear to look at his injuries? He might think I don't care. But in truth, it would be because I care so much."

Martha held her hand. "Then we must pray you will have the strength to bear it. You must be strong for him, as he has been strong for you."

Lydia wiped her eyes again. "Aye."

"Now, let's drink the tea that Mehitabel brought us." Martha poured some into a china cup.

"I hadn't even noticed she brought it in."

"I certainly did, and I am quite anxious to partake." Martha smiled with a mischievous look. "Perhaps we can drink it all if we hurry."

Lydia grinned. "Aye. I shall drink it all with you. With lots of cone sugar."

"A lass who knows how to drink a proper cup of tea." Martha handed her the sweetened, warm drink, and Lydia enjoyed every drop. She savored it, for she'd no idea when she might have another cup anytime soon. Perhaps after the war.

Then she thought how trivial a sacrifice it had been to give up drinking tea. Her husband lay with terrible and painful wounds from fighting for the cause of American freedom.

She would never complain of missing tea again.

HANNAH WALKED Lydia across the street toward her mother's house. She longed to be with Micah yet dreaded seeing him in such a wounded state. Her desire to be with him won out as her steps quickened.

"Hannah, any news of Ezekiel?"

"He's with the body of troops that took more wounded to Tiverton. One of the soldiers say he helped rescue Micah."

Lydia placed two fingers on her mouth and trembled. "Thank you, dear Hannah."

"Let me take the baby, ma'am."

Lydia did not argue but handed the cooing infant to her friend.

Hurrying up the stairs, she flung the heavy front door open and entered. A flurry of activity with strangers everywhere made her think she'd entered someone else's home. But her focus centered not on the other people or the other rooms. She nearly ran into her mother's old bedroom and pulled a chair up next to the bedside.

Micah lay still, his moist face occasionally twitching. His lips were so dry. Grateful someone had placed fresh water in a basin, Lydia took a clean cloth and dipped it into the liquid. She gently touched it to his lips and dabbed it from one side of his mouth to the other.

His left hand, propped high on several pillows, could not be seen because of a bulky bandage. The surgeon had said he'd lost some fingers, and she cringed at the thought.

His shirt had been removed. It was only the second time she'd seen his chest. The first time, on their wedding night, bore far more pleasant memories. She longed to stroke his skin but did not want to disturb his rest.

"Mrs. Hughes?"

She turned to see the surgeon standing in the doorway, drying his hands on a linen. His sleeves were rolled up, and blood stained his waistcoat.

"Aye, sir." She stood and walked toward the doorway to meet him.

"Let's go into the parlor to speak."

When they were out of Micah's hearing, the surgeon stopped. "First of all, how do you fare? You took quite a bump when you fainted."

She smiled, embarrassed about the incident. "I'm fine. 'Twas just such a shock."

"I'm afraid I'm used to speaking with the men on the field and forgot how to speak with a wife of a wounded one. Why don't we sit a moment? I know I am quite fatigued."

"Let me call Cecelia to bring some refreshment for you." Lydia rang the bell, and the woman walked in. "Cecelia, can you bring some cider for the surgeon?"

"Aye, ma'am."

Lydia sat straight in her chair with forced bravery. "First, I wish to thank you for helping my husband. I want to know what I must do to care for him."

His weary eyes had dark circles around them, and his long hair had likely not been combed into a neat queue in many a day. Mr. Bell rubbed the back of his neck, then sighed.

"The sergeant lost a great deal of blood, so he will be weak. That is why his skin is so pale. His bandages will need to be changed every day. Can you do this?"

She hesitated, then held her head high and gave a nod. "If you teach me how, I shall do it faithfully. Whatever Micah needs."

Cecelia brought in a pitcher of cider with a tankard and served a generous portion to Mr. Bell.

He guzzled it, likely parched from the heat and all his work. He wiped his mouth on his sleeve. "We must watch for fever. Our greatest concern is infection in his wounds. I've done everything I can to repair them, but we must keep them clean." He paused. "Another thing."

"Aye?"

"His wounds will be quite painful. But, the injury to his left hand will likely cause him the most pain. Injuries to the hand are notorious for terrible, throbbing misery. Keep that hand propped up on pillows. And, don't be surprised if he still feels the fingers that are missing."

Lydia knit her brow. "He'll still feel them? As if they were there?"

"Aye. 'Tis quite common. Even with those who've lost an arm or a leg, they often feel like the limb is there, whole as before."

Lydia's lips trembled. "I understand."

Mr. Bell took her hand and squeezed it. "Your husband should recover quite well. Especially with the love of his pretty wife."

Her cheeks warmed, and she looked at her lap. "How will I manage his pain, Mr. Bell?" She met his eyes again.

"For a few days, keep him on the laudanum. I'll tell you how much to give. After that, rum is the medicinal of choice. I hear Rhode Island is known for its rum.

"Aye."

Her state was also known for exchanging that rum for slaves in Africa. She squeezed her eyes shut, then opened them.

He stood. "I'd best find some victuals."

"Let me serve you some dinner, Mr. Bell." She arose from the settee. "You have more than earned it. I'll see to it you are given a comfortable bed for the night as well."

She rang the bell again. "Cecelia, please see to it Mr. Bell and all the soldiers are well supplied with food. And blankets for sleeping."

Cecelia nodded. "Yes, ma'am."

Mr. Bell's eyes filled with warmth. "Your husband is a fortunate man, Mrs. Hughes."

"'Tis I who am the fortunate wife, Mr. Bell. Thank you again. Cecelia will see to your needs."

She turned back toward the bedchamber where Micah lay and hurried inside. Even if he were asleep, she longed to be with him. She would tell him how much she loved him and pray he could hear her.

23

The first few days of Micah's recovery were a nightmare of pain and little sleep. Lydia could bear the lack of sleep. But watching her husband in so much agony threatened to drive her mad.

Hannah and Cecelia took turns, insisting they be allowed to drape cool cloths over his fevered form. He often spoke words without meaning. Whether caused by the laudanum or the fever, Lydia could not be sure. When exhaustion forced her to rest, she crawled into the large bed next to him, where she could be awakened at a moment's notice.

Were it not for the necessity of feeding Minta, Lydia would not stop to eat. But Miriam encouraged her, saying her baby needed to eat, even if Lydia felt she could do without. She had nearly forgotten the basic needs of her own body as she grieved over the state of her husband's.

Lydia prayed Micah would recover enough to be aware of her presence. She poured her energy and love into tending his needs.

By the third day, Dr. Caldwell smiled for the first time since he'd treated Micah. "I believe your husband fares better, Lydia."

"His fever's gone?" Lydia feared asking him the direct question, worried she might have false hope.

"Aye. He is breathing far better, and his fever has broken. When he awakens, we need to get broth into him. He needs sustenance."

Lydia leaned over her husband's sleeping form. "You are getting better, my love." She kissed his forehead gently.

Nearly prostrate with weariness, Lydia held onto the bedposts as she walked around the bed, then crawled on top of the covers. She collapsed onto the feather pillow and closed her eyes.

~

A HAND TOUCHED HER ARM, and Lydia startled awake. Sunshine flooded in through the window. She squinted. After pushing herself up on her elbows, she tried to focus her eyes but had to rub them to see more clearly. She searched to see if Hannah or Cecelia had awakened her.

"Lydia." Micah's quiet voice spoke.

She gasped and reached toward him, careful not to grip his wounded hand. "Micah." She tried with all her might not to cry. "Micah, I've been so worried." She stroked his grizzled face, heavy with whiskers left untouched for several days.

He struggled to smile and winced instead. "I hurt." His voice was hardly a whisper.

"Oh, my love." She rolled over and stood, then hurried to the bedside table to grab the laudanum bottle. Lydia poured a small portion into a glass vial, according to the surgeon's directions. Lifting his head, she held the vial to his shaking lips.

He winced with disgust at the taste of the bitter medicinal, and then he fell back onto the bed. He moaned when he lifted his bandaged hand. Looking at it, he cried out with the pain.

"Here, Micah. The surgeon said to prop it on pillows." She helped him lift the wrapped hand with care. His jaw clenched, and he squeezed his eyes shut.

"What happened to my hand? It feels on fire, and pounds like a hundred hammers are banging on it."

Lydia held his right hand and stroked his fingers. "You were shot, Micah. You do not remember?"

He shook his head back and forth. ""Nay. 'Tis all a blur of pain, blood, voices." He glanced down toward his leg. "Why does my leg sear in agony?" He closed his eyes again, breathing in deeply and exhaling forcefully.

"You ... you were stabbed with a bayonet." Lydia's voice trembled.

Micah's eyes flew open. "A bayonet? I remember none of this."

She leaned over him and kissed him gently. "Perhaps 'tis just as well, my love."

"Where am I?"

"At my mother's house in Bristol."

He searched her face. "How long have I lain here?"

"Going on four days." Tears welled. "I've been so worried."

"My dear wife. I kept dreaming I heard your voice telling me to be strong. That you loved me." He stroked her wet cheeks with his good hand.

"'Twas not a dream, Micah. I kept speaking to you. I hoped you'd hear me, even if you could not answer." Exhaustion from days of near-despair and little sleep enveloped her, and she sobbed.

Micah reached up. He pulled her onto his chest, and she clung to him, unable to stop her wails. He slowly stroked her convulsing back with his hand.

"I love you so much, my Lydia." His voice, nearly as weak as his touch, soothed her fears.

She kissed his chest, then his cheek and lay her head on his chest again, reveling in his comforting caress. For the first time in days, hope sprang in her heart. Micah was back.

$\sim$

IT HAD BEEN a week since Micah awoke. Lydia opened the window to allow the cooler September air to flow more freely. Weariness still clung to her, not just from caring for Micah.

Ever since the surgeon visited and Micah asked about his wounds, he'd withdrawn into a shell of silence. Lydia would never forget the look on his face when Mr. Bell told him his hand had lost three fingers. The shock in his countenance surprised her. It seemed as if his self-worth depended on that hand being whole.

When she spoke of it with the surgeon, he said Micah would likely emerge from this gloom with time. He'd also mentioned that oftentimes, the effects of laudanum added to the darkness that afflicted the minds of wounded soldiers.

Lydia prayed this melancholy would pass. She missed his smile and his laugh. His sweet conversations. His sweet kisses ...

Cecelia brought Minta in. She fussed for her breakfast, and Lydia took the hungry baby. After Cecelia left, Lydia pulled a chair next to the side of the bed where Micah sat.

"Micah, is she not getting big?"

"Aye, Lydia. She is growing well." He stared at them for a moment, then turned away.

Minta played with the ribbon from Lydia's shift, gripping the string and waving it outward, back and forth while she nursed. Lydia couldn't help but smile. Minta stopped nursing and cooed at her mother.

"When did she start doing that?"

"Doing what?" His taking an interest delighted her.

"Talking like that to you in baby talk."

Lydia cooed back at Minta. "I suppose about two weeks ago."

His countenance lightened as he watched the lass toy with her mother's ribbon, and Lydia's heart sang.

"Would you like to hold her?"

His expression darkened. "I don't think—"

"Of course, you can hold her. She misses you, Papa."

He looked at his injured hand and scowled. "How?"

"I'll show you." Lydia propped some pillows on his left side. "Now, just support her with your right hand as you always do."

Lydia handed the baby to Micah, and he leaned down and kissed her head. Minta grasped onto his finger and squeezed.

"She's so strong now."

"Minta's not the only one getting stronger, Micah. I see you getting more vigorous each day. Eating better. Gaining strength. Soon, you'll be up and about as before. Mr. Bell says your leg heals well, and someday, you'll no longer need a crutch."

Tears welled in his eyes. ""And my hand? How will that get stronger when 'tis half gone? How will I shoot again, provide for you again? How will I hold you again and ... love you again?"

"It takes two people to love. Do you think your injured hand will keep me from loving you or desiring you? You are the same man I fell in love with, and I will always love you. *Every* part of you. Even your scars."

He set Minta toward the middle of the bed and drew Lydia close. His kisses were every bit as desirable as she remembered them, and they took her breath away.

"If you keep kissing me like that, Micah Hughes, I may need to crawl into bed with you right now."

He looked up at her with passion in his gaze. "Let's go home, Lydia. To the farm, where we first made love on our wedding night. I want to go home with you."

"Then, let's prepare to go back." She stroked his face. "I'll tell Hannah we'll be leaving today."

She stood and walked out the door. Leaning against the closed portal, she couldn't help but think *home* sounded sweet indeed.

24

Micah sat on the porch so he could enjoy the September breeze. He'd been home for a week now, and every day the melancholy slowly drifted from his mind like a tide filtering out the filthy residue on a beach. He still needed rum for the pain, but he tried each day to use a little less. He'd experienced pain before, but none compared to the anguish of these wounds.

He'd never tell Lydia the horror of the surgery, but the memory still lived in his mind, battling for his first thoughts every morning. In the middle of the hand surgery, he'd nearly prayed to die to end the misery.

Now he faced life with a dismembered hand. How could Lydia even look at it when she changed his bandage? The sight appalled him. What did she think of him? How could she ever let him hold her again with these ugly scars of battle?

Hannah came out onto the porch with a tankard of cider. "Here you are, Mr. Hughes. Fresh cider from the orchard." She radiated with the joy of her coming baby.

"Thank you, Hannah. It feels strange to be called Mr. Hughes again." He sighed. "I've been a soldier so long." Taking a gulp of the delicious cider, he settled back into his chair.

"You've done your part, Mr. Hughes. And I know your wife be more than relieved you don't need to go back. I wish my Ezekiel were back home and finished with war." She checked down the road as though waiting for him to return at any moment.

"I do as well, Hannah. I want to thank him for saving my life. One of my mates told me he carried me off the field. 'Tis all a blur to me."

She looked back at Micah and touched his shoulder. "Perhaps it's just as well you don't remember much about it. Well, I'd best be helping with dinner." She returned to the house.

Lydia came outside carrying Minta. "She missed her Papa."

"How did I ever deserve you for my wife?" Lydia's beauty still stole his breath. He held his arms out to receive Minta and set her on his lap.

Lydia kissed his forehead before she sat on the edge of the settee. "Just a fortunate fellow, I suppose." She winked.

"Aye. That I am."

Minta giggled at him and reached for his chin. Who could not smile back at that precious cherub? He played with her foot, and she giggled even more.

Micah grew serious. "Has there been any news of Ezekiel? Any letters to Hannah?"

"Nay. She rarely speaks of it, but I know she wonders. And frets." The baby cried and reached for her mother. Minta sucked on her fingers then cried again. "She is cutting some teeth and seems quite unhappy."

Cecelia came onto the porch. May I take her, Ma'am?"

"Yes. Thank you so much."

After Cecelia went into the house, Lydia gently squeezed Micah's hand. "Before my mother died, she told me a very sad tale about Cecelia. She had been with child and—and my mother sold her baby."

Micah's mouth dropped open, and he did not say a word.

"I'm telling you this, so you will understand Cecelia more and also understand how much my mother changed before she died. God did such a work in her heart. She was a new woman."

"I'm so glad to hear this about your mother, Lydia." He picked up her hand and kissed her fingers.

Lydia leaned toward Micah and kissed him tenderly at first. Their kiss lingered for a time, and Lydia stroked his cheek while he kissed her neck

He leaned farther toward her, nearly falling off the edge of his chair, and kissed her long and deeply. Just when he thought they might need to finish their conversation indoors, Micah heard a horse galloping down the road toward the house.

Micah squinted his eyes. "Is that Henry?"

Lydia dabbed her moist mouth with her sleeve. "Corporal Bearslayer?"

He tried to stand, but Lydia put pressure on his shoulder. "You needn't get up, my love. He'll understand."

Henry Bearslayer slowed his mount and saluted Micah. "Good to see you, Sergeant."

Something gripped inside his gut at the salutation. "It's Mr. Hughes now, Henry." He'd miss the title, but not the fighting. "Or Micah."

Henry dismounted. "How is the baby, Mrs. Hughes?"

"Very well, Henry. It's good to see you." She stood. "I'll leave you two war heroes alone to speak. You will stay for meals and rest, I do hope?"

"Aye, ma'am."

Lydia left, and Henry's expression turned serious. Micah noticed Lydia had not closed the door all the way. She likely listened in on their conversation, as she had worried about Ezekiel for days now.

"So, what brings you all the way out here, Henry? I doubt you're on a casual visit in the midst of war."

Henry removed his tricorne hat and wiped his damp forehead with his sleeve. He slumped into a chair near Micah. "I fear I have some bad news. About Ezekiel."

Micah's heart lurched at the mention of bad news. He shifted on the settee, and the pain in his leg sharpened. He inhaled deeply. "Tell me. No sense in putting it off." While his words were brave, he gripped the side of the upholstered chair arm with sweat-covered hands.

Henry paused for a moment before speaking. "He's dead, Micah."

Micah inhaled sharply and struggled to keep calm. "How?"

"Shortly after the battle, when the regiment returned from the island, several of the privates came down with camp fever. Many of the men succumbed. Unfortunately, Ezekiel was one of them."

Micah lifted his wounded leg up and set it on the porch. He leaned forward and covered his eyes, working with all his might to hold back tears.

Henry cleared his throat. "I found this in Ezekiel's coat. It's addressed to his wife."

Micah looked up and took the folded parchment from his friend. "Thanks." He tucked it inside his waistcoat and wiped his eyes.

Sobbing came from behind the door, and Lydia came back out. "He survived the battle only to be taken by illness? I cannot believe it. I never thought—" She shook her head as she covered her face.

Micah stood on unsteady legs and wrapped his arms around her while she cried.

"I'll go put my horse in the barn." Henry descended the steps and led his mount to the building.

Micah lifted her chin. "Do you want me to tell Hannah?"

"Nay, I shall." She sniffed.

"Then take this to her." He pulled the missive from his pocket and handed it to her. "Henry brought it. 'Twas in Ezekiel's coat." Regretting that he'd recruited Ezekiel into the army, he couldn't help but think this was his fault.

She swiped away the tears on her cheeks and thrust the door open before slamming it shut.

Micah had difficulty forgiving himself. How would Lydia ever forgive him? Or Hannah, for that matter?

∾

LYDIA SHIVERED as she stepped into the kitchen where Hannah cooked.

Miriam noticed her presence first. "What be wrong, Mrs. Hughes?"

Hannah paused in her work at Miriam's words and stared at Lydia. She dropped the knife and gripped the table. Hannah slapped it, then covered her eyes with tight fists.

"I knew somethin' happened to him. I just knew it." Her anger turned to sobs.

Lydia ran over and enveloped her friend in her arms. "I'm so sorry, Hannah. This is all my fault."

Hannah lifted her head. "Why it be your fault? You just did what Ezekiel wanted." She convulsed in between her words. "There be no one, not even me, that could stop him once his mind made up. 'Tis no one's fault. Just the way of it." She collapsed into a chair and wept uncontrollably.

"Let me take you upstairs, Hannah."

She helped her friend from the chair. Tears poured down both women's faces while they went up the stairs with slow, deliberate steps. Comfort and Rose appeared at the top of the staircase and opened their eyes wide.

"What's wrong, Mama?"

"Let me help Hannah to her room, and then we'll talk."

After Hannah lay on her side on the bed, Lydia placed her palm across her friend's growing belly.

"Ezekiel has left his child with you. Try to rest so you and the baby will be well. And Hannah, you will stay with us as long as you want—you and your little one. You are family."

Hannah closed her eyes. Soon grief brought on blessed sleep for her friend.

Lydia kissed her cheek and tiptoed out the door, then found Comfort and Rose waiting for her. "Lassies, let's go downstairs, and we can talk."

Once settled in the kitchen with cups of fresh cider, Lydia relayed the heartbreaking news.

"But, I thought Ezekiel was coming home."

"We did as well, Comfort. But sometimes things happen to change our plans. He wanted to come home, but, like your first Papa, a terrible sickness took his life."

Comfort tilted her head. "I can barely remember my first Papa. Was he kind like this Papa?"

Lydia blinked back more tears and nodded. "Aye, Comfort. Very kind."

Rose reached into Lydia's lap and took her hand. "Can we help Miss Hannah feel better?"

Despite her grief, Lydia smiled at the child's kindness. "Aye, Rose. Perhaps you can find some lovely flowers in the garden to give her. What do you say?"

"I think she might like that."

"I think she might as well."

The front door opened, and Micah hobbled in on his crutch, followed by Henry Bearslayer. Micah's face was drawn.

Lydia hurried toward him and wrapped her arms around his thin waist.

"I'm so sorry, Lydia. This is my fault," he mumbled into her hair.

"Nay." She looked up at him. "'Tis not your fault or mine. 'Tis just what happened. Ezekiel wanted to go into the army. Neither of us could have stopped him."

"But I was the one—"

She placed her fingers across his lips. "Neither of us could have stopped him. He died doing what he felt called to do."

They held each other for a long time, wrapped in grief, and

regretting this day's terrible turn of events. Despite her husband's wounds, Lydia thanked God he had come home.

~

AT DINNER, Corporal Bearslayer surprised Micah with his frequent glances at Miriam. She, in turn, giggled more often than usual. When had this flirtation begun? It seemed much had gone on that he'd missed.

Talk at the table focused on this year's good crop. Cuff and Caesar had hauled in sufficient feed for the horses and food for the family. The extra bounty could be shared with the townspeople, Lydia suggested.

Micah lost himself in thought. Ezekiel had been a good friend to him and had saved his very hide from the Hessians, to top it off. But Lydia had known the man for years. The vacant stare on her face, the swollen eyes, and the way she pushed the food around on her plate rather than eating it revealed how difficult she was taking this turn of events.

He wished he could go back several months and re-do that first visit to the farm when he'd recruited slaves for the regiment. But how would that change Ezekiel's choice that impacted so many, including the regiment that relied so much on his strength and fervor? Might the outcome of that battle on Aquidneck had a different ending?

Micah would never know. Events so often occurred beyond anyone's control—and not always with a happy ending. Yet through it all, he believed Providence still controlled it all. In that, he took some comfort.

Hannah's place at the table remained empty.

"Micah, you've hardly eaten a bite." Lydia tilted her head at him.

"Actually, I was going to say the same thing about you." He pointed at her plate, the food now swirled together like freshly scythed grass.

In humorous defiance, she stabbed a piece of salt pork and thrust it in her mouth, making a show of eating with a hearty appetite.

Micah did the same, which elicited another giggle from Miriam and outright laughter from Comfort and Rose.

"Shall we see who can eat the most?" Lydia challenged him, her eyes twinkling.

"I accept your challenge, Mrs. Hughes."

Lydia tried to chew another bite but kept chuckling, and she had to cover her mouth so as not to spit her food out.

When the laughter subsided, Comfort spoke his thoughts. "'Twas good to laugh,"

"Aye, it was." Lydia's gaze met his. "I think I've eaten sufficiently for this evening. 'Tis near dusk, and I am weary." She pushed her chair back.

Micah and Henry stood.

"Henry, please stay in the house this time. Miriam will see you to your room." She winked at the young black woman, then paused mid-step between the table and the door. "And Miriam, please take some dinner to Hannah and make sure she is well."

"Aye, ma'am. I shall."

Cecelia interrupted. "I can go see to Hannah, Mrs. Hughes."

"Thank you. Lassies, Miriam will see you both to bed."

"May I sleep with you, Mama?"

Lydia grinned at Micah. "Nay, my sweet. Where would your Papa spend the night?" She winked.

"Why, in my bed, of course."

Micah threw his head back and laughed. "I am sorry, Comfort, but I don't think my legs will have enough room in your bed. Besides, I heard you and Rose get to share a bed this night."

The girls hurried upstairs, giggling. They talked excitedly about being able to spend the night together.

"Be quiet, dear ones." Lydia hushed the children at the top of the stairs. "Hannah needs to rest."

"Goodnight, Henry. Rest well," Micah patted his friend on the back as Miriam headed upstairs to show him his bedchamber.

"You too, Micah."

Micah grabbed his crutch and hobbled up, one step at a time. Lydia made her way back down to him and gripped his right arm in order to help him ascend. By the time they reached the top of the stairwell, Micah was breathless.

"Please rest more, my love. The doctor said you lost much blood."

"Sometimes, it seems this recovery will take forever."

"Let's go to our chamber."

After closing the door behind them, Lydia turned to her husband and covered her hands over her tear-filled eyes. "What if that had been you?"

Micah drew her arm toward the bed, and they sat on the edge. "But 'twas not, my love. I am here." He held her tenderly and kissed the top of her head.

Lydia's crying became convulsive, and they sat together for a long while as he stroked her hair.

Thank God 'twas not me.

25

Lydia loved the fall. Especially October. The month brought cooler air, and the warm gold and scarlet hues on the trees delighted her. It also brought Comfort's birthday.

"How shall we celebrate, my sweet girl?" Both excitement and sadness filled Lydia's heart. The five years since her older daughter's birth had passed so quickly. Minta would not be far behind in getting older. Every year galloped by faster than the one before.

Comfort clapped her hands together. "Let's have cake!"

Rose giggled. "Will I get cake on my birthday too?"

"Of course, dear Rose. You will be five *next* month."

"How old are you, Papa?" Comfort grinned at him, knowing such a question should not be asked of an adult.

Micah did not hesitate. "I'll be four and twenty later this month."

Lydia's mouth dropped open. "Your birthday is this month? We must celebrate."

"Mama is already four and twenty, Papa." Comfort giggled.

"Well, I'll tell you a secret, Comfort. I've always liked older women." Micah winked.

"Well, that is good, because Mama is quite old."

Lydia scowled, trying not to laugh at her daughter's seriousness. "So much for respect around here. Suddenly, I'm the aged wife and mother!"

"But you wear your years with such beauty, my love." Micah gave her his mischievous grin.

She threw a linen napkin at him. He ducked as if under attack, which had the little girls howling with laughter.

"All right, enough silliness. Perhaps Papa would like to escort his old wife to the carriage? I've freshly picked pumpkins to bring to town."

"May I go, Mama?" Comfort mouthed "please" over and over.

"Nay, my sweet. I do believe the carriage will be quite full already with Cecelia and the pumpkins."

She stuck her bottom lip out and crossed her arms in a huff. "Why does Minta always get to go?"

"I know you do not remember being a nursing baby, but trust me, you traveled everywhere with me then." She stood, squeezed her daughter's shoulders, and kissed her on top of her head. "Besides, I think you might help Hannah a bit. Do something kind to help her feel your love. Aye?"

Comfort looked at the floor. "Aye."

Cecelia stood in the doorway, holding Minta. "I be pleased to visit Mrs. Varnum's maid. Mehitabel and I, we be friends for a long time."

"I'm glad you get to see her. I'm certain she misses you as well."

Lydia went to help Micah with his crutch, but he held up his arm. "Nay, I need to do this on my own." He grinned, took the crutches from against the wall, then escorted her to the carriage.

"You needn't go down the steps with me." She touched his arm.

"But I want to as a proper husband should."

She leaned toward him. "Well, you certainly were a proper

husband evening last." She placed her arm around his waist and squeezed him.

He paused and grinned at her. "Anything to please my older wife."

She rolled her eyes and shook her head. "You and Comfort give me such trouble."

He grew serious. "And you, my love, give me so much joy." He leaned down to kiss her and nearly lost his balance.

She grabbed him tightly and kissed him deeply. "Perhaps we can share more joy this night. After dark."

"'Twould be my pleasure." Micah reset his crutches and descended the stairs one at a time, the way the doctor had taught him. Leaning on the crutch, he opened the door.

"Thank you, my love." She stood on her tiptoes and kissed him again. "Until later."

"Say hello to Mrs. Varnum for me."

"I shall." After she'd sat inside next to Cecelia, she blew him a kiss. He waited and watched the carriage leave the farm.

As the carriage moved along the rutted dirt road, Lydia glanced at Cecelia, who covered a laugh.

"What?"

"Ma'am, you be like a schoolgirl in love."

Warmth flooded her face. "'Tis exactly how I feel, Cecelia."

Minta fussed and grabbed at Lydia's breast. The infant calmed when given her breakfast.

Lydia stroked the cheeks of her four-month-old and gently squeezed her chubby thighs.

"She be one happy baby, so long as you feed her!"

"True enough."

They both laughed.

"Perhaps one day, you and Mr. Hughes have a baby together. Perhaps you give him a son."

"I'd like nothing better. I know as long as I nurse Minta, that will likely not happen. The midwife told me so."

Cecelia's brows furrowed. "I did not know that."

"Aye. I suppose 'tis God's way of helping women recover from having one baby before having another. In due time, Mr. Hughes and I will rejoice if we have another." *The fruit of our love,* Lydia mused as she looked out the window at the glorious forest of trees turning colors before the onset of winter.

They arrived at the new home of General and Mrs. Varnum. The carpenters had wasted no time in replacing the home burned by the enemy the previous May. To look at this stately two-story mansion, one might never know the previous building had been decimated. Martha must be thrilled to be home again.

Stepping out of the carriage, Lydia held the door for Cecelia.

"Oh my. Such a beautiful home. Mehitabel must love living here." Cecelia stared in awe at the house.

The smell of fresh pinewood filled the atmosphere. Lydia inhaled deeply, enjoying the rich aroma that soothed her spirit. This was far more comforting than the smell of raw ash just six months before.

"Cuff, can you carry the crate of pumpkins to the back door and hand it to the servants? They might want to cook some for tonight's supper."

"Very well, ma'am." He climbed on the step of the carriage and lifted the heavy box down. "Very good crop this year, ma'am."

"Aye." Turning to Cecelia, she said, "If you'd like to go with Cuff, perhaps Mehitabel is with the other servants. I know she'll be quite pleased to see you."

Cecelia picked up her dress and hurried along the path to the back entrance of the home.

Before ascending the front steps, Lydia turned and glanced around the streets. When she'd been here just last month, people were everywhere on the roads. Today, the town looked like the atmosphere before a storm, with everyone taking shelter. She glanced at the cloudless sky. No storm seemed in the offing. Lydia furrowed her brow and went to the front door, carrying Minta.

She knocked. One of the servants answered but did not allow her to enter. "Mrs. Hughes here to see Mrs. Varnum," he called into the home. He turned to Lydia, "You did not come from the army hospital, did you, Mrs. Hughes?"

Lydia tilted her head. "Nay, I only just arrived from my plantation."

He opened the door wide and motioned her inside. "I'll get Mrs. Varnum for you, ma'am."

Such an unusual greeting. Uncertain if she were welcome, Lydia awaited the entrance of Martha Varnum before removing her cloak.

"Lydia." Martha hurried toward her from down the hall. The spry woman rarely strolled, always running somewhere. "'Tis so good to see you. Are all well on the plantation?" The woman bore an unexpected look of worry.

"Why, yes, Martha. Of course, my husband still heals from his wounds. Otherwise, we are all well."

"Please sit down." She rang a bell, and Mehitabel came in. "Coffee, please, my dear."

Mehitabel curtsied and went back to the kitchen.

"Is anything wrong, Martha? There is no one about on the street, and your servant acted quite concerned, even asking if I'd been to the infirmary."

"Oh dear." Her hand covered her lips for a moment before returning to her lap. "You have not heard. Many of the wounded, and even the other soldiers who returned to Rhode Island, carried camp fever with them."

"I know our former slave, Ezekiel, died of some such illness. Perhaps 'twas that?"

"Did he come home to visit?"

Lydia shook her head. "Nay, he never made it home, much to everyone's grief."

Martha leaned toward her and gripped her arm. "'Tis a blessing he did not, Lydia. The men who visited home brought the illness with them. 'Tis highly contagious, and many families are afflicted. Several have died. In Tiverton, whole families have been lost."

Lydia gasped. "Oh, dear."

"'Tis a blessing you took Micah home when you did. Soon after is when the illness erupted, and the hospital—your mother's previous home—is in quarantine."

Lydia covered her mouth and gasped into her hand. "Oh, no!"

"Most residents are staying home, lest the illness spread." Martha shook her head slowly. "The afflictions of war ne'er cease."

They sat in silence until Lydia looked up at Martha. "I'd hoped to take you to the house today. I wanted to give you the opportunity to glean what you need for your new home. I know the fire decimated everything in your previous house."

"I've no need for so many luxuries as my mother had. I took a few things—some jewelry and books and such that had special meaning. But, in truth, there is little from my mother's home that I need. Or want."

Martha narrowed her eyes. "You always refer to the house as your mother's home rather than belonging to your parents. I find that curious."

Lydia swallowed with difficulty and focused on the sleeping baby in her lap.

"Forgive me, Lydia. 'Tis none of my concern." Martha held her hands up and waved them in front of her. "I know your father was not the most ... *affable* figure. Perhaps you've not the best memories of the man."

Memories she wished she could forget flooded through Lydia's mind. Some recollections were too vivid and painful to erase, no matter how hard one tried.

She stared at Minta, who rested peacefully. Could she confide in this woman? She'd no reason to believe she could not. For twenty years, she'd carried the burden of these memories alone. Did she have the courage to share them? An unendurable pain that would only be relieved by revelation erupted in her gut.

"May—may I share something with you, Martha? 'Tis a burden I feel I can no longer carry on my own."

Martha's eyes filled with sympathy. "Of course, you can." The older woman clasped Lydia's free hand with hers.

"I'm not certain where to start. I was so very small—four years old, I believe." Lydia trembled. "My father's ship had arrived in port. I had no idea what he carried in his ships. I knew nothing about human cargo." She swallowed. "I just knew my papa had come home from a very long trip, and I felt excited to see him."

She paused, gripping Martha's hand like her life depended on it. "I could not find my father. Somehow, I lost my mother's hand in the crowd. There were so many people walking around, and I could not see much due to my short height." A strange sense of numbness floated through her veins, as though she were no longer Lydia Hughes but had shrunken back into the four-year-old body of Lydia Warnock.

"I asked several strangers. 'Have you seen my papa? Mr. Warnock?'"

"One sailor—he smelled like fish—pointed to the other side of the wharf. 'Think I saw him headin' that-away,' he said." She paused a moment and took a deep breath before continuing. "So, I followed the man's finger toward the area behind several large crates stacked high."

Her breath would not come as she remembered what she saw next.

Martha stroked her hand. "And did you find him, Lydia?"

"Aye. But I wish I had not." She sobbed uncontrollably.

Martha handed her a kerchief. "Oh, my dear. What did you see? Rid yourself of this terrible memory, so it will free its wretched grip on your heart."

"My father. He lay on top of a black woman. She wore no clothes, and some of his were off. She cried out, but he kept hurting her. I yelled, 'Papa, stop! You're hurting her!' He looked up in shock to see me there. He immediately stood and buttoned his breeches. 'Twas not until I married Jeremiah that I understood what he was doing. But Jeremiah loved me with kindness and gentleness. My father acted with harm and evil intent."

Martha placed her hand on Lydia's cheek and stroked it with her finger like a mother would when consoling a child. "Oh, Lydia, I cannot imagine you carrying this burden all your life. Did you tell your mother?"

"Nay." Lydia shook her head against Martha's hand. "I tried to, but she was distracted at the time, talking with friends. When I tried to talk with her later on, she said I must have misunderstood. But I know what I saw. A while later, I saw that same black woman on the auction block. She looked terrified. I wanted to help her, but what could a four-year-old do?"

She blew her nose. "Years later, I saw that same expression on Miriam's face when she stood naked on the auction block. Jeremiah and I had married recently, and we visited my parents. We were there when my father's ship came in. I saw the way Father looked when he tried to bid on her, and I knew that this would be my chance to do something that I couldn't all those years ago.

"I begged my husband to outbid my father, which caused Jeremiah much consternation, but he did so to please me. Of course, fury erupted on Father's face. But I did not care. I couldn't let Miriam be hurt by him anymore." This revelation of her past sapped Lydia's strength. It had taken every ounce of her being to finally dislodge the terrible memory.

Her wounded spirit, which had festered so long with the putrid secret, had been released of its poison. And with that extraction came the realization that none of this was her fault. Her childish mind had carried that burden these twenty years, and she felt like a seagull with a wounded wing that finally made its way to the sky over the ocean. That freedom brought her renewed strength and even joy.

Perhaps someday she could share the story with Micah. But it would not be today.

Martha had held her hands the whole time Lydia spoke, listening without interruption or judgment. "I am honored that you'd allow me to hear your story. I can see this pained you to speak of it, and understandably so."

The older woman inhaled. "I only wish you'd not been burdened by this horror for so long without finding a sympathetic ear. I do not profess to understand the evil deed done by your father. All I know is, evil dwells in the hearts of many. And you, sadly, witnessed that evil. To make things worse, it was done by your father. I cannot begin to fathom the depths of your hurt.

"But I know one thing. God has blessed you with not one, but two loving husbands. Mr. Hughes treats you well, I assume?"

The question took Lydia by surprise. "Oh, aye. He is truly both kind and passionate without hurting me."

"Good. I'm so grateful to know that. And I pray that now you have shared your difficult story, the words can escape into the darkness, never to haunt you again." She squeezed Lydia's hand.

"Thank you, dear Martha. You are like a second mother to me."

"Well, I've certainly had practice in that calling." She laughed. "But I am here for you whenever you need to speak. About anything."

"I'm so grateful." She stood and dabbed at her face with the kerchief. "I shall wash this and return it to you."

"Nonsense. You keep it—as a reminder your tears were shed to free you. Whenever that nasty memory attempts to return, look at that kerchief and remember you are free."

Martha hugged her, and Lydia embraced her, grateful for this friendship.

"I'd best be going back now. Please write to me and let me know when the contagion is no longer present."

"I shall." Martha rang for her servant to let Cecelia know they were leaving. "And I'll pray your family stays well."

"Yours as well, dear Martha."

"Godspeed, my friend."

Lydia met Cuff outside and climbed back into the carriage, where she waited for Cecelia to join her for the ride home.

When Cecelia returned, her eyes were narrowed. "There be contagion hereabouts, ma'am."

"I know. 'Twill be some time before we can return." Lydia stared out the window. Although sickness thrived in the community, she had never felt so well. Her heart had begun to heal.

26

As the weather grew colder and the leaves fell from the trees, Lydia grew melancholy. For her, the only good thing about November was celebrating Thanksgiving. Yet she feared, with so many deaths these past months, giving thanks could be more difficult than in most years.

She also grew concerned that the camp fever might still be a danger. Having guests could put them all at risk. When she asked Micah what his thoughts were, he agreed they could not take a chance. They would celebrate the holiday without attending services at the meetinghouse in Bristol and without inviting guests.

Lydia forced herself to be grateful for her blessings, which were many indeed. Those on her plantation were well, Minta thrived, and her husband, although wounded, recovered at home, safe in her arms every night.

Hannah's pregnancy progressed without difficulty, and she could get through a meal now without battling nausea. Knowing she carried Ezekiel's child seemed to give Hannah comfort. Although she, at times, was melancholic, Lydia's brave friend took good care of herself lest any harm befall the child.

Lydia rejoiced to know Hannah carried Ezekiel's little one yet felt the tragedy that this child would never know his brave and faithful father. She vowed to speak to the child often about Ezekiel so that his son or daughter would know what a fine man he was.

Miriam only recently started receiving letters from Henry Bearslayer. He'd wanted to write to her previously from camp but worried that the letters could carry illness to their home. His assigned fort had been cleared of the camp fever—for now.

Lydia pondered these musings while lying in bed next to Micah. He got up for a moment and lay an extra quilt atop the other blankets. Crawling back under the cocoon of warmth, he wrapped his arms around her, snuggling close. He seemed more quiet than usual at dinner and, even now, spoke fewer words.

She turned her head toward him. "Micah? Are you well?"

"Aye. Why do you ask?"

"Because you seem very ... preoccupied this night."

He kissed her forehead and held her close. "'Tis nothing, truly. I am well."

Touching his face, she searched his eyes with the illumination from the full moon shining through the windowpanes. "There is something. I can tell. Please share your heart with me."

He sighed. "'Tis quite foolish, really. We have Comfort and Minta. But—" He pursed his lips.

"You fear we shall not have a child of our own?"

"'Tis selfish of me, I know. Please forgive me. 'Tis just that Hannah is with child from their one night together. We have been together many times." He kissed her forehead. "Yet, you've never indicated that you might carry our little one. Perhaps, we will not be able—"

She held her fingers against his lips. "Shh. Do not speak of such. God will send us a babe in His time." She perched her head on her hand, propped up on her bent elbow. "Whilst I nurse

Minta, 'tis not so likely I will carry another child. The midwife has told me such." She stroked his face. "I'm sorry I did not tell you."

His grin widened in the moonlight. "That is a relief. I feared we might not have a child together." He wove his fingers through her long, loosened hair. "I love you so very much, Lydia."

She kissed him. "It should not be too many more months before Minta will nurse less, and who knows what might occur?" She giggled.

He closed his eyes as he drew her toward him. "Who knows, indeed." His kisses covered her mouth, and other desires soon replaced those of babies.

~

THE MORNING of Thanksgiving brought a driving rain to the plantation. When Micah limped indoors from seeing to the horses in the barn, he shivered.

"'Tis like having icicles thrown at you out there." He rubbed his hands together and held them near the hearth then quickly withdrew his left hand, still self-conscious about its appearance.

Lydia came over and grasped his maimed hand, enveloping it with her warm fingers. He looked down at her, amazed by her acceptance of his injury. She kissed him and stood by him until his limbs had thawed.

"Thank you, my love." He kissed the top of her head.

She smiled and returned to help the ladies with the cooking.

Comfort and Rose snuck into the kitchen.

"Unless you lassies wish to help with the cooking, you'd best go play elsewhere."

"But we do wish to help."

"Truly?" Lydia looked at them with surprise. "Very well, then, grab aprons, and we shall make more biscuits."

The two girls bustled toward the rack of hooks and grabbed

two aprons. The adult-sized smocks nearly dragged onto the floor, and Micah squelched a grin at the sight. The serious look on their faces when Lydia and Miriam instructed them on how to make the dough nearly elicited a loud chuckle. He left the room before he hurt their feelings.

They were both precious to him, and he did not wish to discourage their efforts at cooking, regardless of how amusing they both looked.

"I'll be in the parlor if you need anything." He kissed Lydia on her flour-covered cheek.

She laughed and took the edge of her apron to wipe off the white powder from his lips.

He left the room and limped with difficulty toward his favorite chair. He groaned as he lowered himself onto the upholstery. This frigid weather played havoc on his injuries, increasing the pain while the temperatures decreased. He'd closed his eyes a moment, then opened them when his wife's lavender scent wafted into his nostrils.

"I watched you come in and sit, Micah. I know you are still in much pain, and I'm certain the cold makes it worse. Please, let Cuff and Caesar tend the horses for now."

His frustration with his situation grew. "Lydia, I must do something to feel worthwhile." He watched the sleet splatter crystals of ice against the windowpanes. "I cannot do nothing. I've been a soldier near three years. And a farmer before that. Am I to sit around like an old man when still in my twenties?"

She knelt beside his chair and stroked his uninjured arm. "Nay, my husband. We will find a way to overcome this obstacle. Together, we can do this. But please ..." She swallowed back her tears. "Please do not give up."

He stroked her soft hair when she rested her head on his lap. He was not the only one injured in this war. Lydia's wounds were not visible, yet she bore the pain of loss, from the death of her first husband to the death of her son. And now she had to bear with his physical wounds, which tore at her heart. He would keep fighting to find his way in adjusting to what he still had, not focus on his losses.

"I'll not give up, Lydia. I promise."

"Thank you, Micah."

He heard the clatter of a horse's hooves out front. "Who is riding on such a day?"

Lydia stood, and Micah got up from the chair, limped toward the door, and answered it.

An unfamiliar black man stood at the door, rain dripping off the brim of his farmer's hat. "Excuse me, sir, be Mrs. Hughes home?"

Lydia came from behind him, and her mouth dropped open. "Joss? Why ever are you here, and in such a storm? Come in."

The man stepped just inside the portal.

"Micah, this is my sister's servant, Joss."

He'd never met her sister, although he knew about her. Why her servant would be here was a mystery to him.

"I be sorry, ma'am. Your sister be in her confinement, and she's not doing well. She asked me to come and get you."

"Come and get me?" Lydia looked at Micah with narrowed eyes. "Is the doctor not there? Or the midwife?"

"Aye, ma'am, but she insisted you come. She says she needs her sister there."

Micah could only imagine Lydia's thoughts at attending her sister's travail. Why the sibling with the sour disposition would request Lydia's presence confused him, and Lydia's puzzled look suggested she was just as mystified as he was.

She gripped his arm. "What should I do, Micah?"

He looked at Joss and said, "Excuse us a moment." He then escorted her to a smaller parlor off to the side of the main room.

"Lydia, I know how you feel about your sister, and I'm well aware of how she treats you. You do not need to go if you do not wish to."

"But, if I don't go and anything happens to her, will I ever be able to forgive myself?"

"Very well. You should go then." Turning toward the window, he winced at the thought of going out again in this weather. But he would not let her go alone. "But I am going with you."

"Micah—"

"That is all there is to it. I'll not send you into the wolf's lair without a defender."

She gave him a grateful smile. "Thank you, my love. But please, travel with me in the carriage with Minta. Cuff can drive us in the chaise."

"Very well, then."

He had no idea what sort of scenario awaited them with Phila in travail. But after hearing Lydia's tales of her sharp-tongued sister, Micah prepared for the worst.

~

"CUFF, please take shelter in the barn. Then come 'round to the back door, and the servants will give you a warm drink."

"Yes, ma'am."

Sleet stung her cheek, and she pulled her hood over her face, leaving her eyes clear to see. She clung to Minta, who remained safe and snug beneath the shelter of her cloak. Micah took her arm as he led her up the front steps. They could already hear her sister's screams from inside.

Here we go.

Praying for strength, Lydia crossed the threshold of the large, two-story mansion on the outskirts of the town proper. This would be the first time she'd visited since Phila had married Phineas two years prior. Even then, Lydia couldn't wait to wipe the dust off of her shoes when she exited.

The midwife greeted Lydia. By the look on Deborah's face, she had already been on the battleground facing the bullets Phila could fire with her malicious tongue. She was likely to be on the losing side of that war.

"Deborah, how does my sister fare?" Lydia feigned concern.

"She is doing well. Just ... exhibitin' great distress."

"No doubt."

Micah held out his hands, a look of sympathy on his face. "Let me take your cloak, Lydia."

"Thank you. Has Dr. Caldwell come?"

"Aye." Deborah looked at the ceiling when another scream from upstairs jolted the atmosphere. "We sent for him near an hour ago. Poor man."

Lydia nearly laughed at the sympathy usually extended toward a woman during a birthing, not her doctor. To express the concern for the physician seemed ironic, but in Phila's case, understandable.

"I nursed Minta on the way over. I suppose I should go up and see Phila." She handed the baby to Micah.

He touched Lydia's hand. "I pray all goes well."

Lydia rolled her eyes. "I pray so too."

Each step she ascended to the second floor made Lydia feel like she climbed a steep mountainside. She was well used to climbing stairs, but it usually involved visiting her loved ones at home. Here, she faced a female serpent with fire on her tongue and bitterness in her soul. Lydia hoped she wore her spiritual armor securely.

Phineas appeared at the top of the landing as he paced up and down the hallway, running his hands through his long, straight hair. He'd either neglected to secure it back, or the ribbon had long since come off. Either way, the disheveled hair and contorted expression on his face gave the impression of near madness. Not surprising, considering his marriage partner.

Lydia prayed her hateful thoughts toward Phila would cease. According to the Good Book, she needed to love—even her enemies. That would truly take a miraculous intervention.

"How are things progressing, Phineas?"

When he looked upward, compassion stirred in Lydia for the man. His moist, swollen eyes and trembling mouth bespoke the depth of his despair. Did Phila deserve this man's compassion? Lydia hoped so.

"I don't know. The doctor says all goes as expected, but with each scream, it tears at my heart. I cannot bear it."

Lydia squelched the desire to remind him that Phila bore the pain of travail. "I'm certain all will be well, Phineas." She thought better of shaking the man. "Phila is strong and healthy. And both the doctor and Deborah are here to attend her." She gripped his arms with sisterly affection, even though she envisioned slapping him. "You must be strong—for her sake."

"I know." He clasped his hands together repeatedly.

Turning away from him lest she give in to her anger, Lydia headed toward the birthing chamber and knocked.

Dr. Caldwell answered the door. He looked even more distressed than when caring for multiple wounded soldiers at the hospital.

Relief melted across his face when he saw her. "Thank the good Lord, you are here."

Lydia's eyebrows furrowed. "Is all not well?" She kept her voice low so her sister could not hear.

He rubbed the back of his neck. "On the contrary, all goes as expected. She just ... does not bear pain well." He exhaled audibly.

A gut-wrenching scream from Phila startled the doctor, and he closed his eyes tightly. "Perhaps, you can stay with her a bit whilst I call for the midwife."

"Of course, doctor." Who could blame the man? Lydia wished she could turn and run herself. Yet she knew her mother would wish her to be here, and that prompted her to approach the bed and make some attempt to comfort her only sister.

"Phila? 'Tis Lydia here to see you. The doctor says all goes as expected. That is good news, aye?"

Her sister snapped her head toward Lydia. "What does he know? He does not sympathize with my suffering!" Venomous words were alive and well, even in imminent motherhood.

"I'm certain the doctor feels quite helpless with a woman in travail." Lydia reached for her sister's hand when the next contraction began.

Phila clutched Lydia's arm so tightly, her nails dug into her skin. Lydia squeezed her eyes shut and fought back tears of pain. When the tightened belly grew more relaxed, Phila still clutched Lydia's arm. She carefully pulled Phila's fingers from their death grip. Blood emerged from where her sister's nails had impaled her.

Her beautiful sister, with poison in every touch. What kind of a mother would she be?

It hardly seemed like that contraction ended before another one began. This time, Phila outdid herself, shouting curses and language that would have brought embarrassment to their father's sailors. Lydia sickened at the vile sounds that flew from her sibling's tongue.

She raced toward the door. When she opened it, both the doctor and midwife scurried into the room. Once they were inside, Lydia shut the door, leaned against it, and prayed Micah could not hear her sister.

Deborah, the midwife, climbed onto the bed and propped Phila upward.

Phila's face reddened to the ruddiness of a sunburn as she labored. Sweat poured off her brow. "Get this baby out of me!"

"Try to breathe deeply, then push when I say to." The doctor readied his forceps just in case, but Phila's strength in both body and spirit prompted the doctor to set the instrument aside. "I can see the head, Phila. You're doing fine."

Deborah gave a relieved smile as she encouraged Phila. This difficult birthing, nearly complete now, likely elicited deep thanks for the stressed midwife. For her, surviving this birthing would make her even more grateful during Thanksgiving dinner to be at home with her family.

All seemed to be going well—until the baby emerged. Lydia

gasped and clutched at her neck. Dr. Caldwell and Deborah remained speechless.

They all stared at the infant.

The baby, perfect in form and beautiful, had skin as black as Rose's had been at birth. Phila's baby boy was a Negro.

27

"What's wrong? Is my baby all right?" Phila lay back on a pillow. Her knees were bent so she could not see the child squirming between her legs.

Deborah cut the baby's cord, grabbed a linen, and wrapped up the healthy boy, who she cradled in her arms. "The doctor needs to examine him." She hurried out the door with the infant, the doctor close on her heels.

"What's wrong with my baby?" Phila cried.

Lydia walked stiffly toward the bedside. "I'm certain he will be fine." The child appeared healthy. But what would her sister's response be? Surely, she'd not imagined this outcome. What had Phila done? What would she do now? And what of Phineas? Her head fairly swam with unanswered questions.

Exhausted, Phila fell asleep. Apparently, she had no maternal longing to put her infant to breast. Lydia shook her head and exited the bedchamber.

She could not find Phineas anywhere. Had he been told? Lydia heard the low voices of Dr. Caldwell and the midwife down the hall. Her ears also caught the mewling sounds of the hungry infant. Hurrying down the hallway, Lydia joined the conversation.

"What's to be done, Mrs. Hughes?" Deborah bounced the hungry infant and attempted to soothe him.

"Done?" Lydia sighed. "I'd say, 'tis time this infant is brought to his mother to nurse."

The doctor and midwife looked at each other then back at Lydia. "But, the father. What will he do?"

"I've truly no idea. But my sister lives her life the way she has always chosen to. Today, her decisions, however unwise they were, have come home to roost on her doorstep."

Lydia picked up the squirming infant and held him close. "Shh, little one." She carried the baby back to the bedchamber.

Phila still slept.

Lydia inhaled deeply then walked over to the bedside. It took several attempts to awaken her sister before she roused.

"Hmm?"

"Phila, please wake up. Your son wishes to nurse."

"I had a boy?" She grinned, then looked at the infant and screamed. "What is that?" She scooted away from Lydia as though she and the infant carried contagion.

"That, my dear sister, is your child. I'm certain there is an explanation for his color. Although perhaps 'twill not be understood by Phineas."

Phila's face reddened, and the veins in her neck enlarged. "You are lying, Lydia. This is just like you to take my own child and give me a slave's child. Where is my baby?"

"He is here, in my arms, waiting for his mother to feed him." She offered him to her sister.

She shook her head and wagged a finger at Lydia and the baby. "If you think I'll put that black infant to my breast, you are quite mistaken."

Lydia glared at her. "Apparently, you thought nothing of allowing one of your young slaves to be intimate with you."

"It only happened one time." Phila turned away, refusing to look at Lydia. "I thought for certain 'twould be the child of one of the others."

Lydia's eyes widened. She finally found her voice. "One of the others? Just how many men have you shared your bed with? Or have you lost count?"

Whipping back to face her, Phila glared at Lydia. "Who are you to speak? With child while your husband was at war."

Lydia clenched the blanket surrounding the infant. "Minta is the child of Jeremiah, who came home on furlough a year ago in October. How dare you insinuate I've been an adulterer? Does accusing me make you feel better about your own disloyalty to your husband?"

"Phila stared at the wall. "That is not my child. Take him to one of the slaves to nurse. My child was stillborn."

Even for Phila's ignoble character, Lydia could not have been more shocked by her despicable statement. Without saying a word, Lydia left with the infant. After closing the door, tears of outrage warmed her cheeks. Her heart racing, she descended the staircase with care. Micah awaited her in the parlor.

"So, she's delivered her child. Why did Phineas leave in such a hurry?"

Her hands trembled, but she unfolded the blanket to reveal the baby's face.

Micah's mouth dropped open. "This is Phila's child?" His eyes widened, searching hers for an explanation.

"I am as dumbfounded as you." She told Micah what her sister said about disclaiming the infant.

He shook his head and scowled. "Is there a wet nurse among the slaves here?"

"Likely." The infant started to wail. "Let me find someone."

She carried her nephew into the kitchen, where a few of the servants worked. She recognized one of the ladies, an older woman, who'd been in the family for years. "Miss Jessie, may I speak with you in private?"

"Yes, ma'am." Miss Jessie wiped her hands on her apron and followed Lydia into a quiet room.

Inhaling a deep breath for courage, Lydia revealed the baby's face.

Miss Jessie's mouth opened, and she covered it with both hands. "Oh, my!" Her widened eyes flitted back and forth as she stared at the infant. "Where this precious child come from?"

"This— this is my sister's baby, Miss Jessie."

The black woman breathed so hard, Lydia feared she would faint. "Miss Jessie, please sit down."

The servant did not argue but burst into tears when she plopped into the chair.

"Miss Jessie, do you know who the father is?" Lydia placed her hand gently on the woman's large shoulder.

"I fear I do, ma'am. This child, I fear, be my grandchild."

Lydia gripped the baby and bounced him more firmly. When she found her voice, it was strained. "Your grandchild? Your son, Amos? He seems quite young."

"He be eighteen now." Miss Jessie's eyes narrowed, and her lips thinned. "That Miss Phila. She loves to flirt with my Amos. I told him to stay clear of her flaunting ways. But she has that fine form to attract men, and she does all she can to get the young men in the hay.

Nausea gripped Lydia at the thought of her voluptuous sister seducing a young slave. A teen, no less. She closed her eyes tightly to remove the image from her mind. Loud wails from the child forced her back to reality.

"Miss Jessie, I am so sorry about your son. I can only say how sorry I am for my sister's sinful ways. But this baby—your grandchild—needs some food to survive. Can you find him a wet nurse in the slave quarters?"

"I'll go find him a nurse, Miss Lydia." Miss Jessie stood and threw her shoulders back. "Don't you worry. I'll not tell anyone who the mother is."

Lydia stared at the floor. "My sister says to tell everyone her child was stillborn."

"Then, so be it." Miss Jessie took the infant from her.

But not before Lydia gave the child a kiss on his forehead. "Farewell, dear nephew." Lydia scurried away to find Micah.

~

TWO DAYS LATER, Lydia could not get the events at Phila's birthing out of her mind. She knew her sister's morals had been corrupted for years, but she never imagined Phila would stoop so low as to seduce a young slave. She was, like her mother said, becoming more and more like their father.

"I pray the baby is well."

Micah paused in taking a bite of breakfast. "I'm certain his grandmother will see to his needs."

"Aye. Yet he'll be raised a slave. Phila will never free her slaves. And unless the state outlaws this barbaric practice, my nephew will not be a free man."

Micah's face reddened as he sipped some warm cider. "The whole thing is bereft of morals." He spoke little of the birthing, but Lydia knew it troubled him. "It's difficult to believe you and Phila are even related to one another, much less, sisters."

"We've never been close, that is for certain. She's always been an embarrassment to me." Lydia stirred the coffee in her cup. "Micah, I'm so grateful I followed my prompting to go there. I cannot imagine what might have happened to the child had I not been there to confront Phila."

"I try not to imagine it." He looked out the window at the abrupt sound of sleet hitting the glass pane. "The wintry weather is here to welcome in December the first."

"Aye." Lydia sipped her coffee. "Perhaps I'll take up knitting again, now that the air is so chilled. When I found Mother's knitting needles after her death, I decided to keep them. She taught me how to knit at a young age, but I suppose I thought I was too busy as I got older. I haven't held a ball of yarn in quite some time."

"You could make some stockings for Minta. I noticed her

feet felt cool this morning when she awoke." Micah finished his biscuits and wiped his mouth. Pushing back from the table, he stood, then hobbled to her side to kiss her cheek.

"Thank you."

"What for?"

"For loving our children as you do. For noticing Minta's needs. And mine."

His kiss descended, and his soft lips were sweet indeed against hers. "As you see to mine." He grinned.

"Mama." Comfort hurried into the dining room, her eyes filled with fear. "Papa, there's a scary stranger coming to our house."

Micah's eyes narrowed, and he hobbled toward the back door. As he opened it wider, a cold blast of wind swirled into the house, and the chill reached Lydia as she finished breakfast. She stood and hurried toward the kitchen.

"It's a woman." Micah let the stranger in from the storm.

When the woman removed her hood, Lydia gasped. "Miss Jessie! You walked all the way here? Please, come by the hearth and sit."

She feared the woman would not make the distance to the chair, but with her on one side and Micah on the other, they helped her reach the lifesaving warmth of the huge hearth. Lydia removed the soaking wet cloak from around her shoulders and gasped. Miss Jessie held Phila's two-day-old son.

"Miss Jessie, I don't understand. Why—"

The woman burst into tears. "I be sorry, Miss Lydia, so very sorry. But I couldn't let Miss Phila kill my grandson." Her shoulders shook with her sobs.

"Kill your grandson? Whyever—what happened?" Lydia gripped the back of the chair and sought Micah's eyes.

His glare told her he believed Miss Jessie.

"Miss Phila, she became mad somethin' awful when they could hear the baby crying in the night. She had told Mr. Phineas the baby be dead. But when this little one fussed and carried on in the slave quarters, Mr. Phineas got suspicious somethin' wasn't right. We could hear them fightin' somethin' awful.

"Mr. Phineas, he left for the tavern and came home drunk. He told Miss Phila she had to get rid of this baby, or he'd get rid of her. He told her to throw the child in the icy water near the wharf." Miss Jessie sobbed. "I couldn't let them kill my grandchild. You're the only one I knew would take care of him."

Lydia grew dizzy, and Micah brought her a chair next to Miss Jessie. He helped his wife sit.

"I can barely believe this horrific tale. My sister— would kill her own child?"

"The devil hisself be in that woman."

"I often wonder."

The baby awoke, wailing. The infant's cries captured Lydia's heart. The sound brought Cecelia, Miriam, and Hannah into the kitchen. They stood with mouths agape.

Cecelia came over and stroked his cheek. "What a beautiful baby."

"Aye, he is." Lydia smiled and remembered Cecelia's loss. "Would you like to hold him?"

"May I?" Cecelia grinned wider than Lydia had ever seen before. She cooed and comforted the little one, who rooted around for some milk. "He be mighty hungry. I'd be happy to care for this child, but I not be able to feed him."

"I would have brought the wet nurse from Bristol, but I couldn't tell nobody what I intended to do. As it is, I'm in terrible danger from Miss Phila. Iffin' I told anyone else, they be in trouble too."

Everyone looked around, but no one said a word.

Micah finally cleared his throat and spoke. "The answer seems clear. There is only one choice if we are to save this child. Lydia?" His voice held tenderness and resignation.

She captured his gaze and loved him more than ever. "Are you certain, Micah?"

Micah knew by now that nursing even longer would prolong the time they'd have to wait for her to become pregnant with his child.

He took the newborn from Cecelia's arms. "He'll be yours to raise, if you're willing, Cecelia."

Tears dampened her cheeks. "I be more than willin', Mr. Hughes."

"Someone needs you." He carried the infant to Lydia and kissed her cheek gently, then brought her a blanket to cover up.

Loosening her stays, Lydia offered her breast to the infant. The child enthusiastically suckled and relaxed as his stomach filled. Contentment flooded her spirit when she realized her nephew need not fear being enslaved. He would grow up free, mothered by Cecelia, who needed him, just as he needed her to raise him.

Lydia smiled at Micah. "Thank you, my love."

Miriam and Hannah fixed some food for Miss Jessie.

The older woman smiled through her tears as her grandson nursed. "Thank you, Miss Lydia."

After she ate, Miss Jessie prepared to leave. "I best be heading back, or I'll be facing a whippin' for sure."

Lydia shivered at her words.

As Miss Jessie kissed the baby, a tear fell on his head.

"Godspeed, Miss Jessie." Lydia gripped the woman's hand as she walked by.

"Thank you, Ma'am."

MICAH ACCOMPANIED Miss Jessie to the front door, but she insisted he take her to the back. "Someone may see me leave iffin' I go this way."

"Let me have Cuff drive you back in the carriage, Miss Jessie. Please. It's the least we can do."

"Nay, Mr. Hughes. Iffin' anybody see me in your carriage,

they'll know where my grandson be. But I be grateful for your offer." She threw her cloak over her head and descended the mud-covered steps before she hurried away, her shoulders hunkered forward against the driving rain.

Micah stared at Miss Jessie, who had risked her life to save her grandchild—this slave woman whose love had delivered the baby from the same hateful spirit that possessed King Herod to kill the Christ-child so long ago.

A chill filtered through his veins as he realized the depth of evil in Phila's heart—an evil as old as sin itself.

LYDIA HAD JUST FINISHED FEEDING the baby when another knock on the back door startled her and the other women in the kitchen. Micah whisked by them to answer the door, and a frantic voice asked for Miss Jessie. Anxiety needled through Lydia while she awaited Micah.

When he returned to the kitchen, his face had turned ashen. He could barely speak as he knelt next to Lydia. "My dearest, that was Miss Jessie's son. There are men seeking to kill this child. And us, if we resist them. They are not certain where he is for now. But they will surely discover his whereabouts once they are through getting the truth out of Miss Jessie."

Her breathing quickened, and nausea gripped her belly. "Then we must find Miss Jessie and bring her to safety with us.

"Nay, my love. Her son says she insists on returning to your sister's home so she can stall the men who seek his life. It— it will give us a chance to escape."

"Escape?" The words echoed numbly in her head as she contemplated the full meaning. "My sister is after the child? To kill him?'"

"Aye. She has several indentured servants, and she's offered a tidy reward for carrying this out. We must hasten to leave, Lydia. Forthwith."

"We must leave?" Her thoughts muddled through this conversation that her mind tried to comprehend. When her thoughts sorted past the paralyzing fear and realized the danger, Lydia gripped his arm and trembled. "We must go at once."

Micah helped her rise from the chair. He took the infant, then handed the child to Cecelia.

"Ladies, we must escape from here to save this child's life. Hasten to get ready. We must leave, and the sooner, the better."

Eyes wide and voices silent, they hurried to prepare.

Lydia gripped the railing of the staircase as she headed upstairs to gather the children, along with the barest of essentials. She'd already faced danger and heartache in her life. But she'd never imagined such a confrontation with evil before.

The sins of her father were truly at work today.

28

While they prepared for their escape from Bristol, Lydia watched with awe as Micah organized the endeavor. He thought of every detail.

Her love for him grew, as did her appreciation for his ability to remain calm while she fought such terror. What if Phila's mercenaries caught up with them? Grateful that Micah had instructed both Cuff and Caesar in firing a musket and reloading quickly, Lydia still did not know how many men her sister had hired.

Knowing Phila, 'twould be more than sufficient numbers to ensure the newborn would be thrown into the icy waters of Narragansett Bay. Lydia shivered at the thought.

Miriam appeared with blankets filled with the children's clothing while Cecelia stuffed some bread and pemmican into a traveling bag. "I be glad I made this dried pemmican the other day."

Hannah appeared with another sack. "I brung some extra clothes for all the women. Just in case we need 'em."

"Thank you, Hannah."

"Mama, Minta is crying." Comfort hugged her doll and pointed with her finger upstairs.

Lydia gripped the haversack she'd packed with baby garments and inhaled sharply. Such poor timing for a baby's hunger.

"Aye," She started to run upstairs.

Miriam stopped her. "Stay here, Ma'am. I bring her down for you."

"Thank you, Miriam." As she sat down and undid her stays once again to feed her own child, Micah appeared holding a tankard of cider.

"Here, my love. Please drink this. Then we must hasten. You can feed Minta in the carriage." His hazel eyes captured her heart, as did the look of tenderness on his countenance.

Re-tying her stays with trembling fingers, she took the cider and guzzled most of the contents. Inhaling deeply, she stood. "Very well, I'm ready."

Minta's cries grew louder. Hurrying toward Miriam, who had just come downstairs with the unhappy child, Lydia gathered the baby in her arms.

As she opened the door, she paused. This would likely be her last time in this home. She assumed Phila would take it over. Lydia would gladly give the plantation to her sister if it meant saving a little one's life.

Lydia covered her infant with her cloak to protect her from the rain and scurried outside to the waiting carriage.

Cecelia was already in her seat and scooted over to make room for Lydia. Mercifully, Minta had quieted, but when Lydia opened her cloak, the infant was still searching among the blankets for her meal. Lydia, once again, undid her stays to feed her daughter.

Hannah climbed into the other carriage, followed by Miriam hurrying the young girls inside. Lydia wondered what the women would tell the two five-year-olds. How could they explain all of this? 'Twas difficult enough for adults to understand this dreadful situation.

Lydia stared at the infant sleeping in Cecelia's arms. The servant grinned, cooed, and stroked the baby's face.

"What will you call him, Cecelia?"

"I thought Moses be a good name for him since he be rescued from the waters of death."

"That's a perfect name for him. Moses."

As Micah mounted his horse and Cuff and Caesar prepared for their escape from Bristol, a flood of memories swirled through Lydia's thoughts like a whirlwind of both pleasure and pain.

Here is where she'd bid goodbye to Jeremiah for the last time and, months later, delivered his children. She then had to part with her firstborn son, now buried in the family plot nearby. Here is where she'd met Micah, where they'd married, and where they'd shared their love for the first time. There were so many pieces of her heart here.

Yet looking at the group in and around the carriages, with urgency written all over their faces, Lydia realized her heart truly lay with them. They were her family. Love did not exist in a building but in the hearts of those who were faithful and true. No group of people she knew could be more trusted or loved. In that knowledge, she glanced at the house for the last time and did not look back.

Micah rode the gelding up to the side of their carriage.

"We'll stay on the back roads until we're past Bristol. Then head north toward Warren. I believe we can connect with Corporal Bearslayer there. He can guide us for a few miles." Micah pulled his scarf tighter around his neck.

In all the pandemonium and preparations, Lydia realized she'd not asked him where they were going. "Where to, my love?"

"East Haddam in Connecticut. 'Tis my home."

He trotted ahead of the group, leading the way. The carriage thrust forward, and Cecelia held tightly to Moses while Lydia gripped Minta.

The thought of managing two babies at breast seemed

daunting. Yet had little Jeremiah survived, she'd be doing that already.

Lydia closed her eyes while the carriage swayed. She wanted to observe her surroundings as they traveled this little-used road, less familiar to her in its scenery. But exhaustion had its way with her, and she leaned her head back.

~

MICAH SMOTHERED his fears and glanced around at frequent intervals to be sure they weren't spotted by anyone. Since dusk descended earlier now, the chill in the air kept most residents sitting by the warmth of their hearths. Only the foolhardy traveled in such weather—or those escaping a group of killers.

He still could not fathom this first encounter with his evil sister-in-law. He'd met hardened soldiers with less hatred in their blood. What drove this woman—so loathsome in spirit—to such wickedness? The contrast with his beloved wife was drastic. He supposed no logic existed when it came to evil. 'Twas the measure in a person's spirit, not the intellect in their mind, that gave birth to goodness or ruination of one's soul.

Lydia called out the window. "Micah, might we pause for a rest?"

"Of course." He motioned for Cuff and Caesar to halt.

The ladies and lassies poured out of the vehicles.

Comfort danced. "I need to go!"

"Come with me." Miriam guided both young girls behind a tree not far from the road.

Darkness finally fell, and gratitude filled Micah. They would need the nighttime curtain of protection.

The wind whipped the tails of everyone's cloaks, and Lydia strode toward him, covering Minta from the chill. "How long will the journey take?" She shivered.

He closed her cloak to keep her warmer. "A few days."

Her eyes widened, but she did not complain. "How shall we stay warm at night?"

"I'll ask Henry for help in Warren. He'll provide shelter for us the first night. After that, I truly do not know. But I'll make sure we are warm. And safe." He rubbed his hands vigorously over her arms, hoping it warmed her some.

She nodded. When the girls and Miriam returned, she handed Minta to him. "I must relieve myself as well." She pecked his cheek with cold lips and scurried toward the edge of the trees.

Dear God, keep us warm. And far away from Phila's demons.

ONCE MICAH KNEW they were past the town of Bristol, he led the group toward the road leading to Warren. The regiment still encamped there, and he knew Henry should be able to assist them.

When the group approached the fort, they were halted by a familiar soldier. The private paused, then recognition lightened his eyes. "Sergeant Hughes, sir? 'Tis good to see you."

"Good to see you as well, private. But it's Mr. Hughes now." He held up his dismembered hand, and the private grimaced.

"I'm so sorry, sir. I heard you was wounded. Just glad you're still alive."

"As am I." Micah had never been so grateful to be alive. He did not know what might have happened to little Moses had he not been able to help them all escape. He'd rather not think about that possibility.

"I'll hurry and find Corporal Bearslayer, sir." The private said a few words to his fellow sentinel, then left his post.

Micah tried not to focus on the deep ache in his hand. He hoped someone had packed the rum. He'd need it for the pain tonight.

Within a few moments, Henry approached, grinning. "You

planning on moving everyone into the fort?" He slapped Micah's good arm.

"Just need someplace warm for the night. And safe. Even a barn in the fort would do."

"That may be all I can find for you. Come on through."

The sentinels opened the gates wide, while the exiles from Bristol rode in. Micah watched Henry head directly to the carriage holding Miriam. He opened the door, and she emerged, holding onto Henry's hand for support. Miriam watched the ground so as not to stumble. Micah assumed that in the daylight, he might notice a distinct flushing of her cheeks, her smile spanned so wide.

Lydia emerged from the other carriage, and, even by torchlight, the fatigue clearly etched her face. He dismounted and led his gelding toward the open barn door.

On the way, he wrapped his arm around Lydia and escorted her inside the barn. "'Tis not much, dear one, but I pray we will keep each other warm enough." Micah squeezed her waist.

She rested her head on his shoulder as they walked. "I am so tired, even a hay-filled stall is more than sufficient. With you beside me, of course." She gave a sleepy smile. "Perhaps I can eat some victuals, then close my eyes."

"That can be arranged."

Henry approached the group. "Good news. Several companies are out on patrol, and there are cots and hearths available. 'Twill be much warmer."

"Henry, you are a Godsend. Thank you, friend."

"Before you settle in for the night, perhaps you can explain why you are all leaving Bristol. Mayhap, I can help you in some way."

Relief flooded Micah. "I'd hoped you'd say that."

Micah, Cuff, and Caesar attended the horses while Henry led the ladies and children into one of the officer's cabins. "Here you are. This will keep you warmer."

~

LYDIA NEARLY WEPT WITH GRATITUDE. "Thank you so much, Corporal."

"I am much beholden to your husband, Mrs. Hughes. I doubt he has told you how many times he saved my neck in battle. Nor how much the troops respect him. He's not one to boast. So, I will boast for him. He is a much-admired man, and you are a fortunate woman to be aligned with such a one.

"And, of course, he thinks he is the fortunate one to have you. I would not disagree." Henry gave a self-conscious cough and inspected the contents of his cartridge box.

Lydia blushed. "Thank you, Corporal. I very much admire my husband and thank God every day for him."

He bowed and turned to speak in private with Miriam, who continued beaming and spoke softly to him.

A soldier wearing a stained apron knocked and entered, bringing bread, cheese, and cider for the women.

Lydia lay a squirming Minta on the cot and rolled a blanket next to her lest the baby fall off. She ate a portion of the food with a hearty appetite. Micah entered the room, allowing a chilly breeze to swirl underneath Lydia's dress. He sat next to her on the cot and ate the bread and cheese she offered him. Cecelia poured the cider for the group, and soon, everyone's eyelids grew heavy from fatigue and tension.

"I must sleep." Lydia yawned.

"I believe we all must." Micah took a last swig of cider, kissed his wife, and lay on the cot.

Lydia picked up Minta, lay her against herself to keep warm, and snuggled her back up against her husband. Micah's arm embraced her close.

She glanced over at Cecelia in the cot across the way and smiled. There lay Moses snuggled up against his new mother.

29

A light snow fell as the group headed north. Although it barely stuck to the earth, Micah feared any hint of snow did not portend good travel weather.

To avoid crossing the wide bay, Henry instructed Micah on the best route north. They would then head west toward the Connecticut border.

"I can take you to Pawtuxet, and then I'll direct you from there. But you must be on guard at all times. It may be this evil sister has lied to the sheriffs. Rhode Island laws may inflict harsh penalties, even on free slaves." Henry's brow furrowed. "Do you have enough lead balls and gunpowder?"

"I hope so." Micah spoke low enough so the women would not hear their conversation. "I have no idea how many are after us."

He felt Henry staring at him while they rode side by side. "You would do well to leave the carriages hidden somewhere. You could double up the women and girls on horseback."

Micah thinned his lips in a scowl. "I fear the weather is too harsh to travel thus. With two babies and two young girls? There's at least some shelter in the carriages."

"You can hide yourselves better without them. Just bundle

each young one with a woman and blankets. Our native women do so, and they do well."

Micah sighed. "I know you're right. After Pawtuxet, we'll get rid of the carriages. They're slowing us down, and my instincts tell me we need to hasten, or we'll regret the delay."

Henry nodded, and they moved onward.

When they turned westward, Micah heard waterfalls. The temperature dropped as they neared the water, and he clasped the top button on his coat.

"Little Falls. That is where Pawtuxet got its name." Henry stared toward the sound.

"Are not your kin from here?"

"They were. But they have moved farther to the west now." Henry's eyes glistened, though Micah didn't know if he was moved by childhood memories or if the cold stung him.

Henry pointed. "There are many trees that could hide your carriages. This might be a good time to take a rest and make the change."

Micah knew they needed to do this, but he dreaded telling Lydia. It would increase the discomfort for the women, and he hoped they would not object. They truly didn't have a choice if they were to put more distance between them and danger. Micah prayed it wasn't too late for that already.

He directed Cuff and Caesar to follow him and drive toward the tree line. They acted surprised but followed his instructions. He wove his horse through the trees in places wide enough to accommodate the carriages. By now, Lydia must think him mad with this unusual path.

When the conveyances were nestled among the pines, Micah told the drivers to halt. He jumped off the gelding and ran toward Lydia's carriage.

"Micah, what are we doing?" Was she more worried or annoyed?

"We need to abandon the carriages and ride the horses."

"But—"

"'Tis the only way, Lydia. Henry suggested it, and I've been putting it off as long as possible. We are too visible and need to travel more discreetly. The horses can take hidden paths, whereas the carriages must stay on a road. I know 'twill be a sacrifice for all, but we must."

"I understand."

Gratitude prompted him to squeeze her hand with affection when she emerged from the carriage. "Thank you."

She tilted her head. "For what, pray tell?"

"For understanding. I know 'twill be more difficult now. For all of you."

"I trust your judgment, Micah. I know you would not decide this were it not necessary."

The more he knew his wife, the more he treasured her. He'd expected an argument but received understanding, instead. He'd seen two of his married brothers with vexatious wives who fought them at every turn. He thanked God for Lydia's attitude —and for so many other joys in their life together.

Comfort came over to Lydia. "Mama, must we ride horses now? Can I ride with Papa?"

"Well, I think your papa must decide."

"I would be honored to ride with you, Comfort. I believe this must mean you are getting quite grown up now."

"Well, of course." She stood tall. "I am five years old now."

He smiled at Lydia. "Quite grown up indeed."

Henry strode toward him. "Micah, you say you have a farm in East Haddam?"

"Aye, Henry. You know you are always welcome there. And, I think one of our servants would be most appreciative of your presence." He tipped his head toward Miriam as he shook Henry's hand. "Come soon as you're able."

"I shall do that, my friend. Be safe and travel quietly. Godspeed."

"Godspeed to you, my friend."

Henry turned to find Miriam, who stood by herself in a grove of trees a few rods away. Henry walked toward her, removed his hat, and took her hand. They kissed briefly before Henry mounted his horse and bid her farewell. Micah hoped this would not be their last time together.

LYDIA HAD NEVER ENJOYED RIDING horseback, but she refused to complain. Despite the pain in her thighs, she focused on keeping Minta wrapped tightly around her waist. With each jerking motion of the horse's gait, she clung to the reins and told herself this journey took them farther away from her sister. Farther away from the evil that sought to destroy Moses, and perhaps all of them in the process.

Lydia doubted the pursuers would stop at merely murdering a baby. They would not want any witnesses left alive to testify against them. Lydia prodded her mare along at a faster gait.

The wind picked up, and Lydia pulled her cloak tighter. She had Minta wrapped in a shawl and tied snugly to free up her hands. Minta seemed to enjoy the warmth as she slept peacefully most of the ride. Lydia's breasts seemed extra full. And no wonder, with feeding two little ones. It must be near time to nurse.

"Excuse me, Miss," Micah rode up beside her with Comfort in front of him. "Excuse me, Miss, but I found this lovely little lass strolling along the path. I thought you might know who she is?" He grinned in a playful manner.

Comfort covered her mouth to suppress her giggling.

"Why, nay, sir, I've ne'er seen such a lovely lass before. But she looks quite content with you. Perhaps you might keep her."

"I might just do that, Miss."

Comfort burst out laughing. "Mama, you know 'tis me. You and Papa are quite silly."

Lydia smiled. "Yes, we are. But your papa is the silliest of all." She shifted in the saddle. "Perhaps your papa would allow us to stop soon so the babies can eat? And so your mama can get some relief?"

"Oh. Of course." He pulled the reins and held up his hand to have the group stop. After climbing off the gelding, he helped Comfort to the ground. Then, he reached up to assist Lydia.

She winced when his hands steadied her under her arms.

His forehead furrowed. "Lydia, I'm so sorry. We could have stopped sooner. I should not have been pressing us to move onward more quickly."

"I am well. I'll *be* well, as soon as the babies bring me relief."

"Let me hold up a blanket for you whilst you set up."

Cecelia brought Moses, who fussed and rooted. Lydia unwrapped Minta, who was wide awake now. Cecelia took the edges of the blanket from Micah. "I can help her, Mr. Hughes."

"Thanks, Cecelia."

Lydia cringed when both babies latched on but relaxed when the pressure lessened.

Cecelia looked at her with sympathy. "I wish I could feed Moses, for my sake and for yours. I know this is a burden for you, feeding two little ones."

"Cecelia, I'm just grateful God has provided a way for me to care for my nephew. While 'tis at times difficult, 'twould be far more troubling if we had no one to feed him."

"When you are finished, I can bring up a burp and take care of changing him."

"Thank you, Cecelia. 'tis fortunate that anyone can change a baby."

Micah came over. "We've been traveling most of the day, and 'tis near dusk. I think 'twould be wisest to stay here this night. The men and I can set up lean-tos for shelter."

"I shall not argue. My legs are happy to rest."

He spoke with Cuff and Caesar about the lean-tos, and by the sound of it, the men agreed.

They gathered branches and prepared the partially enclosed shelters.

Lydia looked down at Moses. The boy slept peacefully. "I think your baby is ready for you, Cecelia." Lydia covered herself then placed a blanket over the nursing Minta.

Cecelia lowered the blanket and folded it. "My baby." Her voice wistful, she shook her head as she picked up Moses. "I can scarce believe he is my baby."

"And she called his name Moses: and she said, 'Because I drew him out of the water.'" Lydia's eyes welled as she quoted the verse.

"And we saved him from the water, ma'am." Cecelia wiped away a tear.

Lydia lowered her eyes. This whole saga of fear and hiding had its roots in her family's sins. She'd come from a family tainted by the lust of the eyes and the coveting of wealth. Her blood came from those who thrived on blood money and those who shed the lifeblood from others without blinking an eye. She wished she could wash the family filth from her body. But removing that family heritage continued to prove impossible.

How could Micah love her? How could he see past her family's sins to care for her?

Minta slept soundly, and the growing darkness lowered the temperature further. Lydia stared at the fire Micah had started. The flames danced, as though taunting her with thoughts of hell.

"Lydia? Are you not well?" Micah sat next to her on the ground and placed his arm around her. He kissed her cheek with tenderness, and her lips quivered. "What concerns you, my love?"

"I—I am from a wicked family, Micah. Evil and malicious. How can you, a man of integrity and goodness, love me?"

"Oh, my dear, Lydia." He held her close and stroked her shaking back as she sobbed. When she'd quieted, he cupped his hand under her chin. "Lydia, you were born into your family. But, in your spirit, you departed from your family long ago. The spirit of love and gentleness in you has overcome the sins of your family.

"We, each of us, are accountable for what we believe and what we do. You have chosen a different path from those you grew up with, and I rejoice that our paths have joined together. Lydia, you make me so happy. I would not wish to be with anyone else in the whole world. You are the one I love and always will."

Lydia's fears melted away as she rested in his arms.

After a while, Micah shivered. "Let's go into the lean-to so we may warm up a bit." He stood, favoring his right leg where he'd sustained the bayonet wound. He wrapped his arm around her.

As they settled into the enclosed bed with pine needles for a mattress and sheltered by a roof of thick branches, Miriam brought them both some victuals.

"Thank you, Miriam." Lydia smiled at her.

"Comfort wish to know if she and Rose can sleep together in my lean-to. They have already eaten and are getting sleepy."

"Of course, Miriam. Thank you for taking such good care of her."

Miriam nodded and walked back to her bed beneath the stars.

Exhausted, Lydia lay on the quilt, cushioned by a few layers of soft pine branches that protected them from the cold, hard earth underneath. Lydia pulled Minta close to herself. Micah entwined the two of them in his arms, bringing comfort and warmth to the threesome.

Somehow Micah always made things better. And tonight, she could rest in the knowledge that Micah loved her and would be there for her. She did not deserve his love, but she was so grateful for it.

WHEN DAWN'S light shone dimly through the morning mist, Lydia sat up. She vaguely remembered Cecelia bringing Moses for her to nurse during the night. Then Minta fussed, and she had fed her.

Lydia looked at her sleeping husband. He must be exhausted. The pain of his wounds, while better, persisted, and Lydia hurt for him whenever he winced. She bent down and kissed his cheek.

Standing, she shook the dirt off her outer gown. Everyone else lay asleep in their lean-tos. Unsure why she'd awoken, Lydia decided she might as well be useful.

She looked around their campsite, secluded in a grove of trees. "Caesar?" Lydia shielded her eyes from the occasional ray of sunlight streaming through the treetops. Where had he gone? She remembered Caesar took guard duty last night. Perhaps he had needed to relieve himself.

Grabbing a bucket, she headed toward the stream they'd found yesterday. The fresh, clear water enticed her. She couldn't wait to quench her thirst. But before she reached the water, someone pulled her arms behind her back and held a knife blade to her neck.

Gripping pain squeezed through her entrapped arms while horror elicited spasms of trembling. She could barely breathe, yet what air she managed to inhale was tainted with the stench of old rum and sweat. Then a voice, terrifying and deadly in tone, wrought nausea in her belly.

"Make one sound, and you'll be dead—as dead as that Negro on the ground over there."

30

M icah awoke to the clicking of a pistol hammer near his ear. Then he felt the edge of the weapon against his forehead. "Sit up, and put your hands behind your back."

A woman whimpered nearby. *Lydia!*

Not knowing her situation, he complied with the gunman until he could get his bearings. Minta slept next to him, wrapped in blankets. He threw part of his blanket over her to disguise her presence. At least for now, until she woke wanting to be fed.

The stranger bound his hands behind his back and dragged him out of the lean-to. Searching for Lydia, Micah inhaled sharply at the sight of her with her hands held behind her back and a knife against her neck.

How many were there? And what happened to Caesar? He feared the worst.

"Where's that baby?"

He looked up at the hooded man. "What baby?"

A powerful punch to his jaw knocked him onto his side, and the attacker lifted him upright again.

Phila's minion pulled back his hair and held the pistol to his head again. "Don't play games with me, you Negro lover. We want that black baby. Now."

"We left it with a family in Warren."

The hooded face drew closer to him. "I do na' think so. I think you know exactly where that creature is, and you'd best tell us now. Unless a' course, you want us to enjoy your woman for a bit," his captor sneered.

Micah's heart beat at an odd rhythm. "I told you, he's not here."

The man released Micah and walked toward Lydia.

Lydia's look of sheer horror made him ill. "I know where he is."

The scum returned to Micah. "Well, now, that's better. Tell us, and your wife won't be touched."

The desire to strangle the man rose in his heart. Though he strained against the ropes, the knots held fast. "I'll tell you, but only after you release my wife. Then, I'll take you to him." Micah's jaw throbbed from being punched.

"Is that so? Perhaps I'll just take her with us, and then you can show us where he be."

Think of something to say. "So, how much did that woman pay you to kill the boy? I might pay you even more to let him live. You can even tell her you did the deed, and she'd never be the wiser."

He slapped his hands against his legs and laughed. "Oh, she'd know all right. On account a we're supposed to bring part of him to her."

Bile rose in his mouth. Part of the baby? He wanted to vomit but struggled to keep his wits about him.

God, help us.

Just then, Minta woke and began to cry.

The blaggard pointed his pistol at the moving blanket.

"No!" Micah thrust himself at the man's legs, and the gun dropped at his feet. Before the attacker could pick up his weapon again, a shot fired from the woods. It hit the intruder in the shoulder, and he fell to the ground, cursing. Blood poured from his wound, and he couldn't get up.

Musket fire exploded all around the camp. "Get down, Lydia!"

When the knife-wielder tried to take cover, he freed his grip from Lydia. She ran toward Micah.

"Get down!" He repeated his cry.

She reached him and sank to the ground as she wept.

"Are you hurt?"

"Nay." She gripped his hands behind his back and pulled the knots apart with both fingers and her teeth, all the while keeping low as the reports of gunfire continued.

With the ropes looser, Micah freed himself, then half-dragged Lydia along the ground toward the lean-to. He crawled inside and placed his body over the two of them while he waited for the shooting to end.

Minta wailed, and Lydia tried to soothe her.

He searched for his musket to no avail. Likely their weapons had been taken while they slept. Where could Caesar be?

Micah listened to the shooting. No bullets had been aimed at him and Lydia. Were they shooting at the bounty hunters? Confusion cluttered his mind as volumes of black smoke shrouded the area. An occasional ball of lead must have hit its mark, because he heard groans. Were these their rescuers? Or new enemies bent on finding Moses?

Suddenly the firing ceased, and Micah heard Lydia's muffled whimpers and Minta's terrified screams. Unfamiliar voices yelled at each other. He crept near the entrance of the lean-to and listened. He dared to look outside at the two men speaking.

"You'll be the only one left of your gang, you fool. You can tell whoever hired ya, that I'll be collecting the fee as soon as I find that black baby you spoke of. Now be on your way, lessin' you want to join your mates in an earthen pit."

A younger man, bent downward, backed away toward the woods, then turned and ran.

"We won't be seein' that blaggard 'round here again."

Micah squeezed his eyes shut. Captured by yet another group of bounty-hunters. Hardly what he'd hoped for.

"You folks can come out now."

"So you can shoot us?" Micah licked his dry lips.

"Nay, we saved your hides, man. Come on. You're safe with us."

"How do we know you're not lying?" Micah's heart raced.

"Cause you've just been rescued by God-fearin' Swamp Yankees. Now come on out. I hear two little 'uns crying for their breakfast."

Could this be true? "Then put your muskets on the ground. I don't want to be your easy target."

The two men placed their muskets on the dirt and weeds.

Micah crept out of the lean-to. He'd heard of Swamp Yankees but never met one. Now he would meet two. By the looks of it, a father and his son. Both men wore heavier beards than most, and their clothes looked like they'd not seen a woman's care in many a year.

Micah stood, legs still quivering. "We're grateful. We weren't sure we could trust you after what you said to our attackers."

The older man chewed on his corncob pipe. "Figured 'twas the only way to keep them vermin from coming after you again. Now, will someone please feed those screamin' babies?"

Cecelia emerged from behind a tree holding Moses. She rushed toward Lydia's lean-to.

The stranger took off his tricorne hat and wiped his forehead with his sleeve. "Whew! Never could stand the screech of a crying baby."

Micah laughed in relief. "Not to mention *two* crying babies." He took a step back and fell when his right leg gave way on the uneven ground.

"You all right, mister?"

"Aye. Just a wound from the war."

He looked at Micah with suspicion. "Which side you fight on?"

"American, of course. Hessian took a bayonet to my leg."

The Swamp Yankee jutted his chin toward Micah. "Looks like that's not all they did to ya."

Micah stared at his crippled hand. "Nay. They did some damage." He lifted his chin. "But we threw it right back at them."

"Hah!" The stranger smiled and strode toward Micah, holding out his hand. "My name be Lusher Fry. This here be my son, Gaius Fry. A pleasure to meet a war hero." He pulled Micah to a standing position.

"I'm Micah Hughes." He shook his head. "But I'm no hero."

"Not wantin' to be disagreeable, sir, but any soldier gets wounded like that, be a hero."

Micah looked around. "Caesar? Cuff?"

Miriam came out of the woods with the two little girls. The terror on her face disconcerted him.

Comfort saw Micah and ran in tears toward him. "Papa!"

He held his arms out and gripped her tightly. "You're safe now."

She pulled away enough to look at him. "Where are Mama and Minta?" She shook from her sobs.

"They are safe, in the lean-to over there." He pointed, and she unwrapped herself from him and ran to the shelter. He could hear wails from within.

Miriam approached Micah, looking sideways with suspicion at Lusher Fry. "Cuff be over there. He be weeping over Caesar."

Micah's heart skipped a beat. He squeezed Miriam's arm. "And where is Hannah?"

"She still be hiding in the woods from all the shootin'."

"Can you find her and bring her back to the camp?"

"Aye, Mr. Hughes." She kept her arm wrapped around Rose's shoulder and headed back toward the thick trees.

Micah sat back on the ground and put his head in his hands. Forcing his shoulders back, he wiped the moisture from his face.

Lusher held his hand out to him and helped him stand. "Come on. I'll help you bury your Negro. Gaius is already digging a hole to throw those vermin in. We can make a separate hole for your friend."

"Aye." Micah set his focus on the task at hand and strode with purposeful steps toward the grave digging.

~

THEY HEADED down the hill toward the Fry's cabin, and Lydia asked Micah how many men they'd buried.

"Seven. Counting the one that returned to Bristol, there were eight that hunted us."

Lydia could not speak for a moment, shook her head slowly. "Could Phila be that determined to carry out her wretched plan?"

"Aye." The ground was steep, so Micah held her arm steady.

Ice formed on the marshy swampland on their left. A bitter chill whipped the hem of her gown, and she pulled her cloak tighter around her neck.

Micah looked at her. "We should be there soon. Lusher said 'twas not far."

"I'm fine." She wanted to reassure him, but in truth, she felt anything but fine. Fear from the attack engulfed her, and the stress of the journey sapped her strength beyond measure. Would she ever recover?

"There it is." Micah's voice held the same relief she felt.

A house with a steeply slanted roof appeared in the distance. It was a humble dwelling with a large addition, no doubt for a growing family. The smoke that curled from the chimney invited her freezing limbs to quicken their pace.

She turned slightly to the group behind them. "We're here."

"Thank the good Lord."

Hannah sounded so weary. Poor woman. Lydia would find a warm bed for her pregnant friend as soon as they were indoors.

"Here we are, folks." Lusher Fry opened the creaking door and held his hand out in welcome. "Come in and warm yerselves by that hearth."

No one needed encouragement to take him up on the offer. Comfort and Rose hurried over and held their hands over the flames.

"Not so close, lassies. Watch your gowns." Lydia gently pulled the girls back a few steps.

Gaius Fry pulled a chair next to the fire. "Here you are, Mrs. Hughes."

Surprised yet grateful, Lydia thanked him and sat on the wooden rocker with a pillow seat. She sighed and rested her head against the back of the rocker. "This is delightful. Thank you, Mr. Fry."

His face turned red in the firelight. "Mr. Fry be my father, ma'am. You can call me Gaius."

"Thank you, Gaius. I am most grateful." She remembered Hannah. "Is there a bed my friend Hannah could rest upon? She is with child."

"O' course, ma'am." He scurried into the other room and came back in a moment. He motioned to Hannah. "Come with me, ma'am."

Hannah looked at her in surprise. Lydia doubted anyone had ever called her *ma'am* before. Her friend grinned and followed Gaius into the other room.

It wasn't long before Gaius closed the door behind him and returned to the hearth. "She be asleep already, ma'am."

"Thank you." Lydia wished she could sleep next to this warm fire, but first, she looked around to be sure everyone was safe and accounted for. Satisfied that all were well, including Minta snug in her lap, Lydia gave in to her fatigue.

LYDIA AWOKE to the smell of something delicious. When she opened her eyes and sat up, she watched Lusher flip over some kind of fried cake.

He noticed she'd awakened and grinned, his tobacco-stained teeth nearly matching the brown of his beard. "Hope ya had a nice rest there, ma'am. You appeared to need it. And no wonder, after all you've been through."

She rubbed at her eyes. "Thank you, Mr. Fry. Not certain what you're making there, but it smells wonderful."

"Pshaw. 'tis just Johnnycakes made with corn. Don't tell me you've ne'er had some afore?"

"I'm afraid not, but I can see I've been missing out."

Minta stirred.

"Before I partake, might I use the other room to feed my daughter?"

"A course, ma'am. I think your friend might need to feed her babe as well." He jerked his head toward Cecelia, holding a fussy Moses.

"Cecelia, we best go feed the little ones." Lydia stood and headed for the door, then paused. "Where is my husband, Mr. Fry?"

"Aw, he insisted on helping with the horses in the barn. I told him there was no need. Gaius could do it. But I could see he were determined to help. I thought it best to let him."

"Thank you, Mr. Fry. My husband is finding his way with his wound. I appreciate you not making him feel he could not do it."

Lusher grinned. "He be one lucky husband, ma'am."

"I am one lucky wife, Mr. Fry." Lydia walked into the back room, bouncing a squirming Minta, who grasped for her mother's breast.

After the women sat in the bed across from Hannah, Lydia undid her stays, which had tightened against her breasts to the point of pain. Cecelia helped her get the babies attached, and Lydia nearly cried with the discomfort. She exhaled with relief after she nursed the children for a moment.

Cecilia frowned. "Maybe when we get to Mr. Hughes's home in Connecticut, we can find a wet nurse to feed Moses."

"Perhaps. I'm not certain why 'tis so painful. I'm sure I'll get used to the extra milk." Lydia tried to reassure her friend, although she also wondered if perhaps finding someone to nurse the infant would help. "We'll see."

Hannah woke. "That rest felt so good. I did not realize how sleepy I was." She sat up and stretched.

"Dear Hannah, I'm so sorry for all you've been through whilst being with child. I pray when we arrive at my husband's farm, you can rest all you want."

Cecilia suddenly cried. She waved a hand in the air at the ladies. "I am sorry, ma'am. I miss Caesar so much. He became like a father to me."

"Oh Cecilia, I am so very sad for you. Caesar held a special place in our hearts, and I know you will miss him terribly. We all will."

A knock sounded on the door. Cecilia wiped the tears off her face and held up a blanket to cover Lydia.

"Who is it?" Lydia tried to sound cheerful.

"'Tis I, my love. May I come in?"

"Yes, Micah." She longed to see him after their terrible night in the woods. How did he fare? Had he suffered injury? She'd fallen asleep by the hearth before she'd had a moment to ask him.

He entered then closed the door behind him. "How are the little ones?"

"They are well fed and warm. How do you fare? Are you injured from that scoundrel?"

"I'll be fine."

"You always say that, even when you're not."

Cecelia took a sleeping Moses and left the room, followed by Hannah.

Micah sat next to Lydia and stroked Minta's head. "I'd hoped we could leave at first light, once we'd all been warmed and had victuals." He paused.

"But?"

"It's snowing."

Her heart sank. "No! How badly?"

"Bad enough. It does not seem to be wind-filled, but trying to travel during any storm is too dangerous. We'll have to wait it out here. Lusher has already invited us to stay."

She leaned toward him and kissed his cheek. "At least we have a safe home in which to take refuge."

"Aye." He stared at his hands in his lap.

"Micah? Are you truly well?"

"I—I keep seeing that varmint heading toward you to molest you. And me, bound and unable to protect you. Then, when he pointed his pistol at Minta, I thought I'd go mad."

Her heart grieved at the sight of tears flowing down her strong husband's face. "You saved us, Micah. You did everything you were able to do, and you saved us." She placed the sleeping baby on the bed next to her.

He wrapped his arms around her and held her closely, protectively. "I do not know what I would have done if anything had happened to you and Minta."

She enveloped him in her embrace. "But nothing did happen. We are well. We are here. And we love you so very much." She kissed his tears away and kissed his lips. "I am so very blessed to have you as my husband."

He kissed her forehead and continued to hold her tightly, as though afraid to ever let her go.

31

Gratitude grew in Micah's heart at the provision of their welcoming hosts. This home with enough beds for their large number of travelers was truly a blessing. And the Johnnycakes were like manna in the wilderness for their hungry group.

"I cannot thank you enough for your help, Lusher."

Gaius tended the breakfast over the hearth, and the scent of pork and corn cakes whet Micah's appetite.

"Happy to help. Not every day my son and I get to help fellow Yankees escape the dirty hands of Tories."

"Well, you certainly saved our lives, and we're beholdin' to you. Just sorry we lost Caesar." He frowned as he watched the fire.

"Wish we'd a come five minutes sooner, and we mighta saved his hide too." He turned toward Cecelia. "I be sorry your friend be gone, ma'am. But grateful you and your baby survived."

"Thank you, sir." She rocked baby Moses to sleep in her arms.

Micah didn't want to go into all the details of Moses' birth. He wanted to spare Lydia from the shame of her sister's sins.

Best to let the story stay as it stood. The Frys need not know that Lydia nursed her sister's baby.

Lydia held Minta close and spoke to Comfort and Rose while they played a game Gaius had taught them. Micah noticed that Gaius had shaven his face this morning. He'd revealed a handsome countenance that had Micah a bit jealous, especially when the man kept looking at his wife.

Gaius brought her a plate first, stacked high with corn cakes, and set it on the table board. "Here you are, Mrs. Hughes."

"Thank you, Gaius." She licked her lips and sat on the bench, still holding Minta in one hand. With the other, she picked up her spoon and took a bite. She closed her eyes and smiled. "Mmm. This is quite delicious." She swallowed. "Thank you, Gaius."

The man's face turned red. "Pleased you like it, ma'am." He returned to the hearth and served up more plates. He carried them to the table and set them down, inviting the other women to partake. Then he served Micah and Cuff.

Micah had to give him credit. He liked that he served the women first. He was rather well-mannered for living near the swamp. Micah squeezed next to Lydia on the end, placing one arm around her and eating with the other.

She smiled at him and squinted her eyes in a way that questioned his familiarity with her at the table. He glanced at Gaius, kissed Lydia on the cheek, then ate.

Miriam and Hannah watched their interaction and grinned, trying to hide their laughter.

His jealousy must've been obvious. He knew he was being ridiculous. Of course, Lydia would be fed first, feeding an infant and all. He tried to shake away his insecurities.

The occasional burst of wind that clicked snow against the window panes concerned Micah. The longer they put off leaving, the more it increased their chances of running into foul weather. He prayed they could start their journey to his home soon.

"Lusher, how far to the Connecticut border?"

The man swigged a gulp of cider and wiped his mouth off on his sleeve. "About twenty miles or so." Lusher placed a whole Johnnycake into his mouth.

"Twenty miles? The sooner we leave Rhode Island then, the better. I hope this storm passes quickly."

Lusher's cheeks bulged with the corn cake. He talked before he swallowed. "It don't look like a nor-easter. You should be fine 'morrow or next day."

The next day? Micah desperately hoped for tomorrow. But he tried to be grateful. They were, after all, safe, warm, and well fed. But he'd keep his eyes on Gaius.

After they finished breakfast, the women stood to clear the plates. Micah slid off the end of the bench and took Minta from Lydia. She helped gather the trenchers and walked toward the basin of water to clean them.

Gaius followed Lydia with his eyes while she bustled around the room.

Micah cleared his throat. "So, Gaius, mayhap you have a young woman you've set your eyes upon?" He nearly added, "other than my wife."

The now-smooth-faced rescuer turned toward Micah. "Nay. Not too many women folk around here."

Lusher joined in the conversation. "I keep tellin' him he needs to stop playin' fiddle at the dances and do a bit o' dancin' instead. The ladies don't want to hold onto a fiddle, but warm flesh and blood." He laughed and put his pipe in his mouth.

"Pa, you know I be too shy to ask a lady to dance."

"Well, lad, iffin' you ne'er get over it, you'll be spending plenty o' cold winter nights alone in yer bed."

Gaius stared at his breakfast. "Aye."

Micah tried to be sociable. "So, you play the fiddle? Perhaps you can entertain us a bit. I'm certain we'd all enjoy it."

"Thank you, sir." Gaius drank the last of his cider. "I'd best head to the barn and tend the animals."

"I'll go help you." Micah stood. "You needn't add our six horses to your tasks."

Lusher stood. "I'd best bring a rope to stretch to the barn. No sense in anyone getting lost in case snow gets too deep."

"Good thought." Micah handed Minta to Lydia.

Instead of taking the baby, she drew his face toward hers and gave him a long, moist kiss. "Take care in the cold, my love." She took the baby and walked toward the extra room, looking back at him with a flirtatious sweep of her gown.

Micah warmed inside. When he refocused on the company in the room, Lusher and Gaius were staring at him.

"Now, there is a woman who knows how to kiss her man." Lusher laughed as he drew his coat on.

Cuff grabbed his jacket from the hook on the wall, and the four men exited to the barn.

Despite the cold snow and falling temperatures, Micah grinned at the passionate kiss from Lydia. She certainly did have the key to his heart.

ALTHOUGH A FEW INCHES had fallen during the day, the snow let up near nightfall. Micah could not have been happier about that. They still had a hundred miles to go to get home, and the next twenty were the most critical. Once in his home state, he would breathe with more ease.

Lusher leaned toward Micah from the chair he sat upon. "Gaius and I be talkin' about the travel tomorrow. It might be better for you to make it to the border right faster iffin' we take you all in our two sleighs. At least 'til you be in Connecticut."

Micah furrowed his brow. "Your sleighs? But that would be a burden for you and your son. You've already done so much for us."

"Nay, nay. If we leave first o' dawn, we'll make it back home by nightfall. That way, the ladies and young ones can ride more comfortably. We can tie their horses to the backs of the sleighs. You and Cuff can ride faster on your horses. What say you?"

He felt as though he had taken advantage of the Fry's hospitality, but it didn't take long for Micah to ponder the benefit of Lusher's offer. Besides, Moses' life depended on it. "I say, thank you. I am most beholdin' to you."

Lusher sat back in his chair. "Nay, nay. Call it following my duty to help a veteran and his family. 'Tis the least we can do for the cause."

"I'm grateful, Lusher."

That evening, the two Fry men slaughtered a couple of chickens for the meal. They called the night's feast "a belated Thanksgiving."

"Our Thanksgivins these days be sparse with folks at our table. All o' you make us remember how much we miss a large family." Lusher looked at his son with raised eyebrows. "O'course, young Gaius here could remedy that with a family of his own."

"I know, Pa, I know." Gaius stared at the food he cooked over the hearth. He looked back at his father. "I can't help that all my brothers married and moved away." He shook his head with disgust. "Puts the pressure on me, I can tell ya."

Micah felt some sympathy for the young man. "I had the same pressure at my house, only from my older brother. I kept remindin' him he could have married and started a family, but he claimed no woman would want him, which wasn't true. I think he just wanted to come home at night to the quiet. But," he looked at Lydia and gripped her hand, "he didn't know what he was missin'."

Lydia blushed, picked up his hand, and kissed his fingers. She released his grip to tend to Minta.

"So, what drew you to leave home and join the Continentals?" Gaius paused in his cooking to look at Micah.

"Word had gone out Washington's Army hurt for men. Still

not married, I felt I needed to answer my country's call. Simple as that." He looked down at Lydia, who held a cooing Minta.

Lydia held the baby's arms and bounced her up and down, eliciting giggles from the six-month-old.

Micah stroked Lydia's hair. "If I'd not gone in the army, I'd ne'er have met my wife."

Lusher laughed. "And now you're a papa."

"Aye, the girls' father died in service of our country. I fell in love with Lydia the first time I saw her. I don't know how I came to be the fortunate recipient of her affections."

"Don't sell yourself short, Micah. She seems to be quite happy with the arrangement."

"Well, I know I am. More than happy."

Gaius held a ladle up and pointed to the clean dishes at the table. "Dinner is ready. Iffin' you bring a trencher this way, I'll serve you up forthwith."

One by one, the guests took a trencher and allowed Gaius to fill their bowls with a chicken dish that caused Micah's mouth to water.

When they were seated with their bowls, Lusher prayed a prayer of thanks for the food, the guests, and for future grandchildren to fill up his table. Micah stifled a chuckle when Gaius shifted in his seat.

At the "Amen," everyone ate with ravenous appetites.

More candles were lit as the evening darkened into night. When the guests had settled onto benches and into chairs, Micah suggested to Gaius, "Perhaps you could share some of your fiddling with us. You must be quite good if the locals ask you to make music for the dances."

"I don't know about that. I think they just need anyone who can sort o' carry a tune on the fiddle."

"Nah, son, you be a fine fiddler. Come on, show us yer tunes."

Gaius pushed himself up from the floor and went upstairs. He returned with his fiddle and bow. After tuning up the strings, he slid the bow across the neck of the instrument and began a song worthy of a joyous dance.

Comfort and Rose immediately stood and, holding one another's hands, danced together in the center of the group.

Lydia covered her smile, then laughed and clapped her hands to the music. One by one, the rest of the company joined in the clapping. For the next few minutes, the song carried a curing medicinal with the lilting melody that brought joy to their souls, despite the pain in their lives. It brought Micah blessed comfort and hope that healing could begin.

When the upbeat reel ended, Gaius began a romantic ballad called "Fare Thee Well, Ye Sweethearts." Not only did he play his fiddle, but he sang the words with a clear, resonant voice. The verses described a young man going off to war and leaving his loved one behind.

It sobered Micah to think that, had he not been so wounded, he'd be bidding his Lydia goodbye to return to war. While he hated the wounds he bore, he could not bear the thought of leaving her behind again.

Lydia may have been thinking the same thoughts as she looked at him with tears in her eyes and gripped his hands. So many unspoken words flowed between them—grief at all the sadness borne, relief he did not have to return to battle, the pleasure of sharing their love, the hope for a future together. He held her hands to his lips and kissed them.

After Gaius played a few more tunes, Comfort and Rose both yawned.

"Perhaps we should retire for the night. Dawn will arrive before we know it. And I think some young ladies might just perhaps be a wee bit tired." Micah tipped his head in their direction.

"They are not the only ones who are tired." Lydia yawned.

He noticed dark circles under her eyes. "Aye, my love. Let us get some rest. We still have a long journey ahead. Thank you for the music, Gaius. I know it did my heart good to hear it." Micah reached out to shake his hand.

He placed his fiddle under his arm and shook Micah's in return. "Glad I could offer you thanks for serving this fledgling country. I think you've inspired me."

Lusher paled, and his jaw dropped open. "Ye're going to join the militia?"

"Nay, Pa. I'm going to find me a wife!"

32

The cold that usually set in after a Rhode Island storm chilled to the bone, and today's temperature took Lydia's breath away. Grateful the Frys insisted they place foot warmers in each sleigh, Lydia pulled the extra quilts they'd provided more snugly around Cecelia, the babies, and herself.

Lusher Fry seemed unbothered by the cold. When Lydia offered him part of the blanket, he declined. "My body be used to this cold, Mrs. Hughes. I'm a tough old bird." He flicked the reins to keep the horses moving a bit faster.

They slid quietly across the wide path. Micah followed them when the road narrowed. Gaius drove the second sleigh with Hannah, Miriam, and the little girls. Cuff, on horseback, brought up the rear.

Occasionally, the road widened to allow Micah to ride along beside them. With each exhalation, both he and the horse's chilled breath sent clouds of smoke through the air. Lydia ached for both man and horse.

This frigid air would nearly incapacitate Micah with pain by the time this journey ended. Relieved she'd brought rum for him, she still fretted that even the strong spirits offered insufficient relief under such conditions. She prayed the rum might at least make the agony tolerable.

"There be a tavern just past the Connecticut border. I imagine you'll be ready to stop and get a room for the night by time we get there."

"Aye, Mr. Fry. I'm so grateful there's a place to stay near the border."

What would they have done without Lusher Fry's help? Lydia couldn't bear to think of it.

The frigid hours drug on, and it seemed they'd never reach the state border. When concern in Lusher's countenance attracted Lydia's attention, however, she became hypervigilant.

"We're nearly there now," Lusher said, almost under his breath. "Well, look at that." Sure enough, there were official-looking men standing guard in the distance. "Rhodie Tories, no doubt."

Lusher smiled and kept his voice low when they drew closer. "Whatever you do, ma'am, keep that black baby quiet. And let me do the talkin'."

She'd not been prepared for this kind of difficulty. Did her sister's evil never cease? She quickly attached Moses to her breast and covered him tightly with her shawl then half tucked him under one arm. She placed Minta under her other arm, and, half laying her daughter across Moses, concealed the black infant with the chubbier Minta.

Lusher put on his most congenial face. "Good day, gentlemen. How fare ye this freezing afternoon?"

"Sorry to bother you folks, but we have to ask you about a missing slave child. Seems an infant from Bristol was stolen a few days past. I don't suppose you know anything about it?"

"Stolen baby? Who'd steal a slave baby, sheriff? This white woman be travelin' with her freed slaves and her children and husband."

"I understand, sir, but theft of property be a serious charge, as you know. I'm afraid I need to check the sleighs."

Lusher started to object, but Lydia touched his arm. "Let him search the sleigh, Mr. Fry. We've nothing to hide." She met the sheriff's gaze with a smile.

"Sorry about this, ma'am." He lifted the outer quilt, then the next.

"Please take care, sir, as my daughter might chill." She revealed Minta's face to the man, and he grinned.

"Fine looking baby you have there, ma'am." He turned to Cecelia. "I need to make sure you're not hiding a baby in there."

Cecelia took off several layers and shivered. He felt around beside her, making sure no baby was tucked under the folds of her clothing.

"Please, Sheriff, you can see my servant is cold. Allow her to replace her warm covers." She glared at the man.

He reluctantly stopped searching. "No Negro baby here." He walked to the next sleigh.

Lydia turned her head toward the other sleigh and prayed Hannah and Miriam had warned the little girls not to say anything. Her heart pounded, and the cool air she inhaled through her parted mouth dried her throat. She coughed then forced a smile when she looked at the other sheriff, who watched her and Cecelia closely.

Comfort's small voice broke through the stillness of the day. "Why would we steal someone's Negro baby? It's wrong to steal. My mama said so."

Lydia nearly laughed at her daughter, making such a show in front of the sheriff. She would have to smother her in kisses after they arrived at the inn, where they could rent rooms for the night.

The men searched the second sleigh and the haversacks of both Micah and Cuff. These men obviously didn't know an infant would never survive the cold or lack of air in a leather haversack.

Disappointed, but finally satisfied that there was no stolen slave baby in their company, the sheriffs released them. Lusher tipped his hat at the uniformed men and snapped the horse's reins to get them moving. No one said a word. No one dared draw attention to them for a long distance.

After some time passed in silence, Lusher glanced her way. "You can breathe again, Mrs. Hughes. We be in Connecticut."

Lydia burst into tears of relief. "Thank you, Mr. Fry."

"Nothing to fear now." Cecelia handed her a handkerchief and pulled out another for herself.

Micah rode up beside the sleigh. "We're in my home state, Lydia. We're safe now."

Moses had been cramped beneath Minta for so long, he now voiced his objection. Lydia removed him from her shawl, kissed his cheek, and handed him to Cecelia, who bundled him beneath her cloak.

"Welcome home, precious child." Cecelia leaned down and kissed his head.

~

MICAH HELPED LYDIA, Cecelia, and the babies out of the sleigh. Lydia touched his arm. "Please allow the others to stall and feed the horses, Micah. I know you are in pain."

"I'll not argue with you today." He took Lydia's arm, and they walked into the ordinary. He limped toward the hearth in the food area then collapsed into a chair, grimacing from the throbbing in his hand. His leg felt little better.

Lydia sat in a chair next to him. "Can I order you some rum, Micah?"

Normally he would take the lead in these matters, but the pain had drained his ability to cope with such a simple task as ordering a drink. "Aye, Lydia. I'm so sorry."

"Don't apologize for being in pain. I understand."

The taverner came over. "Are you hurt, sir?"

"War injury." The pain spiked to nauseating proportions as the thawing began, and he scrunched his face in reaction.

"Let me get you some rum, sir. No charge for veterans." He hurried away.

Lydia stroked the sleeve on his right hand until the taverner returned with a tankard. "One generous portion of flip for you, sir. Made special with extra rum."

"Thank you, sir." Micah sipped the rum mixed with ale and molasses that had been warmed instantly with a hot poker. "Much appreciated."

"And may I get your lady something as well, sir?"

Lydia answered, "Perhaps cider would warm me up. Thank you, sir."

The Frys came inside with Cuff, the ladies, and the little girls. Cecelia carried Moses underneath her cloak.

"Negro folks stay in the barn." The taverner's voice had changed from congenial to annoyed.

Micah stood. "Then I shall as well. If my servants are not welcome inside on this frigid night, then I'll not pay one shilling to remain here."

The taverner's face contorted. "Very well. But they'll only use one room. In the back of the tavern. I'll serve them meals upstairs, not in this common room."

Hannah slightly shook her head at Micah, then put her shoulders back and looked the tavern owner in the eye. "That be just fine, sir. We can stay in the back room." She smiled, although he didn't deserve her pleasantness.

Heat rose in Micah's face, and not from the fiery hearth. He felt Lydia's hand on his arm.

"Please don't object, Micah. We cannot afford to draw attention to ourselves. We're not that far from the state line." She kept her voice low and gave him a pleading look.

"Very well. But we'll all eat in our rooms."

Lusher and Gaius walked toward them. "'Tis been a pleasure makin' yer acquaintance, Mr. and Mrs. Hughes." They bowed and tipped their hats.

"I don't know how to thank you both. We owe you so

much. I—"

Lusher held up his hand. "You owe us nothin', my friend. Besides, you've inspired my son here to finally find a wife. I couldna' be a happier man." He laughed and tipped his hat again. "Godspeed, friends."

"Godspeed, Lusher. Gaius. I hope we meet again. I'll ne'er forget you both." Micah bid them farewell with regret.

"Farewell, Mr. Fry. Gaius." Lydia curtsied. After their new friends left the tavern, she turned to her husband. "Micah, do all of them have to sleep in one room?"

"I suppose 'tis better than the barn. I'll not have any of them out in the cold." He guzzled the flip in a few swigs and slammed the empty tankard on the bar. Refusing to look at the taverner, he walked up the stairs with Lydia and the baby.

When they arrived at the room the taverner had assigned them, Micah fairly fell onto the covers. That was strong flip. And on an empty stomach.

Lydia answered the knock at the door, and she took the tray of food handed to her. "Here's your dinner, my love. I need to slip down the hall and make arrangements to feed Moses during the night."

The door closed, and he looked at the tray of food. Famished, he picked up the spoon and inhaled the thick stew of beef and vegetables.

He grew sleepy and wondered how long before Lydia returned. Where had she put Minta? He clumsily sat up and saw the baby sleeping in a basket on the floor. He fell back onto the soft feather mattress and wondered why the room seemed to spin.

Lydia walked in and looked at him with a strange expression. "Are you well, my love?"

"I am quite well. Jus' waiting for you, my dear," he slurred.

"Oh dear. I wonder just how much rum that man put in your flip."

"I don' know. All I know is, I'm quite dizzy."

"Perhaps you should rest, my love." She kissed his cheek.

He smiled, sleepiness nearly overwhelming him. "You have the sweetest kisses." He closed his eyes.

"MICAH." Someone shook him. "Micah, 'tis near dawn. We must awaken and have breakfast. The sooner we start our journey, the quicker we can arrive home."

A hammer pounded inside Micah's head as he tried to open his eyes, but the flickering candlelight increased the headache. He rolled onto his side and moaned. It took all his energy to sit up.

"Here, my love, drink this cider. 'Twill help you awaken." Lydia held his hand over the handle of the tankard.

Gripping the vessel, Micah took a sip. It tasted sweet and soothing to his dry throat. He guzzled the rest and smacked his lips.

He finally opened his eyes halfway and looked at Lydia. "What happened evening last?"

Lydia shook her head and tightened her closed mouth. "That taverner gave you a strong brew that knocked you off your feet. You went to sleep almost immediately. At least you were not in so much pain." She took his hand and kissed it.

"Nay, I just have pain in my head now. And a most foul taste in my mouth."

She went to a small bag she carried and brought out a pouch. "Here. Some dried parsley leaves to settle your stomach." She handed him a small portion, and he tossed them into his mouth.

Chewing the herb, he twisted his mouth in disgust. "Are you trying to kill me, Lydia?"

"Nay, my love." She covered her mouth, attempting to smother her laughter.

"Well, I'm glad my distress amuses you."

"I'm sorry, Micah." She kissed him. "I am not trying to make you more miserable, truly." She kissed him again.

"There's only one thing you can do to alleviate my distress."

"What's that?"

He drew her onto the bed and kissed her. He undid her hairpins, and her hair fell onto the bed.

"You do know, I just did my hair for the day."

"Well, 'tis not yet day. So perhaps we can lie abed awhile. And keep one another warm." He smothered her with kisses then blew out the candle.

~

LYDIA APPRECIATED RIDING in the sleigh even more now that she was on horseback. But knowing they were on a Connecticut road helped relieve the anxiety of their escape.

Minta had grown so much that her added weight tied to Lydia's torso in the front caused discomfort in Lydia's lower back. After several hours of travel, she ached more than she cared to admit.

Micah rode up beside her. "Are you in pain? I noticed you rubbing your back."

"Minta is growing so much. 'Tis more difficult to bear her weight on horseback."

"Let me carry her for a time. I'm certain Comfort would enjoy riding with you awhile, and she can bear her own weight." Micah looked around. "I think it's time we stopped for a rest before we get to Norwich. And the snow is sparser here."

"That sounds quite agreeable to me." Lydia looked around. "Where is a good place to relieve ourselves?"

"Follow me." He sped up his gelding and headed toward a copse of trees off the main road.

Lydia directed her mare to follow, grateful the snowy precipitation barely covered the ground. The air, although chilled, did not carry the bite of the previous day. The sunshine lifted her spirits, and she realized that she smiled, despite the ache in her back and legs.

Micah wove a path to a secluded area, and Lydia turned to be sure everyone in the group followed. By the looks on their faces, they all were ready to stop for a break.

Lydia drew on the reins and awaited Micah's help in taking the baby and dismounting the horse. Plopping onto the ground, she undid the shawl around Minta and held the baby underneath her cloak.

"I've got to go! I've got to go!" Comfort did her dance of distress.

Lydia rolled her eyes. "Then go."

Her daughter took off, running into the trees.

"Don't go too deeply into the woods." She hoped Comfort heard her.

"Mama, can you take me?"

Miriam smiled at Rose's request. "Of course." Rose took her hand, and they walked toward the woods.

Lydia watched them, aware that Rose had become more insecure since the attack by the bounty hunters. And no wonder. It had left its mark on all of them.

She took a canteen from Micah's outstretched hand. "Thought you might be thirsty. After this morning." He gave her a mischievous grin.

Her cheeks burned. "You are quite the romantic admirer first thing in the morning."

"I admire you any time of day, my love." His look caused her to grow warmer yet.

A scream in the distance sent abrupt shivers down her spine. "Comfort!"

"Stay here." Micah grabbed his firelock and ran toward the sound.

She covered her mouth with one hand and cried. Hannah came over and wrapped her arms around Lydia's shuddering shoulders.

"I should have gone with her."

Minta began to cry, and Miriam came and took the baby from Lydia's arms.

Cuff grabbed his firelock and ran after Micah into the woods. It seemed an eternity of waiting, but then they heard the loud report of a musket, followed by another.

Lydia buried her face in Hannah's shoulders.

Miriam pointed toward the woods. "There be Mr. Hughes. He has Miss Comfort."

Lydia pulled away from Hannah and ran toward Micah. The closer she got, the more she panicked. Blood covered Comfort's leg.

"What happened?"

Her daughter cried inconsolably. "A bear. A bear. Mama!"

"Oh, my precious daughter."

Cecelia had found some linens and brought them over. Lydia's hand shook so much, she had difficulty wrapping the wound tightly.

"I must get her to the surgeon in Norwich. Lydia, I can go faster if I take her myself."

"But Micah—"

"Lydia, Cuff will lead you all the rest of the way. 'Tis perhaps another mile or so. But I must hasten to a doctor."

"I understand." She swallowed and kissed her daughter. "I'll see you forthwith, my dearest. Be brave. Go with Papa."

Lydia had never heard Comfort wail in such pain before. Her mother's heart shredded with each cry. She forced herself to inhale deeply. Lydia followed Micah to his gelding, took Comfort from his arms, then handed her back to him after he was seated in the saddle. His eyes fixed on the roadway west, and he went at a full gallop toward Norwich.

Cuff approached her. "Best be on our way, ma'am. I know you want to be with your daughter."

"Aye." Swiping away her tears, she climbed onto her saddle, took Minta from Miriam, and tied her snugly back in her shawl.

While Lydia's mind wanted to gallop toward Norwich, she knew she'd never keep up with Micah and Comfort.

When everyone had readied themselves in their saddles, Lydia turned to Cuff. "Lead the way."

Although they did not gallop, Cuff led at a brisk canter. Lydia prayed for her daughter. And that she, herself, would be strong enough to bear whatever lay ahead.

33

A town appeared in the distance, and Lydia squeezed her legs against the mare's side, encouraging her mount to a canter. She was desperate to reach her daughter. Arriving at a village green, she slowed her horse.

Micah's gelding stood tied in front of a small cottage, so she guided the mare there. Holding tightly to Minta, she held her breath and slid toward the ground, reaching the snow-covered dirt safely and without harming her daughter.

Not bothering to tie the mare to a post, she ran up the front steps of the cottage. She could hear Comfort crying inside and burst through the front door.

The doctor met her gaze. "This is the mother, I assume."

"Is she all right?" Lydia breathed in gasps and stepped toward Comfort.

"We've just given her some laudanum, Mrs. Hughes. Then I can stitch up the wounds. They should heal well."

"Thank the Lord."

Micah came toward her, his eyes narrowed. "Lydia, you must sit down."

"Aye." Weakness riddled her limbs, and she all but collapsed into the chair Micah held.

He rescued Minta from her grip and held the baby up on his shoulder.

Comfort had stopped crying, the laudanum doing its work. Micah held onto the baby while holding Comfort's leg for the doctor.

"That bear scratched me with its big paws." Comfort's face contorted at the memory.

"Must have been a younger bear, because these claw marks are smaller than a full-grown one. Where did you see the bear?" The doctor questioned her while sewing up the lacerations.

"Inside a tree hollow. Digging in the ground."

"Ahh, getting ready to hibernate, no doubt. He must have been annoyed that you showed up to interrupt him."

"He came after me, and I ran away." Her lips quivered.

"Well done, young lady. A bear must not be trifled with."

"My papa came and saved me."

The doctor raised his eyes to look at Micah. "You have a good papa, little lady." He tied off the last stitch. "There now. She should recover quite well. Will you be in town for a bit?"

Micah licked his lips. "Likely just overnight. We're on our way to East Haddam. That's where my farm is."

The surgeon tilted his head. "What did you say your name was?"

"Hughes. Micah Hughes."

"I believe I know your family. Your older brother, Ben, runs the farm."

"Aye." For the first time since Lydia had arrived, Micah's expression softened.

The surgeon glanced downward, then faced Micah. "Have you been in touch with your brother of late?"

"I've not heard from him in a bit. I've been in the army since early '76. I recently finished service after being wounded."

"I can see that, son. Sorry about your hand."

Micah looked to the side. "I get by."

"I'm certain you do." The surgeon paused. "Your brother has been quite ill these past months."

His face paled. "Ill? How ill?" Micah swallowed with difficulty.

"Your brother's time on this earth is numbered, Mr. Hughes. I'm sorry to be the one to share this with you."

Lydia stood and put her arm around him.

Micah said nothing.

Comfort touched his arm. "Papa, what's wrong?"

"I—I just need some fresh air." He turned and left. The door slammed shut.

Lydia fought back tears and looked at the doctor. "This has been such a difficult time for my husband. And now, to find his brother is so ill. I pray he can bear so many griefs."

"Mrs. Hughes, in my work, I have seen many dreadful wounds, both in the body and in the spirit. We all carry scars. But some of the strongest people I know are the most wounded —scarred vessels, as it were, looking for all the world like they will sink in the waves of adversity.

"Yet those very waves become the power that lifts them up to save them through the worst storms. The hurtful swells of this life lift us closer to God if we entrust ourselves to Him and His purposes for us." He paused. "And God sends helpmates like yourself to share the burden and bring joy amidst the sorrow."

Her eyes welled. "I pray I can be a help to him."

He grinned. "By those very words, I know you *are* a help to him."

Micah came back inside with a fussing Minta. "Lydia, I'm sorry, but Minta—"

She took the infant from him. "Don't be sorry, my love." She kissed his moist cheek. "Doctor, is there somewhere I might feed my little one?"

"Of course. We have a large house next door. My wife got tired of having patients being treated inside our home and begged me to do my practice elsewhere." He chuckled. "In fact, why don't you folks spend the night with us? We have lots of room since the young ones have moved on."

Micah and Lydia looked at each other.

He wiped off the remaining tears of grief from his face. "You see, we have a larger group than just the four of us. We have several servants who need lodging as well."

"Well, they can stay."

Lydia swallowed forcefully, remembering the taverner. "But, our servants are Negroes." She looked at him with hope that he wouldn't reject them as others had.

"That is not a problem. 'Tis about time the states banned slavery. It's a blot on the revolutionary cause to demand freedom whilst enslaving people of a different color."

Lydia looked up with wide eyes. "Aye. Thank you so much, Doctor—"

"Huntington. Dr. Richard Huntington. Too old to serve in a war camp, but not too ancient to still help my patients." He laughed. "Well, young Miss Hughes, I believe my wife might have some chocolate in our home that will help your leg feel better."

Comfort's eyes widened. "Chocolate? My favorite."

He whispered in her ear. "My wife's, too."

"I cannot thank you enough for helping my family, Dr. Huntington." Micah shook his hand.

The doctor patted Micah's shoulder. "And I cannot thank you enough for serving our country, Mr. Hughes. Godspeed in your new endeavor."

"Thank you." He picked up Comfort and carried her out the door that Lydia held open.

She looked back at Dr. Huntington and smiled. "Thank you, doctor. For everything."

"My pleasure, Mrs. Hughes."

~

THE LARGE HEARTH at the Huntington home brought soothing warmth to the travelers. Mrs. Huntington bustled around, serving everyone with pleasure and ensuring all were well fed.

"My wife has missed having our children under our roof these last years. When they all come on holiday, she is at her happiest. Having you all here is like an extra day of celebration." Doctor Huntington grinned while his plump wife served chocolate desserts to everyone.

"This chocolate is delicious, Mrs. Huntington. It was considered a luxury to find it in Rhode Island." Lydia licked a dollop of the gooey pudding from her thumb then realized her manners were little better than her daughter's.

"We have our own chocolatier right here in Norwich." Mrs. Huntington's rosy cheeks glistened. "Mr. Leffingwell, God bless the man, is quite brilliant in manufacturing so many things. But my favorite is his finest chocolate."

"I wish we were moving right here to your town so we could have as much chocolate as we wanted." Comfort lay on a settee, covered with a blanket, her leg elevated.

Mrs. Huntington chuckled. "Well, East Haddam is not so very far away. Perhaps your mama and papa can bring you all for a visit sometime."

"I would like that very much." Comfort yawned.

"Thank you for everything, Mrs. Huntington. You've been so gracious. I think my family must retire for the evening. It has been a very long day."

Mrs. Huntington stood. "Let me show you all to your rooms." The gracious woman guided them all to rooms both upstairs and down. Lydia noticed their hostess had given Cecelia the room next door to theirs.

Lydia wondered if Mrs. Huntington knew about baby Moses and that Lydia nursed him. Word could have filtered through from Rhode Island about the "stolen" black baby.

Although their hostess appeared to be a simple country doctor's wife, she was a Yankee woman who interspersed her generous hospitality with words of firm convictions concerning slavery and freedom. Lydia took her for the kind of friend with whom she could entrust her life.

While she lay in bed that night surrounded by her husband, her injured daughter, and her hungry infant, Lydia counted her blessings. Then she prayed her own faith in God would grow—no matter how strong the waves of adversity.

34

W hen they approached the Hughes farm late the next day, Micah tensed. He'd not had an opportunity to tell his brother they were coming. He imagined Ben, although an easygoing sort, would be quite upended by the arrival of not just his war veteran little brother, but that brother's family and a slew of servants as well.

Under the best of circumstances, this could be nerve-wracking for a single man in his forties. But considering Ben's state of health, Micah greatly worried about how their arrival might upset him.

Ben strode toward Micah's horse. Micah slid off the gelding, and his brother smiled and hugged him tightly.

"Welcome home." Ben's raspy voice and thin cheeks sunk in a disturbing, cavernous depression concerned Micah. His eyes moistened. "So glad you're here."

"You don't seem—"

"Surprised? Nay. Received a post from Dr. Huntington in Norwich letting me know my little brother was comin'." He looked past Micah. "And, he had quite a family group with him."

Lydia's shy smile and blush only made her look more

beautiful. Micah hurried toward her and took Minta from her arms, then helped her dismount.

She brushed off the dirt from her cloak and walked toward Ben. "So pleased to meet you." She curtsied.

Ben slapped Micah good-naturedly across his chest. "Where'd you find yerself such a beautiful lass?" He walked toward Lydia and swept her up in his arms with a hug. "And what exactly did you see in this little brother of mine that made you want to spend yer life with him? He is one lucky dog."

Lydia grinned. "I am the lucky one."

He peeked at the baby in Micah's arms. "Sweet lass. She yours, Micah?"

"Not by blood. But by love, for certain sure."

Micah went over to Cuff, who held Comfort. "Come on, lass, and meet your Uncle."

His brother grinned. "And who be this little lady?" Seeing her bandaged leg, he drew his brows forward. "And what got you? Dr. Huntington said he dressed your wounds."

Comfort puckered a sad face. "A big bear got me with his claws. Big, nasty claws."

"I bet you fought him off like a brave lass."

"Well, Papa shot him and saved me."

"I remember helping your papa learn how to shoot a musket."

Comfort's eyes widened. "You do?"

"Aye. Come inside where 'tis warmer, and I'll tell you all about it."

Micah put his hand on Ben's arm. "First, I need to ask. Can all our servants stay inside?"

Ben met his gaze with saddened eyes. "Brother, this house will soon be yours. You can have anyone live here that you wish." He turned, took Comfort's small fingers in his large hand, and walked inside.

Lydia turned to glance at him, tears welling in her eyes.

Micah cleared his throat. "Come on, everyone. Please come in and warm yourselves. I'll help Cuff bed down the horses."

THE FIRE DREW in Lydia like a welcoming embrace. They were finally home.

Years before, Lydia had seen such a cabin in the countryside and asked her mother, 'How can anyone live in such a small house?'

Her mother stared at the dwelling for some time. Lydia would never forget her answer. 'Small in size does not mean small in love.'

As she looked around the large main room with the huge hearth and an abundance of chairs, Lydia could almost feel the love that had existed in this house for so many years, starting with Micah's father and mother. For the first time, Lydia understood her mother's words.

She saw a huge kettle cooking over the fire and automatically went toward it to stir the soup. Lydia reset the ladle on a hook and inhaled the inviting fragrance of home cooking.

Cecelia came up to her and whispered, "I'm sorry, ma'am, but Moses be hungry."

"Nothing to apologize for, Cecelia."

Minta also fussed.

Lydia turned toward Ben. "Is there a room where Cecelia and I can sit to feed the babies?"

"Of course, Lydia." He walked toward a closed door and opened it. "I had enough time to fix up this room a bit for you. Didn't have quite enough time—or strength—to get the other rooms ready."

What a dear man, so like her husband. She placed her hand on his arm. "Ben, you needn't trouble yourself. The other ladies and I can prepare the rooms. We don't want to—" She stopped and bit her lip.

Ben looked downward. "I see Dr. Huntington has let you know. About the cancer."

"I am so sorry, Ben. Micah is sick with sadness."

"Well, he has you to comfort him. And, I think he's chosen the perfect wife. I can see you love him."

"With all my heart."

"That does my own heart good to hear." Ben leaned down and pecked her on the forehead.

She could see a resemblance to her husband, especially in the hazel eyes. "Thank you, Ben."

The babies fussed louder as their hunger increased.

"Haven't heard that since your husband was a baby."

Lydia laughed. "That's hard to imagine."

"Harder to imagine he's a father now. But I am so happy for him."

Lydia stood on her toes and pecked his cheek. "We'd best go feed them."

She sat on the bed inside the cozy room and put the babies to breast. Again, the latch-on proved painful, bringing her near to tears.

"Cecelia, I don't know if something is wrong. Perhaps you're right. We may need to find a wet nurse to help."

"I think that be wise, ma'am."

"I'll talk to Micah about it. Perhaps one of the neighbors will know of someone." She sniffed back the tears and closed her eyes, praying the pain proved to be nothing serious. What if she were ill? Had cancer?

She'd known of women who'd died from it, even while they raised little ones. Her mind took her to a place of fear, a place to which she did not wish to travel. What would Micah do if he had to raise these children by himself?

Cecelia tried to comfort her, but Lydia's tears continued.

By the time she heard Micah enter the house, she had Cecelia worried.

"Let me get Mr. Hughes to find someone for you." Cecelia collected Moses from her and left the room.

Lydia lay Minta next to her and fastened her stays. But first, she inspected her breasts to see if there was anything unusual. She could find nothing out of the ordinary.

A moment later, Micah came in, his eyes dark with worry. He shut the door. "Lydia, what's wrong?" He wrapped his arms around her. "Cecelia says you might be ill."

"I don't know what is wrong, Micah. I've ne'er had such pain before. I think we need to find a wet nurse for Moses. I can't keep up."

"Of course, my love. I will find someone right away to help you."

"Thank you, Micah."

He held onto her and rocked her gently side to side. "This has been a journey unlike any other. No wonder you are so distressed, even ill about it. It has taxed my endurance, and I can only imagine what a strain this has been for you."

She shuddered. "Thank you for understanding, Micah. I love you."

"I cannot imagine my life without you, Lydia." He kissed her gently. "Please rest. I'll find someone from our congregation at church, first thing on the morrow. They'll know someone who can help you."

THE NEIGHBOR in the farm closest to Micah's dropped her bucket of pig slop and hurried toward Micah. "Praise be, you are home, Micah Hughes! And look at you, so tall and filled out. And I heard you have a wife and family. Well done! Of course, we are so sad to hear of your brother. He's so young." She shook her head.

"Aye, Mrs. Warner. 'Tis a heartbreak to my homecoming."

She noticed his hand for the first time and covered her

mouth. "Oh, Micah. I am so sorry. Those nasty regulars!" She spit on the ground.

"Actually, 'twas Hessians that did this damage."

Her mouth turned into an *O*. "No! Those mercenaries should go back where they came from!"

"I agree. Mrs. Warner, perhaps you can help me. Or more exactly, help my wife. We've only just arrived, and I'm not certain who to ask about such things ..."

"Oh. She needs womanly help." The kindly neighbor nodded knowingly.

"Yes, but—"

"No need to worry a bit, Micah. I'll find someone to send over right quick."

Before he could explain about a wet nurse, she had disappeared into her home. Oh well. Surely, she could help find a wet nurse.

Micah headed home.

As he approached, he noticed an unfamiliar horse tied to the rail. After putting his gelding in the barn, he returned to the house.

When he entered, he nearly collided with Cecelia, who swept the floor of the cabin. His brother was nowhere to be found.

"Where is Ben?"

"I think he couldn't take all this 'woman-cleaning,' as he called it, so he escaped somewhere to read." Cecelia grinned.

"And whose horse is that outside?"

Cecelia paused from her sweeping. "Oh, that's the woman Mrs. Warner sent over."

How did word travel so fast that it had beat him home? Women had a mysterious and unseen connection that acted like a postal system all its own.

An older woman exited their bedroom. "Are you Mr. Hughes? I'll be sending over a wet nurse forthwith. Poor woman has enough troubles without feeding two babies." She glared at Micah as though he were guilty somehow.

What had he done?

He escaped her stares by heading toward the bedroom.

"And let her be." She pointed her accusatory finger at him, then shook her head and rolled her eyes. "Men."

Cecelia stifled a laugh as she opened the door for the woman.

Micah waited for her to leave before entering their bedchamber. He felt like an intruder. Lydia lay on the bed while both Minta and Moses slept in cradles. She seemed far more at peace today.

"You look well, my love. Is everything all right? The woman who left here seems to think everything is my fault. I felt like an accused convict trying to enter our bedchamber."

She grinned.

"What? Why are you laughing at me?"

"I'm not laughing. I'm smiling."

"Can you tell me what's going on? Yesterday you thought you were seriously ill, and today you're grinning like you have some deep, wonderful secret."

"Well, perhaps I have. But I'll tell you only if you kiss me first."

He pointed toward the door. "Are you certain I have that woman's permission?"

"You have my permission."

"Then let me accommodate you, Mrs. Hughes." He kissed her slowly, deeply, with enough passion to make him want to lock the door. He kissed her neck, enjoying the feel of her soft hair across his cheek

"By the way, that woman happens to be the town midwife."

He stopped kissing her mid-nuzzle. "The town midwife? Why was she here?"

Lydia placed his hand on her belly. "Because, my love, you have given me another baby."

"What? You said 'Twas not possible. How?" He narrowed his eyes at her.

"Well, I think you know the *how*, but why I am with child

whilst still nursing, I cannot answer. This midwife says she's seen it before. And that's why I've been miserable nursing two babies."

"You're with child?"

"Aye."

"By me?"

"Most assuredly by you." She laughed. "Now, I *am* laughing at you."

"Lydia." He stroked her cheeks with trembling fingers. "Lydia, I am so pleased. When?"

"The midwife says in June."

"I am beyond pleased. I want to kiss you, but I fear I might hurt you."

"You will not hurt me. Or our baby."

He grinned. "Our baby. It sounds wonderful."

"I think so. I cannot wait to see him."

He grew serious. "And I cannot wait to kiss you."

"Then, lock the door, and I just might kiss you back."

"I just might do that."

"I love you, Micah Hughes."

"Not as much as I love you, Lydia Hughes."

EPILOGUE

The wet nurse fed baby Moses until he could eat and drink on his own, and Cecelia reveled in raising the child. No one knew his past, and Lydia and Micah would never tell. Cuff grew to love Cecelia, and they married that spring, making the family complete.

May of 1779, brought new life to the town of East Haddam, Connecticut, when Hannah delivered baby Ezekiel. He looked so much like his war-hero father that no other name seemed appropriate to give the handsome child.

That June, Benjamin Micah Hughes was born to Lydia and Micah. As Micah had promised his brother Ben before he died that spring, they named their first son after him.

Benjamin came into this world just as Minta turned a year old. Both Comfort and Rose fussed over who he liked the most. With some help from Lydia, they decided he liked Minta the best.

After fighting in several more battles, Henry Bearslayer retired from the army when he lost a leg. He found his way to the Hughes farm and reunited with Miriam. They wed in the spring, and now Rose looked forward to becoming a big sister.

Micah gave Henry and Miriam a few acres of land on which to build a home and raise their family.

Lydia, Micah, and the children often made their way back to Norwich to visit the Huntingtons. Comfort always managed to get some chocolate.

The war was not yet over, but, for Micah and Lydia, it was in their past. They prayed it would never revisit them or their children, and that their many scars would heal. They longed for renewed strength and faith. And for many more years in each other's arms.

AUTHOR'S NOTE

Although the official vaccine for Smallpox was not created by Edward Jenner until 1796, a very crude version of inoculation was practiced during the American Revolution. George Washington knew first-hand the dangers of smallpox, especially in the close quarters of a war camp. He could not take the chance of losing nearly a third of his army to the illness.

In a risky and dangerous move, Washington determined to use mass inoculation which would provide his troops with some protection from the disease lest the natural form of the illness nearly wipe out his army. A few of the patients did in fact die of the process, but most survived.

By choosing this plan for massive inoculation, Washington accomplished the first state-funded immunization campaign in American history and helped to win the Revolution against England.

ABOUT THE AUTHOR

Award-winning author Elaine Marie Cooper focuses her writing on the era of the American Revolution. She has authored Love's Kindling, Saratoga Letters, Fields of the Fatherless, as well as several other historical novels. She has also has been published in numerous magazines and anthologies. Her one non-fiction memoir is Bethany's Calendar, the journey of her daughter's battle with a terminal brain tumor. Although she has not lived in New England for many years, her heart for history was birthed there and continues to thrive.

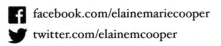

facebook.com/elainemariecooper

twitter.com/elainemcooper

MORE HISTORICAL ROMANCE FROM SCRIVENINGS PRESS

Under This Same Sky

She thought she'd lost everything –

Instead she found what she needed most.

Illinois prairie – 1854

When a deadly tornado destroys Becky Hollister's farm, she must leave the only home she's ever known, and the man she's begun to love to accompany her injured father to St. Louis. Catapulted into a world of unknowns, Becky finds solace in corresponding with the handsome pastor back home. But when word comes that he is all but engaged to someone else, she must call upon her faith to decipher her future.

Matthew Brody didn't intend on falling for Becky, but the unexpected relationship, along with the Lord's gentle nudging, incite him to give up his circuit riding and seek full-time ministry in the town of Miller Creek, with the hope of one day making Becky his bride. But when his old sweetheart comes to town, intent on winning him back—with the entire town pulling for her—Matthew must choose between doing what's expected and what his heart tells him is right.

Dreaming of Tomorrow

Love leads them to a lifetime of commitment where the dreams they have held onto for so long start to come true.

Popular and eligible, Logan De Witt must convince the women in town that he is engaged to be married. A quiet, simple ceremony is what he has in mind for his wedding day, but when the date and time of his bride's arrival is published in the newspaper, the whole town joins in the celebration proving to Logan and his new wife their sincere friendship and support. Added to the excitement of Logan's marriage is the question of what the congregation should do with the unexpected donation of an orchard.

Karen Millerson is counting the days until her long-distance engagement comes to an end and she may travel to Oswell City to marry Logan. More than anything, she wants to share in his life as a help and support, but keeping a house and finding her place in the community requires much more work than she ever expected.

Learn, laugh, and love with Karen and Logan as they start a new marriage and work together ministering to the citizens of their small town.

(Coming November 2020.)

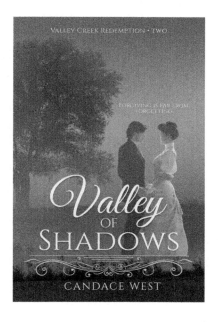

Valley of Shadows by Candace West

Valley Creek Redemption Book Two

A shattered heart.

A wounded spirit.

A community in crisis.

Lorena Steen gave up on love years ago. She forgave her long-time estranged husband, but when circumstances bring her to the Ozark town of Valley Creek, she discovers forgiving is far from forgetting.

Haunted by his past acts of betrayal, Earl Steen struggles to grow his reclaimed faith and reinstate himself as an upstanding member of Valley Creek. He soon learns that while God's grace is amazing, that of the small-town gossips is not.

When disaster strikes, the only logical solution is for Earl and Lorena to combine their musical talents in an effort to save the community.

But even if they're willing to work together, are they able to? Or will the shadows that descend upon Valley Creek reduce it to a ghost town?

~

Safe Refuge

Newport of the West—Book One

In two days, wealthy Chicagoan, Anna Hartwell, will wed a man she loathes. She would refuse this arranged marriage to Lyman Millard, but the Bible clearly says she is to honor her parents, and Anna would do most anything to please her father—even leaving her teaching job at a mission school and marrying a man she doesn't love.

The Great Chicago Fire erupts, and Anna and her family escape with only the clothes on their backs and the wedding postponed. Father moves the family to Lake Geneva, Wisconsin, where Anna reconnects with Rory Quinn, a handsome immigrant who worked at the mission school. Realizing she is in love with Rory, Anna prepares to break the marriage arrangement with Lyman until she learns a dark family secret that changes her life forever.

~

Connie Lounsbury

A Hobo's Wish

After a tragic mistake during The Great Depression, Dr. Pete Walters becomes penniless, forced to ride the rails along with thousands of other unemployed men and women, surviving by trading labor for food, or asking for handouts. Will he find the trust and the love he doesn't believe he deserves when he hops off the train at Kathleen Creek, Minnesota, or must he leave again when someone exposes his past?

Scrivenings
PRESS
Quench your thirst for story.
www.ScriveningsPress.com

Made in the USA
Middletown, DE
24 July 2021

44679468R00179